Swimming Through Air

by N. K. Hart

Tangible press

Dedicated to my one true love…
JMH

Works By N. K. Hart

The Innocence Of Power

Up The Crime Ladder

Swimming Through Air

Part One

Nariantha's Journey

As I walk slowly through the field of wild flowers and late summer clover, my steps deliberate and my eyes searching left and right of my path, looking for the tiny green and yellow leaves of the Thymum plant that grandmother requested I find before returning, my mind reviews the events of my day.

I've turned the soil where the last of the legumen had been harvested just days before, readying it for the caboche seeds that grandmother intends to plant there next week. I've studied the next five pages in my "Book of Herba and Pharmaco", committing to memory another six medicinal plants. I'll review them again tonight after supper for good measure. And, after a painstaking search, I've found three rare herba down by the stream. Grandmother will be proud of me but if I don't find the Thymum for her flatbread, any goodwill my studies may garner might come to naught.

The sun is lowering in the afternoon sky, bathing the air in an almost white light and brushing the high clouds, leaving them tinged with pink and yellow. I know it's getting late and think to pick up my pace when I spy the tiny-leafed herba not one measure from my path. Happily I cut several stems, careful not to destroy the little patch in doing so and make a mental note as to its location for my future reference. I make the leaves safe in among my other finds in my gathering basket, and step lively toward home.

Home is a modest structure, tucked along the outskirts of my village. It's situated next to a wonderful wild field that gives way to a lush, green woodland where I spent a great deal of my childhood quietly observing nature or searching for rare plants and flowers. I wake every morning to a most pleasing view. My window frames a huge and gnarled Bilboa tree whose leaves shimmer with the slightest breeze.

I can still recall when life in the village was rather simple. Chores and responsibilities were divided among all those able to work, with the very young and the elderly doing what they could. Everyone worked at what they did best and all essentials were shared equally. Everyone had enough food to eat and the right clothes to wear; light weaves in the warm summers and heavier fibers for the harsh winters. My people divided the labor according to ability and need. The fields were always tended, small gardens looked after and dwellings erected and maintained. There were those who knew how to fashion tools and those who could weave. Everyone had a part and everyone a share in the rewards.

A typical day would consist of work, home, and family. On warm summer evenings it wouldn't be unusual to find family groups gathered in the village center around a small central night fire. I recall neighbors and friends greeting each other with jovial hellos and asking about the day's activities and quietly telling about family or new adventures. Eventually, all would settle down and as everyone became sleepy from their day's toils, a hush might gather over the group. As a child, I would sit quietly and look into the fire and let my thoughts go quiet and my mind wander where it would. As the flames danced about, I remembered many a time when a voice would call out to one of the Elders entreating them to tell a story. Sometimes they would ask which story was desired and other times they would fall silent and wait for everyone's attention. At those times, I could clearly hear the crackling of the fire and see the fire-lit faces all turned to gaze at the elder storyteller so as not to miss a word.

The eldest among us remembered the tales told them by their parents and their parent's parents. They told the stories handed down to them from generations gone by. And they told stories that they themselves had created during their lifetime, sometimes changing a word here or a place there, but always including a small gesture or quiet whisper to emphasize a point or a feeling.

I remember most of those stories. They have stuck in my mind and have stayed with me all these years. Frozen there as if it had been etched upon a stone and placed along the path of my memory garden so that I may revisit it again and again.

One story told about our past, in a time when only a few humans had existed on the Earth. These few humans had gathered together into one clan to share the labor and the rewards of a rich life they built together. The name they gave to themselves was simply the Genii. The life they led was modest but not without small pleasures. They celebrated new life, remembered life ended, and lived by the seasons and by necessity. Those people were our ancestors. We are the Genii.

Another story, told for the children, was of days when plump sweet berries hung on the vines and children were allowed to eat as many as they wanted as long as they filled their baskets before the mid-day meal. Friends would tease each other by stuffing two or three fat berries into their mouths, puffing their cheeks out and laughing until the juice ran down their chins.

The storytellers would puff out their cheeks and wag their head while trying not to smile. It was funny and would make the children laugh and squirm with joy. I never tired of that story.

I think the Genii have been very fortunate. We have stayed together through the generations and across an untold number of seasons caring for one another and developing ourselves into a thriving and productive society.

From among our ancestors, certain individuals became known as more skilled in areas not necessarily requiring muscle but definitely requiring their minds. These individuals became our teachers. They would patiently observe and meticulously refine their skills and pass on their knowledge to those who showed promise and interest. Many, many years ago, six Masters arose from among the teachers who held and taught the knowledge for all: horticulture plant care, astronomy, medicine, storytelling, art, and essentials.

The Horticulture Master studied the seasons and taught which plants grew well at what times. She learned which plants eased suffering and which helped to heal all kinds of ailments and distress. Through her care, plants thrived and crops were bountiful.

The Astronomy Master watched the night sky and learned which star patterns followed each season. He recorded all the findings that were kept for the village, adding to their treasure of knowledge.

The Medical Master, worked with shrubs and herbs, reducing them to their most powerful distillation and studied the effects on ailments. She found healing stones and earth powders that aided in those efforts.

The Storyteller Master used his memory and voice to tell stories from history and to tell tales of learning and power. With each tale that he told, the daily lives of the Genii were transformed into a living history. He recorded his stories on scrolls of parchment in his finest hand and adorned them with beautiful pictures to add life to the tale.

The Art Master would create fantastic drawings recorded from life so that anyone could see a spring flower in the midst of a harsh winter. She was inspired to draw and to explore her dreams and was very fond of extracting color from plants and minerals to color her art. Her pictures took on a life of their own, inspired from the Earth and from her imagination.

The Essentials Master found knowledge and power in discovering which methods were best for each task. From the loom to flint tools to the delicate crafting of baskets and bowls, he could instruct anyone in the proper handling of the necessary materials and tools and from time to time he would create a new tool or revise one to improve it.

For generations the Earth responded generously to the care and kindness of the Genii people. It had always yielded its bounty and refreshed with each passing season. Peace, tranquility and the comfort of life's pattern continued for time after time, story after story.

Then, in the summer of my eighteenth year conditions began to change. The Genii would need to adapt and endure. They would have to survive because trying times lay ahead.

The sky watcher noted small, almost imperceptible changes among the star patterns. Small groups of stars that had never changed, that were always to be found at certain times in the same location of the sky, had suddenly started to move. The shifting of stars in the night sky brought a deep concern to the Astronomy Master. In all the known history of the people, he had never observed a change in the patterns and he carefully recorded each change. As the star changes continued, the watcher became more and more concerned. He observed and consulted records and his memories and when he was certain of his findings, he brought his observations to the Elders.

After the star changes began, other changes also became apparent. The following mid-season harvest was barely enough to fill the storage jars in preparation for the harsh late-season when the Earth slept. The Elders managed to quell the early fears of the people by telling them that small changes could not mean anything serious. They would be fine. Everything would be fine. They would make up for any shortages during the next season. The Elders told the people not to worry.

But things were not fine. The night sky had stopped shifting, true, but other changes still occurred. The late-season was colder than it had ever been and food and fuel supplies ran dangerously low. Supplies had to be rationed and families grouped together to ensure that everyone survived. The early season brought with it lightning storms that came without thunder with its fury raging for days and nights without ceasing. Dark clouds gathered and swirled about overhead but brought no rains. Gradually the rivers and streams that flowed throughout the land bringing life waters to plants, to animals and to the people started to dry up. Their movement slowed to a trickle, the thirsty Earth gobbling up what little water remained in the streams leaving behind dry cracked fissures that were the only trace of its fleeting existence.

This time became known as the Darkness.

The Darkness lasted for several seasons and many of the people suffered and died during this time. The strongest among us continued to labor in the fields past the time of hope into a time of desperation. They could not coax even the smallest of buds from the parched earth. Women walked for long distances in the drying heat of the sun searching for water, only to return at the end of the day with their jars holding small amounts of muddy liquid that they used in their meager kitchen gardens. The men left the dead fields and spent their days wandering the landscapes scratching at the earth gathering stunted plant life and catching insects hoping that it would sustain their families for just one more day.

As the time of Darkness wore on the people started to lose all hope. Many became depressed and walked along with dull minds and empty eyes. Others became angry. The number of squabbles had started to increase daily and the people argued over ration portions and who deserved more because they had worked harder or longer than the others. On occasion, a violent fight would erupt with blows exchanged. Inevitably someone would get hurt.

The Elders worked tirelessly to quell the fears that had permeated every aspect of life but the people feared no end to their suffering and feared that their resolution would perish with the Earth, that they would turn to dust and blow away on the hot winds.

The Elders contemplated the events and spoke to one another in an effort to understand the different facets of the burden brought upon the people by the time of Darkness. While maintaining hope that life would return to normal, that the rains would fall and that the crops would grow, the Elders continued to study the Darkness and to discuss possibilities.

Many scenarios were brought forward and each one was discussed at length and looked at from every angle before laid to rest or reserved as having merit. The Elders fell into a natural rhythm of discourse that gradually led them toward a result that in the end produced one conclusion: two would be chosen who would lead the remaining people to a better life. To salvation.

The Elders contemplated their final decision for days and discussed it among themselves to make sure that nothing was left unnoticed. They meditated and consulted the ancient runes. And when they were absolutely sure that their choice was the right one, they called for a council.

Council meetings were considered to be very important and for this reason, were rarely held. When word spread that a meeting was to be held, the people shook off their apathy and became more alive with a strange mixture of emotions. At once, anticipation of a council meeting stirred curiosity... *what could the Elders have to say?* Mixed with apprehension... *will it be troubling, more troubling than no rains?* Further complicated by the sheer weight of hopelessness... *will they tell us what we already know: that the people are doomed?*

The Elders sent word that the council would take place in

three days in the village center. The people should gather as much fuel for the night fires as they could and the village leaders were to prepare the meeting area in the prescribed manner. When all was ready, the Elders would assemble and address the people.

The village center was a place that inspired quiet meditations and invited gatherings of friends and neighbors, boisterous and jovial. It was also the hub of all activity. It was a large space many feet wide by many feet long and easily held all the Genii of the village.

In its center was a tall irregular shaped jasper boulder. It was and still is, buff brown, filled with veins of milky white quartz and pockets of petrified red algae from an ancient seabed. Many of its surfaces and facets had been rubbed smooth, some by tool and some by touch. The large boulder is topped by an opaque, red spinel crystal, its sharp facets shone flawlessly atop and melding gently into the jasper base. Elders often told stories of the crystal's power of revitalization, its inspiration, and how it would instill new hope in those who sat quietly with their private thoughts.

Radiating outward from the spinel and jasper boulder centerpiece was a flat stone surface. Builders had quarried stone from a nearby mountain and brought it to the village. It was carved and cut into many flat stones and laid to fit, stone to stone, to provide a wide stable surface.

Interspersed among the flat stones, were designs done with contrasting pebbles, representing the Genii's ancient symbols of knowledge. These were arranged in a circle surrounding the center and linked together by a series of tourmalinated quartz inserts the size of a man's fist.

The plaza had four main boulevards and each one was signed as to its direction, as indicated by the Elders at the time it was built: North, South, East, and West. Ancient symbols, done in corresponding energy stones (trigonic quartz, pink tourmaline, fire agate, and vanadinite) graced the boulevard entry points.

Additionally, Above and Below were honored by their symbols and celebrated by amber and garnet inlays.

There were four gardens at the four corners of the plaza that were planted with tall trees with spreading limbs that provided shade from the hot sun. Flowering shrubs gave visual rest and large boulders provided places to sit and were often used as playthings by children.

The plaza was surrounded by structures done in the architecture of the Genii and adapted to their needs. Some were places of learning where the Masters would hold sessions to teach their knowledge. Others were home and hearth to village families. Some of which would trade their crafts and home wares from their front porticos.

The village plaza was a place of vibrancy. A place that mattered. A place very important to the Genii.

The village leaders met and quickly agreed among themselves who would guide which activity. The meeting might last for days, maybe for a quarter turn of the moon and there should be enough fuel and herbs for the fires. Everyone in the village understood the importance of a meeting of the Elders and pitched in where they could.

It took two days to complete the necessary preparations.

Several of the men moved the braziers into place while women brought baskets of fuel and dried herbs and arranged them nearby. The entire plaza was swept clean and the small gardens raked into order. Everyone contributed what food and water they could and when the leaders were satisfied that all had been put to right, they thanked everyone for their work and retired to their homes to rest.

On the morn of the third day, the villagers woke as usual and set about their home duties. But on this day, no one went to the fields, no one went hunting and no one walked for water. The day of the Elder's council meeting had arrived.

The morning air was cool but as the sun moved to mid-day, it became still and dry. The sound of buzzing insects and the hum of locust could be heard. And as the sun continued to move across the sky, the late afternoon air became hotter and seemed to sit on one's chest like a large stone. As the afternoon wore on, a slight breeze from the north revived the people from their listlessness and they started to quietly assemble in the village center where many had labored for two days to make everything ready for the Elder's meeting.

They sat or stood in small groups, whispering quietly or admiring the transformation of the village center. Changed to an opulent stage for their council meeting from the ordinary plaza it had been.

As dusk started to deepen and the shadows began to fade into the gray of the landscape, the Elders sent a runner to the plaza with a signal that the meeting had begun.

The runner was brilliant with color and lithe as he made his way through the streets to the plaza. His hair had been braided with ribbons and festooned with gold cords. His tunic was decorated with beautifully crafted flowers and leaves, woven from dried petals, pine needles, and sewn with thread, gold as the sun and as fine as a spider's web. His face was flush with anticipation and when he reached the plaza, he spoke no words. He moved his body in a sort of dance until he was assured of everyone's attention. When everyone was silent and all eyes were upon him, he took his torch and lit the night fires that stood aligned with North, South, East, West, Above, and Below, moving slowly, deliberately and with a touch of pageantry. When he had lit the fires, he took his place by the northern boulevard, made a graceful bow to the gathering and pointed in the direction from which the Elders would appear.

Music started to play. Soft flutes and piccolos at first, followed by the whispers of wood blocks and as the melody flowed, lyres added their notes.

As the six Elders slowly made their way through the village streets, the soft murmuring of their chanting and prayers became more tonal and distinct. The people that were gathered in the village center could hear them approaching and fell silent, taking their places around the outskirts of the plaza.

Each of the six Elders held a torch over their heads and in the deepening twilight shadows the light flowing over them made them seem ethereal and singular and to float above the Earth as they walked.

The ceremonial garb worn by each Elder was exquisite. Each design was marked with deep sensitivity and far reaching understanding of the ancient values they portrayed.

Each of the Elders had adorned themselves in the likeness of one of the ancient emblems of life and knowledge that the people held in sanctum: service, honor, passion, kinship, wonderment, and security. They were dazzling in their appearance.

Elder North led the procession

North is Service and the token is arctic wolf whose likeness was sewn on his ceremonial tunic using many layers of light and dark gray thread that create a fantastical dimensional portrait whose eyes shone bright and seemed to move in the firelight. His garb resembled the northern landscape with light skies, clouds of snow and the creatures that inhabit that land.

South followed a few paces behind. She is Honor and her token is sea creatures. About her garb were portrayals of wild grasses and an arctic tern. Her dress was made of flowing cotton that reached to her calves and as she moved it seemed to shimmer. Creatures that populate the great oceans adorn the whole of the dress: a marine turtle, small fishes, and anemones. Along the bottom, where the ocean turns the deepest blue, swims a large sea creature with pearlescent fins and tail made from silk and mesmerizing scales made from flecks of pink tourmaline.

East came next. She is Passion whose tokens are trees and plants. She wears crafted likenesses of flowers, flower buds, and leaves in her hair. Her dress is long and flowed about her ankles to almost cover her soft, dark brown slippers. Above the hem are renderings of trees and shrubs, plants and grasses with a large and stately ancient oak just above the hem. A symbol of perseverance and longevity.

West is Kinship whose token is bees. Her dress is made from a fawn-colored suede and is cut just below her knee in the front and hangs to her ankles in the back. The hem is encircled with the images of every flower imaginable. The bodice has garlands of beautifully crafted bees. Dozens of them. She wears a cape made of the sheerest silk that is decorated with dark thread to mimic the gossamer of bee's wings.

Above is wonderment. Her token is a wildcat. Her long flowing sleeves are of azure blue silk and her dress wraps loosely around her middle to end in large pleats at her ankles. From her waist to the hem, the midnight blue material is covered in constellations and ancient symbols that are crafted in amber and silver thread.

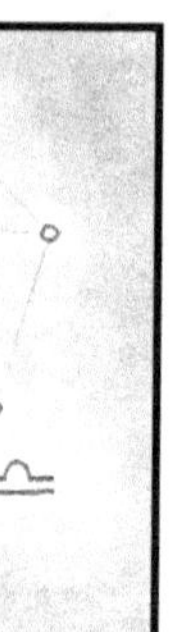

Below is last of the Elders to enter the plaza. Below is Security whose token is the sun. His tunic has square shoulders and hangs past his waist ending in loose trousers. His arms are bare and strong. The sigil at his chest is a large raw ruby situated atop many

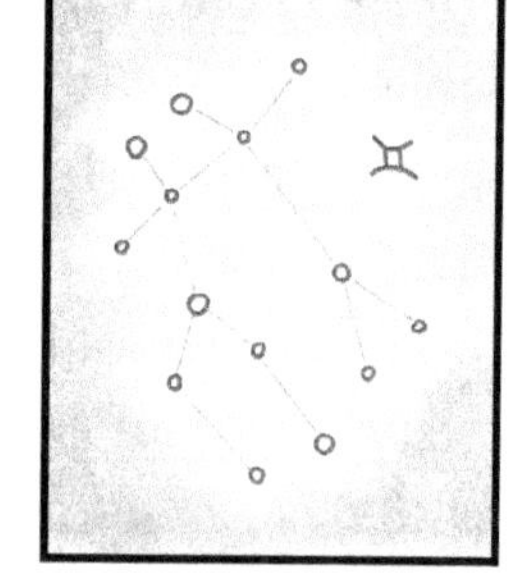

bright sunflower petals sewn of a fine yellow silk to represent light. Red threads at the hem represent the warmth of the earth and the fires from which security is fashioned.

The six Masters follow, flanked by a dozen torchbearers whose job it is to light the path and then place their torches throughout the gardens to help illuminate the plaza.

The six Masters are not garbed in the same splendid manner as the Elders but simply, in dresses or tunics of pale green, cream, blue, and smoky gray as related to their disciplines. Each Master carries a token of their knowledge: herbs, artist's brushes, boughs of leaves, a rolled parchment, a star chart, and a piece of flint. Each takes their place among the tourmaline symbols in the plaza and stand quietly, waiting for the ceremony to begin.

A hush fell over the gathering. People stood quietly along the walkways and throughout the plaza gardens. The entire plaza was awash in firelight from the six braziers that burned steadily in the square and the raised torches, sputtering at their spindles of oiled rag that had been arranged in the gardens.

The music had softened until barely a note could be heard and then slowly it faded into the night.

Elder North raised his arms heavenward to command attention and after a moment relaxed them back to his sides. He gazed around at the expectant faces turned his way, smiled a sad sort of smile and spoke.

"With harmony and grace we've come unto our place
of security and vastness above.
Of our plight we will strive with lightness and small divide
to come to the end and with peace."
The Elders called, "May the universe bestow its gifts."
The people responded, "Keep us worthy to receive."
Elder North continued, "The storms rage against the land but bring no rains to quench its thirst or fill the rivers and streams. Our sun stays hidden behind dark clouds, keeping its warmth and energy from everything."

Elder South spoke next, "Our seas are changed. What was once thought to be a small irregular happening has not changed back to what was. Fish and turtle are not seen and the ocean tides have turned the shores to bone yards."

Elder East spoke, "The Earth no longer yields its bounty and many Genii have suffered, some have gone and some might not have lived at all. The ancient oaks still stand but many flowers have not been seen for two seasons."

Elder West slowly moved her arm across the expanse of night sky and said, "The living creatures that once were found throughout our land are seen no more, seemingly disappeared from us. Birds do not grace the sky. Bees no longer labor in our fields. Animals have left us, too. All have left to seek survival elsewhere."

Elder Above, her voice low, spoke, "Our stars have moved in the heavens. They look upon us from another place. Perhaps they send knowledge that everything has begun again. Now is new. The Genii can never go back."

Elder Below took two steps forward, closer to the firelight. His movements made the red almandine garnet of his headdress flash brilliant.

"The Elders have held many discussions of the problems the Genii are now facing. And while numerous answers have come to light only the value of one withstood our meditations and our thoughts."

He stood motionless, with his eyes closed, breathing deeply and then, opening his eyes, spoke once again, "Two will be chosen who will lead the Genii to a better life. To salvation."

The gathering immediately erupted with murmurs and whispers among themselves, neighbor turned to neighbor with looks of astonishment on their faces, questions on their tongues, and doubts in their minds.

Elder Below passively observed the crowd to give everyone a moment to take in the proclamation.

When the initial shock of such news wore down, resignation took its place. It was agreed. We had no choice.

Elder Below raised a hand, motioning for the group to quiet themselves. When the people had turned their attention to the Elder, he spoke in a calm but reassuring tone.

"We have lived here in peace and plenty for many generations. This land and its waters have sustained us beyond our needs and desires. We have reciprocated by treating the land with respect, helping it to survive, ensuring that together, the land and the people, would continue. In this we have been diligent.

"The Elders have come to believe that something greater than the land and the people has caused the profound changes we have been observing for the past three seasons. It is not fully understood but we agree that the solution to our problem is to move forward. If we stay still, we will surely perish."

Elder East stepped forward and turned to face the majority of the gathering. "We can not stay here any longer. But all of us leaving at once would pose many problems and hardships that for some, would be more than they could endure."

Smiling she continued, "It is better for two to go in search of a new home for the Genii. There will be others that will go also, to help with the daily needs, but for certain, the two that the Elders council have chosen will lead, will consider, will decide, and will have the only word as to all matters concerning the journey and the outcome."

Elder West, her voice soft and kind said, "We have confidence that these two will succeed. The two that have been chosen are Nariantha Hygea and Jeon Aculata."

Instantly the gathering broke into excited chatter. Everyone looked around to see if Nariantha and Jeon were among them and had they heard the news: they were the two chosen by the Elder's council. Within moments the two had been surrounded by their friends and were being ushered to the plaza's center. Both looked stunned and their faces were flush in the firelight but both still had their wits about them and were steady on their feet.

The six Elders and the six Masters now left their ceremonial positions and moved to receive Nariantha and Jeon from their friends. When the two had been brought forward, the others took a few steps back so that the small group stood alone. A hush fell over the gathering and everyone looked expectantly, waiting to hear anything more.

The meeting went on for several more hours. The Elders and the Masters mixed and mingled, answered questions, and gave advice. By the early morning hours, most everyone had taken their leave and only the most stout hearted stayed on.

When the first light of the new day streaked over the horizon, the last of the Genii in the plaza tended the six ceremonial fires, tossing dried bundles of herbs onto the last of the glowing embers, then left for home and to bed.

My name is Nariantha Hygea. I am the granddaughter of Liri Leyana, known to everyone in the village as Elder East. I have lived here, in this place, my entire life. I am a young woman of twenty plus seven years.

My parents died when I was young. My father from injuries sustained while on a gathering trip out in the vast wilds beyond the mountains. The men that were with him at that time performed a ceremony and buried him among the flowering chaparral. I like to think that his spirit watches over our plains and rivers. From his place on the mountain.

My mother died a short time after. Some say from a broken heart and this may be so but I know that she loved me because she left me in the care of her mother, my grandmother, before she left to join my father in eternity.

My grandmother has raised me to be a strong, knowledgeable woman. She has taught me the names and uses for many trees and shrubs and seasonal flowers. She taught me how to coax blooms and gather seeds. She taught me many things about edible and medicinal herbs and because of her knowledge and her infinite patience in teaching me her way, I have become known as an expert in my own right. Some day, I may take my grandmother's place as Elder East.

Let me take a moment to tell you something about Jeon Aculata. He is thirty plus one years of age. Jeon is tall, tan, and muscular from his work as a builder. As a student of the Master of Essentials, Jeon's skills with tools are excellent. He can fashion the right tool for any task. His fingers are both nimble and strong, his mind both open and singular, and he possesses the knowledge to know when either is needed. He is kind, intelligent, and steady. And I have known Jeon my entire life.

After the shock of hearing my name called out at the council meeting, time seemed to slow. Smiling faces, most of them my friends, immediately surrounded me. Everyone talked excitedly and offered their thanks and surprise. Several hands propelled me forward from my place by the large beech tree where I had stood silently, mesmerized by the pageant and the words. The guiding hands were welcome because my feet seemed to be rooted to the spot where I stood. As I moved toward the plaza center, I saw that Jeon was also surrounded by friends and was moving through the crowd to the center. He was smiling and nodding his head to the well-wishers that surrounded him and called out from afar.

The Elders and the Masters who reached out with soft words and kind smiles joined us. When the crowd had stepped back and hushed their excitement, Elder West spoke.

"The decision to send these two and a small group of others to find a new home for the Genii did not come without thought and contemplation. After many hours of talk and many hours of quiet, the choice was clear.

"The effect of these two and their small number of companions are bound by the fates and their own knowledge and strength, to succeed. The Elders have spoken."

My grandmother had come to my side and slipped her cool hand into mine. And as I turned to look at her, her smile and her touch were enough to dissipate any fears or doubts that had been building inside me. I stood next to her confident and calm.

Then her words sounded in my ear even as she addressed the villagers, "The Masters have been tasked with preparing the group for their journey. This may take a few days and we ask for your kind cooperation."

Elder North raised his arms and gestured for everyone to

step up. His voice kind and reassuring, "Please come and wish Nariantha and Jeon success. The Elders and Masters will answer any questions you may have."

Elder South leaned close to Jeon and me; I could almost smell the sea in her hair. And then she said, "We will meet with you both for the noon meal, tomorrow. Don't worry. Everything will be fine."

I woke early the next morning and dressed quietly so as not to disturb grandmother. I could hear the soft sound of her steady, slow breathing and knew she was sleeping restfully.

I banked the softly glowing embers of our night fire, added twigs and sticks and gently blew on the pile until it smoldered into life. I then set cooking stones among the coals and while waiting for them to warm up, set about preparing my mug of dried herbs for tea. I added the hot stones to a standing pot of water and when it had heated, poured a small amount into my mug.

The sky had brightened as the sun started the new day. Grandmother stirred in her bed and softly called my name.

"Good morning, grandmother. Did you sleep well?"

"Yes, child. I did. And I had interesting dreams, too."

Grandmother's dreams were almost always of the future. I smiled with remembrance when, as a small child, she told me she had dreamt that I had a large bruise and a puncture on my foot and that I couldn't walk. I laughed. I told her that I was too fleet-footed, I would jump and run from anything that could harm me. She had smiled and nodded but told me to take care all the same. I said I would, but in truth, I had not yet learned to listen to my grandmother's dreams. That afternoon, as I walked in the fields gathering herbs and nettle, my left foot slipped into a pocket gopher burrow and was impaled by a ragged torn tree branch. I yelped with the pain and surprise and pulled my foot free and took note, clear note, of the hideous puncture wound and the bright red and purple bruise growing under my skin that started to mark the spot. I never doubted my grandmother's dreams again.

I prepared a second mug of tea and waited for grandmother to join me. "I was going to sit at the edge of the field and watch the sun. Would you like to come with me?"

Grandmother, her robe pulled about her shoulders, answered, "Not just now. You go ahead. I'll sit a moment by the cooking fire and then start the pottage. Come back in an hour and we'll eat and I'll tell you my dreams."

I smiled at her, noting her kind face, trying to sear it into my memory, then quietly went out the back door.

I sat on a large boulder with my knees pulled up and holding my mug just under my nose to catch the steam as it rose. I wanted my thoughts to focus on the enormity of my situation, to reason through it, and to start to plan the future. But they wouldn't come. All I can truly remember of those moments was the sun warming my face and the smell of herbed tea in my nose. No thoughts came unbidden and no thoughts frightened me... nor did they comfort me.

I finished my tea and returned home.

Grandmother and I sat quietly together spooning her delicious oat and dried, wild apple pottage into our mouths. When we finished and were about cleaning the bowls and cooking utensils, grandmother spoke.

"I slept well last night. I thought I would be overtired but that wasn't so."

She moved about the cooking area, fussing with this and moving that. As I watched her, she seemed to be wrestling with her thoughts. Then she stopped, invited me to sit with her and spoke.

"I had three dreams last night. Two were clear and one was shadowed, hard to see. I think it best to tell them as I had them. But first, I would like you to know that I dreamt of you weeks ago. I knew that the Elders would choose you. You and Jeon. I saw it clearly in a dream but didn't say anything to anyone, thinking that it would come to pass or not, as it should. But I knew."

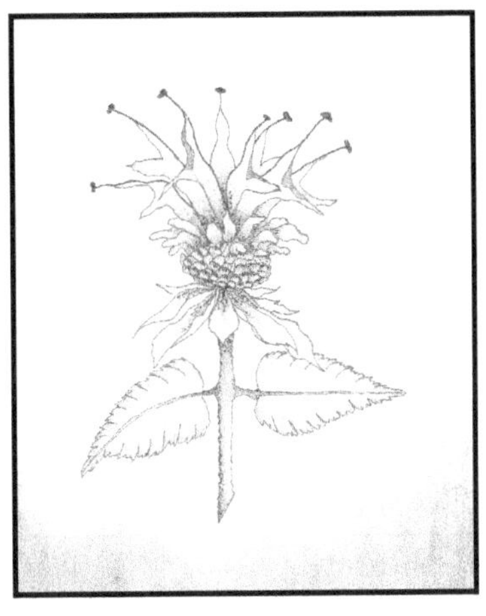

She looked thoughtful for a moment then went on, "Last night, in the first dream, I was waving goodbye to you as you left this house. Smiling, you told me that you loved me and that all would be fine. As you walked into the field, you stopped to pluck a wild bloom and fixed it into your hair. A feeling of assurance came over me and I knew that your skills with plants would carry you and your small troop. I watched as you walked on until I couldn't see you, only the place in which you disappeared. And as I watched the spot for a last glimpse of you, a beautiful flower arose and opened its petals to the sun. It was the bloom of Monarda. From this I knew you would be safe."

She shifted in her chair and gazed out the window but then brought her attention back and continued. "I slept for awhile, I don't know how long, but another dream soon unfolded. It was dark and a storm was rising. I was standing, looking to the east, the winds whipping my robes, my hair twisting about my eyes. I was afraid. I had a sense that you were lost. That I had lost you. And as I called out your name into the dark swirling fog, a face started to take shape. The fog swirled and brightened and came together into the face of a woman. I addressed her. I said, 'I don't know you, by what name are you known?' She replied, 'I am known by many names. You may call me Gaia.' 'How is it that I see you in the storm?' 'Tis not a storm, good woman, it is a distant memory obscured by the passions of your mind.' 'I'm looking for Nariantha. Is she there?' 'She is always here, close to you, bound by love and through time by a silver thread.' The face of Gaia faded and then was taken by the fog to swirl about into nothingness. My worry left me and I awoke in the dark, no longer afraid. Peaceful. I don't remember falling back into sleep but I must have."

I was listening intently to what grandmother was telling me and thought to ask her a question, "What do you think the dream is telling you?"

"I think the dream tells of you being lost for a time. For how long, I couldn't say. It wasn't clear. However, the appearance of Gaia gave me hope and took my fears away. I believe that something will come out of the fog to help. Further, I can only think that that means all will be well in the end. Nothing more can be seen from it but I can hope that I may dream further of it some night soon." She sighed and continued.

"I had one more dream that I can put words to. I was standing at the edge of the garden, gazing up at a huge bright moon. This moon filled a fourth of the night sky and was so close that I could see the lines and spots that scarred its surface. I knew that I was waiting for something but didn't understand what it might be. The sky darkened and the moon and stars shone bright; brighter than on any other night. And still I stood. The sky turned from black to blue to purple and then to pink. And still I stood. As the sky blazed to yellow I had to turn my eyes away to the land beyond my garden. Then I saw six figures emerge from the mountains. I couldn't make them out but as they moved closer, one faded from view and only five moved on. I cupped my hand over my eyes straining to see but the sunlight was too bright. As I peered at the figures, another faded from view. Then there were four. I searched for meaning but only questions came. I watched the four and they came closer still. And as I watched, you came forward. I saw you and my heart soared. It was you, Nariantha. You had come home. You and Jeon and two others had come home.

The dream grew brighter still and then faded altogether. I awoke with a clarity that I would see you at journey's end. I am confident of it."

We sat silently for a moment with grandmother looking at me with a mixture of love and curiosity. At last she spoke, "Take my hand, sweet one." Gently holding my hand, "Know that I love you."

"I do, grandmother. Know that I love you, too."

Jeon arrived to accompany grandmother and me to the Elder's meeting that was to take place at noon. Elder West had offered her garden as the meeting place and had set a fine table for the group. Provided were dried fruits, root vegetable stew flavored with oregano and thyme, two loaves of poppy seed bread, and pots of herb tea.

As we entered the garden, I took note of the faces assembled. All the Elders were now present, my grandmother the last to arrive. The six Masters were there, standing in small groups and talking softly to one another.

There were several men and women among the group that I knew to be village leaders who I have worked with, on and off, over the years.

On seeing Jeon arrive, two men called out and moved to join him. It was Adain Pedat and Ronnan Taraxa, Jeon's good and best friends. The three held a lifelong bond and truly enjoyed each other's company. They frequently hunted together. Adain was skilled with a bow and Ronnan's tracking skills were incomparable. It's said that he could track with his eyes closed... at night.

As I joined the group and made my greeting to those who received me, I happened to see, standing in the garden, my friends Serri and Sella Crass. I was happy to see them and I could feel that my face held a huge smile as I greeted them.

Serri and Sella are twin sisters. Sella has trained with the Master of Astronomy and Serri with the Master of Medicine. Both are adept in the art of cooking, fabrics, and gathering wild edibles from forests and shores.

"Good noon to you both, so happy that you're here!"

Together, smiling, they answered, "Nariantha, hello to you! You look well."

Nodding, I said, "Yes, surprising to me, I slept well and woke early feeling in good health."

Serri spoke, "We had a fitful night... by our own cause. We were so excited we could barley sleep."

Sella added, "The news that we have been chosen to go with you and Jeon on your journey delights us to no end."

Together they said, "This makes us both happy and honored."

I stood for a second, absorbing what the twins had just said and a feeling, almost of relief came over me. In the brief moments between last night's council meeting and now, when I've managed to think beyond today, into tomorrow, the unknown has managed to govern my thoughts. Nothing of consequence has shown itself. But now that I know Serri and Sella will be with me, I at last can see a bit further. I can see companions.

I threw my arms around them and hugged them close to me and felt their arms encircle me. We stood for several moments murmuring our joy and excitement to one another and then stood back looking from smiling face to smiling face to smiling face.

Serri said, "Adain and Ronnan have also been called to serve."

I looked around and caught Jeon's eye. He was smiling and raised his hand to me, then clapped both Adain and Ronnan by the shoulders, at which they turned to see what Jeon was looking at. They saw me, standing with Serri and Sella, looking back at them.

Immediately, our two small groups, gazing across the patio at one another, recognized that our final group was accounted for and acceptance and joy spilled across our faces.

The Master of Astronomy tapped his fingers lightly on the tabletop until he had our attention, and then said, "We are here to honor our chosen travelers and to prepare them for their journey. But first, let's commune over the humble repast that has been set out for us."

Smiling the Master said, "We'll all think better on a full stomach." He patted his stomach and looked around at who would agree with him. "I know I would!"

I heard twitters ripple though the group and then Master continued, "May the universe bestow its gifts."

The gathering replied, "Keep us worthy to receive."

We made our way to the tables to help ourselves to the noon meal foods.

The meeting lasted several hours. It broke up at dusk with Master of Art telling everyone to go home and rest, that our labors would start in earnest the next morning.

My mind was active from all the information and the myriad of discussions that took place at the meeting. Many, many things were talked over and I tried to bring them into order. Preparation for travel was critical. It had been decided that everyone would travel on foot and that everything needed for long-term survival would have to be carried in packs. It was too much to ask that a cart or a litter be used. Heavy and slow was not a wise choice. Meager shelters of leather, wool and rope, and basic tools and cooking utensils would be needed. Dried food stores and as much water as could be managed was paramount. Hunting and trapping would be done along the way and if successful, then the dried beans, dried pemmican, oatcakes, and berries that we carried would supplement. The bulk of our stores would be used sparingly and reserved, as much as was possible, for necessity. Our group would forage and hunt as we moved forward. It was the Elder's expectation that the Darkness did not reach on and on and that we would quickly find our way to a new home.

The villager leaders worked tirelessly to ensure that everything was as ready as was possible. Sleeping blankets and small tents were to be inspected and repaired if needed. A small kit was assembled containing needles, thread, patches of leather and cloth for quick repairs, and cutting knives. Cooking utensils were assembled that were to be distributed among the travelers so to spare any one member the full load. All the food items and water would be divided among them, also.

Jeon, Adain, Ronnan, Serri, Sella, and I were instructed to pack our personal belongings, being careful to pack warm season and cold season clothing. Surely we would travel beyond the territories known by the Genii and it was smart to be prepared for either hot or cold and anything between.

Jeon spent time sharpening his tools and fashioning pointed digging sticks to be carried as we walked. He inspected his tool kit and refreshed or replaced various tools as needed, being careful to add a new whetstone and a good amount of chert to its contents. He instructed Adain and Ronnan to add strips of leather and lengths of rope to their packs, for use in repairs or modifications as needed. All three men brought their hunting tools as well as tools for building and digging.

I spent my time gathering a variety of herbs and ointments into leather pouches and arranging them as neatly as I could into my gathering basket. The basket would fit nicely next to my share of the food stores and cooking pots and both would fit snugly under my bed and clothing roll. Everything was fixed to a bent birch wood frame that had a net woven across its sides. The packs and tools I would carry could be tied to this frame netting and the netting could be used to catch fish from a stream... if we had the luck to find a stream with fish.

The sky darkened to dusk. I was confident that I had packed just about all I would need and as I slowed down, I realized how bone tired I was. There was still one more day to make ready, so I left my chore and started to prepare a meal for grandmother and myself.

After we had eaten our meal and had cleaned the cooking area, we made ourselves comfortable among the cushions thinking to relax and wind down before bed. I had made us mugs of tea and we sat silently for a time.

Grandmother spoke, "This has been quite a day. The energy and expectations among the villagers and especially among the leaders has run very high. Everyone has wholeheartedly grasped the importance of this plan and are doing their utmost for its success." She sat smiling at her memory of the day's activities.

I looked into my mug of tea, turning it around once to watch the herbs float at the edges of the hot liquid. "Grandmother," I asked, "do you know the meaning of Gaia, the face in your dream?"

"Only vague notions and meanings, much like the dream

itself. However, the dream gave me cause to think on your journey, and while nothing clear comes from the dream, something clear came from my thoughts."

She reached into a pocket of her skirt and brought out an object and held it out to me. It was a talisman pouch made of supple suede.

I rolled it between thumb and forefinger and felt lumps and bumps that moved about inside. "May I open it?" I asked.

Nodding, grandmother said, "Yes. I thought about your journey and what you would need beyond the goods and tools you will carry in a pack and beyond the knowledge you have in your being. Each talisman has a purpose."

I brought out the contents of the pouch and laid them before me. There was a smaller pouch that made soft clinking noises as I handled it. I opened it and dumped its contents into the palm of my hand and counted eight small stones and crystals. Each of them had been polished smooth and shone with clarity. I recognized them all. A frosted white beryllonite crystal to find light in darkness. Tourmaline, black threads trapped in golden quartz, for strength and stamina. Fulgurite, also know as earth lightening, for purpose. Rutile, with its golden threads in a golden crystal, for inspiration. Clear quartz for healing. Labradorite, with its shimmering blue lights, for higher guidance. Orange calcite, as orange as a sunset and flecked with black, for courage and confidence. And peacock obsidian, a hypnotic black stone glowing with blue and green that moved in the depths of the stone, for lucid dreaming.

I contemplated the meaning of each and looked up at grandmother. She was smiling and said, "You will carry items for your body on your back. These items are for your mind."

"Thank you grandmother. Their meaning is not lost on me and I'm sure I'll have need of them as the days ahead are past."

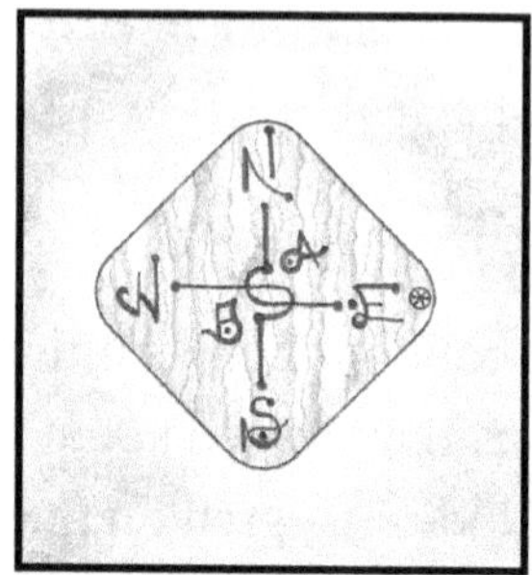

I held the stones a moment longer to feel their energy then returned them to the little pouch.

I noticed a small piece of oil rubbed and carved oak wood and picked it up to examine it closer. I saw right away that the markings burnt into its face were of the six Elders symbols copied from our village plaza. I rubbed it between thumb and forefinger before setting it down.

There was a small bundle among the objects that lay on the table. It was a rough spun material tied around with silver thread and wheat stalk fiber. I held it up for grandmother to see and fixed my face with a silent question.

"That my sweet, is a tiny dried flower bud from a Monarda plant. I dreamt of a Monarda bloom at your departure and thought it fitting to include it. It's wrapped in a piece of my smock that I cut from the place over my heart. It will tie us together even though we're apart."

I almost cried, my heart rang with joy. "Such a small token filled with meaning beyond words. I'll wear it next to my own heart."

Grandmother leaned over to me and patted my hand. "Everything's going to be fine. I know it." She pointed to the last object on the table.

It was a small length of parchment that had been rolled into a cylinder and tied with a piece of leather. I undid the strap and carefully unrolled it.

Grandmother spoke, "Elder Above made this for you. It's a star chart. She says you will be able to locate your directions by comparing her markings to the stars in your night sky."

"Thank Elder Above for me if I don't see her myself. This is very valuable and I appreciate all her work." I studied the small chart for some time. The translucent paper crinkled with my touch as I rolled it out to its full length. Holding it down with my fingertips, I started at the left side and moved my eyes across the pictures to the right. Ursa Major, representing north, was first, followed by Orion in the south, Gemini in the east and Cassiopeia and Taurus in the west. All were expertly drawn and carefully labeled. The scroll was adorned with symbols and decorative text. It was beautiful and thoughtful and I used a considerate hand to roll and tie it back up.

I placed all the talismans back into the black suede pouch, looked at it for a moment and then slipped the supple braided cord around my neck. "I feel that with this gift, I am ready to start the journey ahead. I feel safe and sure."

Grandmother picked up our tea mugs and stood up, stretched out her body, then stepped to the cooking area. "We should sleep now. Get rested for the work to come. Goodnight. Bank the fire before you go to bed and we'll see each other in the morning."

She kissed my cheek and stroked the hair from my face. "Sweet dreams."

The next day was a blur. There was a seemingly endless stream of well-wishers, friends, and neighbors who stopped by for a moment to congratulate and encourage me. Amid the chaos, I managed to complete my packing, although I don't know how. Throughout the morning, random thoughts would occur to me, *Take a warm jerkin* or *Wear three layers to start* or *Don't forget boots.* In the midst of the day, Elders and Masters came to offer advice and support, the most valuable of which was this: Stay true to the journey, your group, and yourself and everything else will come.

I slept fitfully that night, my dreams filled with dark and swirling images and scenes that made no sense.

I awoke before dawn and as I was rubbing the sleep from my eyes, I realized that the designated departure day had arrived all too quickly. In my anxiety I went to my grandmother's room and crawled under the covers next to her. She put her arms about me and I lay like a small child tucked next to her, feeling for the moment warm and safe.

I burnt that moment into my memory and hold it there still.

When the sun was full up and the air had warmed, everyone gathered in the center of the village. There was to be an informal salutation and then the small group would depart. It was expected that in the remaining daylight we would be able to make it to the foot of the mountains where we would camp for the evening.

Jeon and I stood with our travelling companions surrounded by the Elders and Masters and, really, the entire village.

Elder North raised his hand to indicate that he would speak. When the group had quieted he smiled and spoke, "We have done our best to prepare for this day. Surely there is nothing we have forgotten except to say," and turning to Jeon, Adain, Ronnan, Serri, Sella, and I, "that you take our hearts with you. May the universe bestow its gifts."

The six of us replied, "Keep us worthy to receive."

There was a moment of frenzied chatter from the villagers and then it seemed that without me knowing quite how, my pack was on my back and almost in a blur, we were standing at the edge of the fields, facing the village and saying our goodbyes. I almost couldn't let go of grandmother's hand but she gave it a squeeze and reminded me once again that everything would be fine.

Jeon and I took our places at the head of the troupe and as we stood, silently looking at all the faces turned our way, the only noises I could hear were those of a few insects in the field as they searched for a meal.

We stood, all of us, quietly, in a sort of trance. I turned to look at Jeon and watched as his eyes scanned the faces of the villagers. I noted the deep breath he took into his lungs and then let slowly out. We turned our backs to the group and Jeon took my hand and looked softly into my eyes. Raising his other hand into the air, he gave the signal and the troupe moved forward, following our lead.

We made the foot of the mountains and camped in a place that protected us from the winds that had started up at dusk. We built a small fire and ate sparingly. We were bone tired from the day's trek and fell to sleep within minutes of setting the lean-tos and wrapping up in our blankets.

The next day we climbed a mountain, one that looked to be smaller and less rugged than the others around us. Climbing was hard and frequently we had to go singly and in places our feet slipped on loose stones. It took nearly the whole day to climb and we made camp near the top in order to get a fresh start the next day.

The following morning, we broke camp and started to climb again. We made the peak within four hours and as Jeon and I pulled ourselves over the final ridge, the view from the top was disconcerting. At the bottom of the mountain we stood upon ran a vast expanse of more mountain peaks separated by the briefest of valleys.

Most of the days that followed fell into a sort of pattern. Wake, eat a light morsel of food with a mug of tea, clean the campsite, climb, rest, climb, eat a mid-day meal, walk and climb, set up camp, sleep.

Days turned into weeks and it seemed that the mountains would never end. They were steep, rocky and treacherous. Sella slipped on an unstable outcropping and almost fell. She was fortunate that she didn't injure her foot but did have a bruise that ached her foot for several days.

The mountains were cold and windy most days but always cold at night. We frequently slept huddled together under the lean-tos. Sometimes Serri, Sella and I would whisper quietly, talking about our day, that is, anything beyond climbing and gathering. And when the others had drifted off to sleep, I would find comfort in listening to the soft breathing and yes, sometimes muffled snoring, of my companions. Then I would drift, too.

Cooking pots were not as full as they were at first. The mid-day meal, the main meal of sustenance, was frequently made from whatever roots and grubs we had gathered from the rocky earth as we walked on. These, along with small bits of Cambrianese bark were mashed into a sticky pulp. Dried herbs or fresh herbs, if found along our path, were added to the mix to give it a palatable flavor. If baked in a lidded clay pot, the mashed pulp would harden into a sort of quick bread. If stewed with a bit of water, it would thicken to a pale, orange slurry. If you closed your eyes, you could almost imagine it was a hearty stew. Either way, quick bread or imagined stew, the meal would sustain our lives. To our delight, we found peppermint and dandelion in abundance and used them for tea. There was a profusion of low growing shrubs clinging to rocky slopes. They bore small fleshy berries that I could not identify. I ate a small handful and waited for any changes to come upon me. Not experiencing any, I allowed the others to eat small handfuls and watched them closely. We found no ill effects so gathered and ate as many as we pleased.

This was the last of our fresh finds along the way. As the season turned colder, less and less herbs and berries were found. The Earth was preparing for fall and the shrubs were more and more bare as their leaves turned red then brown and fell from their branches.

Most evenings after the camp was set, Jeon and I would sit together and talk about the day that had finished and plan the day to come. He would check supplies and I would track our direction of travel, careful to make notes in the hand-sized bound parchments given me by grandmother. She had been adamant that I not be remiss in my notes and observations so I took care in its keeping. Together, Jeon and I would consider the food reserves and the reliability of finding daily food sources against the number of days it would provide.

As our days went on, our stores looked less and less hopeful. At first we kept this news from the others, trying to spare them any discomfort, but soon realized that they were quick enough to grasp the meaning of meager rationing. From that point on, Jeon and I kept nothing from our companions except our private fears and misgivings about the journey.

One morning, it was mid-day, on what I thought to be the one hundred thirty fifth day of our journey, we made the crest of the climb we had been on since daybreak. The distance to the mountain peak was short and gently sloped upward through short dried grasses that shook in the light cool breeze and crunched under our steps.

Jeon advised that our curiosity would be satisfied if we stood at the top to see beyond, but that we would break for our mid-day meal in this place before moving on.

Everyone took their packs off and placed them in a relatively flat space that would serve as our resting area. Jeon and I were the first to stand at the top, followed by Adain, Ronnan, and Sella. Serri had lingered and was starting to retrieve a cooking pot from her pack.

The five of us stood transfixed by the view on the other side of the mountain. Sella called out to her sister and waved her to join us. Jeon lifted his hand to shade his eyes from the pale sun that hung low in the fall sky and scanned the vista from far left to far right before he spoke.

"It's long and it is wide and appears to be empty. I don't see trees. But look down there." He was pointing to a spot directly below us, at what appeared to be a cloud of dust rising from the valley floor.

Adain said, "It looks like a herd of running animals. I wonder what has frightened them so much as to make them run so fast."

Ronnan added, "I can't see anything clearly from this distance but maybe they just run from place to place. Jeon, do you recognize them?"

"No, but if we get a chance to hunt, it will mean meat in our bellies and a benefit to our stores."

I added, "Let's have a meal, rest and then climb down to the valley. We could find a place to camp and then," addressing Jeon, "you and the men could look around before it gets dark."

Ronnan said, "Yes, we might have time to track those animals."

Jeon nodded and said, "Ok. We'll start down after we break."

That night the men returned to camp with the news that they had lost the trail due to darkness but thought to go out again at first light.

Sella and Serri and I set up the lean-tos and had foraged enough roots and seeds to make a hot soup. Within an hour of finishing and clearing the meal items, all six of us were fast asleep, although I slept fitfully.

I woke before dawn and lay in my blankets alert to the sounds of this new place. I heard the wind as it moved through the low shrubs tickling the dried leaves that still clung to dormant branches. Light puffs of wind made the dry grass quake as it ebbed and flowed down the mountainside and out across the wide expanse of... nothing. I sat up to watch the cooling season sun rise in the east and was taken with the beauty of the pinks that came from the darkness and the pale disk of sun rays starting to lighten the sky.

Serri was the first to stir and she raised herself up to her elbows and looked around through bleary eyes. She spotted me sitting up and awake and smiled. Then, as if we were one, we got up, stretched out and set to making the morning tea. For break fast, Sella had added a small handful of oats to the remainder of last night's soup, along with a handful of mountain berries to sweeten it up. This along with herb tea was enough to get everyone going.

Before the men left to hunt, Jeon and I took a moment to get our bearings, gazing up and down the vast expanse. We had decided, early in the journey, to travel to the west. That direction now lay across the expanse. We had no idea how far it was to the other side and looking across to the small looking mountains that rose in the hazy distance, Jeon judged the trek across might take a week. I wasn't as sure. As I gazed out, the air seemed to shimmer and move as a gauzy curtain might in a light summer breeze. I did, however, spy a shorter mountain further down the range, where I thought climbing might be easier. We decided that that was our next objective.

Sella cleaned the food preparation items and I reorganized the backpacks to even the loads. Serri spent time repairing one of her shoe straps that had torn as she climbed through the mountain rocks.

The remainder of the morning was uneventful. The men were out less than an hour and on their return, told us that they were not able to track the animals as they had moved up the mountainside, leaving no tracks.

We began the day's trek later than usual but there didn't seem to be any harm in that. We walked in silence, my eyes scanning the ground for anything we might use. At one point I did see, for a moment, a flash of brilliance just steps ahead. And I saw, as I got closer, that it was an irregular shaped pebble so I picked it up. It was a piece of clear quartz that I know is used to promote healing. I held it in my hand as I walked, rolling it between my fingers and pressing it to my palm. When I thought to clear my hand, I slipped the little stone into my pocket.

For days our trek across the tremendous plane had been fairly uneventful, although we were happy to be out of the mountains and walking on flat ground. The sun shone down and we walked on. As the journey progressed, I started to lose all sense of time. Everything started to blur and if not for the sun replacing the stars and the dusk slowly cooling the afternoon air, I may not have known the passing of days.

Jeon started to worry that our trek through the vastness to the mountains beyond was taking too long and that our supplies might not last.

First, Adain twisted his ankle when the earth seemed to disappear from under his step. He had tried to bear up and hobbled as he walked but I could see that the pain was too much and decided that a day of rest was called for. I kept his ankle wrapped in warmed mud and made sure to gently move his foot every few hours to avoid stiffness.

Then, Serri and Sella returned from a short foraging trip and told me that a large flying insect had either stung or had bitten Sella. She had heard a loud buzzing just before a burning sensation had stabbed at her left shoulder. Neither she nor Serri had gotten a good look at the bug but both agreed that it was big and it was fast.

I examined the mark and saw that it had raised a big red welt that was by that time, surrounded by a dark red splotch. I had to poke at it, which caused Sella to wince in pain, but I determined that the large fast bug had indeed stung her. As I gently pushed on the welt, it oozed a clear liquid from a neat little puncture hole. I immediately fashioned a heated poultice from a bit of the starchy flatbread I was carrying and applied it, re-warming it over our campfire every few minutes. I thank the six gods that within four hours, the swelling had showed signs of improvement and by evening had almost returned to flesh color. However, Sella complained of a stiff and aching shoulder and a shooting pain down her arm for days afterward.

After two days in the same camp, we all became very restless and when Jeon suggested we move on, I could almost hear the cheers.

The next morning, we resumed our trek without a glance back.

Days and days and still more days passed. And while the mountains came closer, it was slow going. Our water stores were running low and our food supplies lower. We counted every step and foraged for grubs and small crawling creatures to sustain us. We grew weaker but still held out hope that we would reach the mountains soon and kept to our determination, as faded as that was becoming.

On the one hundred fifty fifth day of our journey, the twenty first in this vastness, Jeon decided that he and the two men would move on to test the distance and that the women would stay in camp. The men would travel with their hunting weapons and blankets only; it would be faster that way. They would return within two days no matter what they found so we were not to worry.

After the men left, we gathered dried fuel and started a fire but none of us had the energy to do much else. We sat around the fire wrapped in our blankets, not really speaking, not really thinking. Sella and Serri sat snug and after a short time, fell asleep.

I couldn't sleep. I sat staring into the fire, watching the flames dance about and listening as the fire caught hold of a dried twig and crackled as it moved along, consuming its fuel. As I looked deeper into the flames, I imagined figures moving about. Their movements mesmerized me. It was as if a form was trying to take shape but before it could, the fire danced on it, taking the opportunity with it.

As the fire hypnotized me, aimless thoughts flitted through my mind. *Did I make the right decision about our direction? Look what I have brought us to. For the first time during our journey, we are separated from the men. Our water is low, our food almost gone. We can't go on eating grubs. We will sicken and die. Oh, six gods…what have I done?*

No answers came.

It was past dusk when I roused myself. I thought to erect one of the lean-tos and gather our belongings around us for the night. The packs would provide a bit of shelter from the chilling air. Serri woke and came to help and did the best she could even though she moved as if in a daze.

Looking at her and her sister, I noted their pale and drawn faces and that both had lost weight. And I knew that looking at them, I was also seeing myself.

I let the fire die and crawled into the lean-to and wriggled up next to the girls, pulling my blanket around me to cut the chill. As I tucked and pinched the blanket tight, I was reminded of the times when I was a child trying to get snug in my bed. I was a bit frightened of the dark and thought to hide under my blankets so that anything bad, out there in the dark, wouldn't get me. If I couldn't see 'it' then 'it' couldn't see me. I now hoped that was true, out here in the vastness, with no real protection. I thought about my belief in myself, my grandmother's lessons, my two companions, and in the vibration of the universe and felt comfort in those things. After some time, I fell into a deep dreamless sleep.

When I awoke next, I was momentarily disorientated. My eyes winced in a bright light and for the briefest of instants, I thought that the moon had come too close to the Earth. I sharpened my mind and came fully alert. At once I grasped it. I had slept past sunrise and the dull light was not the moon but the cool fall sun.

Serri and Sella had been awake for some time, had started a fire, gathered more dried fuel and had warmed three sips of tea for us.

I greeted them, "Good morn. I'm happy we made the night without trouble." Serri handed me a mug and I took a swallow of tea. "I thought I heard noises, like the steps of large animals before I fell to sleep."

Sella said, "That may be. Earlier I was in that direction," pointing off to the south, "and noticed hoof prints in the dirt. All were pointing the same way so the animals were moving."

Serri added, "Maybe our great smell offends them!"

We laughed at that. It was good to hear the sound of our laughter. It was something that had been missing for many, many days.

The following two days were the same. We only ate what we could forage, to leave the stores for as long as we could. And to be safe, we never foraged out of sight of the camp.

Busying myself with digging roots, I came across two fleshy ones that I thought to smash up into a pulp and bake over the fire. But digging up the roots gave me the idea to dig deeper to see if I could bring up more of them. To my surprise, as I dug a hole a hand-width wide and maybe two deep, I found very moist soil. Sniffing at it told me it was clean, so I retrieved a cooking pot and a piece of cloth and managed to strain a couple mugs of water from the sandy earth. We dug two more holes and by the end of the day had filled our water skins, ate large portions of a hot thin soup, and sat, fully satisfied, drinking mugs of hot weak tea.

Toward the end of the second day the men returned. After the joy of our reunion settled down, we, all of us, chattered news and energy.

The men made the foot of the mountains after dark on the first night. At first light the next day, they saw that the mountains were sparse and rocky but had shrubs at their base and small trees further up. They marked the spot by piling up flat stones into a totem and ventured to the north, following the valley floor, in search of game. They saw the herd of animals way off in the distance but dared not veer too far off their path, so let it pass. On their return to the totem, they spied two birds.

Ronnan took one as it pecked the earth and Jeon the other as it took flight.

They saw our campfire that night. It was a tiny dot of yellow light way in the distance and Jeon said, taking my hand for a moment, that when they saw the fire, they knew we were all right.

They started back that next day.

When they presented us with the two game birds, scrawny as they were, they were a welcome sight. Moments after producing the birds, Serri started to clean them and Sella and I set up the cooking area.

We made a hearty stew from one bird along with dried beans and herbs and I put an oven pan in the fire to bake up my smashed root and seed bread. The other bird was roasted dry in a covered pan and added to our stores, along with the rendered fat that Serri mixed with flatbread crumbs so it would last for a couple of days.

We entreated the men to sit and rest and told them to drink as much water as they wanted.

When Serri, Sella and I finished the cleanup and refueled the fire, we joined the men to rest beside the fire before we slept.

As we wound down and the tension left our bodies, I found myself watching the fire's flames and again my mind spoke. *We seem fine in this moment, but it would be foolish to believe this will last and that hunger has been banished. If we continue on this journey we may die. I feel terrible when I look at my friends, pale and weak, to know that I am responsible. Should I bring this out to them? Should I speak my doubts?* I looked at the faces of my companions, my friends, shining yellow with firelight, everyone sleepy and lost to their thoughts. *No. This is not the time for me to speak my fear. I'll talk with Jeon in the morning. I'll see if he has doubts, then that would be the time…not now.*

I calmed my mind enough to go lay down and to sleep, but I tossed and turned and woke several times before the dawn came.

Over morning tea, Jeon and I talked.

Jeon spoke to me softly, "Nariantha. We've come a long way and some of us have suffered injury while all of us are near starved, but I think our journey may get better."

"What makes you think that, Jeon?"

"The mountains we are to climb, on our path west, don't look as barren and hostile as those we climbed to get here. And we found birds, something we did not see on the other mountains." He sipped at his tea and gazed westward, then continued, "We need to push on. The nights are getting colder and the mornings start with frost. Soon the storms will start and we should be far from here when they do."

"Ok. We have come a long way and I don't have a better idea of how to carry on. We'll clean the camp and start for the mountains. Maybe you'll find more birds?" I said hopefully.

"These mountains should be easier than the last." Jeon took the last swallow of his tea and rejoined the others.

I stood for minutes, staring at the mountains in the west. The mountains that stood in our path. I was a little upset with myself, that I hadn't told Jeon my thoughts, my fears. He seemed resigned to continue, as if thoughts of failure and possibly hopelessness had not occurred to him at all.

I rejoined the others after reconciling my thoughts… maybe Jeon had enough confidence in the journey for both of us.

The two days to the mountains were uneventful. Our meals meager, our conversation sparse. We were tired and losing strength but managed to climb a small part of the way up the mountain before making our night camp among the boulders where we hoped for a little protection. There was still enough dried brush for fire kindling and Serri managed to stew up some roots to give us a warm thin broth for our stomachs. Even though it was bitter, it was enough to put us in mind of food.

The next day we climbed. It wasn't too difficult at first. The mountain was low and long, not tall and steep like its neighbors. We made it up and over the top before we stopped for a mid-day meal. The wind had started up that morning and seemed to have gathered speed as it whipped through the valleys. The hard-packed earth and stones were as bare as if it had been cleared by hand. The wind had blown all the loose leaves and twigs… I don't know where… away.

Serri and Sella gathered fire tinder as they climbed, careful to pack it securely. The ground was so hard that I had broken my digging stick and had to use Jeon's metal digging spade to bring up roots and unearth beetles and grubs. I gathered roots when I could, thinking that each precious one was guarantee of a meal. One more day closer to our goal. One more day to be alive.

And I counted. Another day and one more day. The days in these mountains faded one to the other and this morning I had counted fourteen.

The mountains and the weather were taking a toll on every one of us. We were getting weaker by the day. Our food consisted of roots, dried leaves of bay and sage, and the occasional lizard or beetle.

It was bitter cold at night. We wore layers of clothes and huddled close under the lean-tos. In the mornings we scraped frost from the lean-to roofs to fill our water skins and tea mugs, although our mugs were only warm water as our herbs had run out days earlier.

One late afternoon as we climbed down a mountain side, Ronnan lost his footing on a ledge as stones crumbled away and the ledge boulder loosed from the mountain's grip and fell straight down, taking Ronnan with it. Serri and Sella, who had been behind Ronnan, both screamed in surprise and panic. I jumped with fright and turned in time to see Ronnan disappear from sight as he scrabbled for a hold, but found none.

Adain and Jeon had stripped their packs off and had sprinted to the spot where Ronnan had fell and peered over the edge. Jeon called out to Ronnan, who lay sprawled on the rocks some distance below.

"Ronnan! *Ronnan!!* Are you all right? Don't move, we're coming down to you."

Adain pointed to a tight path and both men started carefully down.

Serri, Sella, and I stayed at the edge watching. I realized that I held my talisman bag in a tight grip and prayed to the six gods that Ronnan would be fine before I loosed my grip just a bit. Sella was crying in an uncontrollable, muffled way, gulping air and sobbing. Her sister was trying to sooth her with shushing sounds and stood close with her arm around Sella's shoulder for support.

I looked at them with a wan smile and said, "He'll be alright, you'll see."

Then I looked back over the side and called out to Jeon, "Is he awake?"

"Yes, although in a lot of pain," he said.

Adain called up, "It looks as if Ronnan has a broken leg, just below his left knee."

I could feel panic starting to rise in my chest but pushed it down with a deep breath. I looked around for an easy way down and saw an opportunity, but before I started for it, I called down, "Don't move him."

I told Serri and Sella to stay with the packs, no sense all of us crowding down. I took my medicine bag from my pack along with a water skin and cautiously picked my way down to the men.

Ronnan was fighting to stay conscious and Adain was carefully holding his leg down in an attempt to hold it still and to stop some of the bleeding that trickled from the wound.

I meticulously looked at Ronnan's leg. It was broken. I could see a lump of tissue raised under the bruising skin.

"Ronnan. I have to touch your leg. It's going to hurt. I'm sorry."

Through gritted teeth, Ronnan said, "Ok, I'm ready."

I touched, as lightly as I could but as deep as I needed. *Thank you, six gods,* I thought. It was a clean break, the bone was shifted under the muscle and skin and I felt that I could manipulate it back into place but preparations were needed.

"Jeon, I'll need two, maybe three sturdy shrub branches about this long," holding my hands apart to give him an idea, "for a splint and cloth for bandages as well as leather straps to bind it with."

Jeon had been looking around and spotted a flat area off to the right. Pointing to it he said, "That spot looks as good as any for a night camp. Adain and I will climb up, get our packs and help guide the girls down. They can set up camp while we tend to Ronnan."

As I touched Ronnan's leg, he winced in pain and as I felt along behind it, he briefly cried out.

I touched his forehead, brushing his loose curls from his eyes, "You'll be fine, Ronnan. Can you hear me?"

He rolled his head and whispered, "Yes but by the six gods, the pain is overtaking me."

I said, "I need to bind your leg but before I start, I'll give you an herb potion to ease the pain."

The next hour moved slowly.

The camp was set up and a fire started.

I set Ronnan's leg, although it took me two tries to do it. On the first try, the bone slipped out before I could bind it in place but once I had one leather strip wrapped, the others neatly followed.

Ronnan passed out, I think from the herb potion and the pain. It was just as well because Jeon and Adain had to carry him down a short distance to the camp and the footholds proved to be unsteady causing the two men to jostle Ronnan in their efforts.

We got him situated in a bedroll with his left leg resting in a slightly raised position. Sella and Serri had put the lean-tos together around the fire, to provide the most protection from the wind for both the fire and us, capturing as much warmth from it as possible.

By that time it was dark and we were able to assess our situation more clearly, without all the stress and fear we had experienced earlier.

Sella stayed with Ronnan, watching him for signs of pain and periodically, gently raising his head to put a drop of water on his tongue.

The rest of us grouped around the fire and sipped at mugs of weak root and sage broth. The firelight made us appear as ghosts of ourselves. Our eyes shone dark in shadow and our skin pale and sick looking. Our thoughts... depressed, concerned, anxious.

I spoke, "Ronnan can not be moved for at least two days. His leg needs rest."

Jeon was staring into the fire when he spoke, "Two days. Adain and I will start out tomorrow to hunt game and look at the way ahead. We could all use a bit of a rest, we've been pushing hard."

Serri tossed more twigs onto the fire and poked it back to life. "Two days will give me time to look for winter berries and fleshy tubers. Will one of you let me use your digging spade while you're away?" She looked expectantly at Adain.

Adain immediately reached for his spade that he kept on his belt, and handed it to Serri. "Be careful, I've just sharpened the tip."

Serri smiled and said, "Thank you. I'll take care of it and I'll save the fattest root for you."

We fell silent and when the fire burned down, all went to

bed.

I had a dream last night. I dreamt I saw six lights on a mountainside. One flickered but steadied. I gazed up at the clear night sky and saw hundreds of bright stars, all clear on that cold night. The light on the mountain that had earlier flickered, burned so bright I had to shield my eyes. Then it rose slowly into the night sky. I stood watching, not in amazement but with great fear and was confused by this. Why should I fear a light off in the distance? Suddenly the light pulsed brightly one more time, almost to blind my eyes but I watched it steadily as it shot up and away into the firmament, taking a place among the stars.

I woke at first light and immediately set the fire. By the time I set stones to heat, the men were stirring. My dream faded from my mind as the sky grew lighter and I had all but forgotten it by the time Jeon came to sit by my side.

"Adain and I will leave as soon as we're ready. We should return within two days, maybe as long as three but in either case, we should continue on. Do you think Ronnan will have recovered enough by then?"

I was staring into the fire, silently planning the next two days when I heard Jeon's question. I looked up at him so that he could see the concern on my face, then answered, "I'll see to him and we'll do the best we can." I took a sip of broth, "The break was clean and Ronnan is strong. We'll do the best we can."

I felt Jeon's eyes upon me but I went back to staring at the small fire with its dancing yellow flames.

Jeon set his mug down and got up and I roused my thoughts

and my body and set about my day.

I checked on Ronnan and saw that he was still sleeping. I felt his forehead and noted a fever was upon him.

Sella came to his side with a mug of cooled broth and said, "The fever came in the night. I've kept chilled cloths on his head and given him drops of water. It's a steady fever, it hasn't gotten worse, although it hasn't gotten better, either."

We sat for a minute looking at Ronnan's face. It was distorted as if he was in pain and his chin moved slightly as he clenched and unclenched his jaw. No doubt he was in a fever dream. All I could hope was that he won his dream battle and woke soon.

Sella said, "Leave a bit of dream tea and I'll see he gets a few drops of it if his fever dream gets worse. I'll watch him so you can do your other tasks."

"Thank you, Sella. Call me if he wakes. I'll return in a couple of hours to check his bandages."

Serri was by the fire watching Adain and Jeon ready their gear. She looked up hopeful at my joining them and asked, "Is Ronnan better?"

Both Adain and Jeon stopped their activities and turned to listen as I answered, "Ronnan is fighting a fever dream. It's up to him and the six gods and time will tell if he has the strength to win. Sella and I will watch over him and see what we can do to ease his battle."

Jeon said, "Ronnan has a strong heart, I have no doubt he will prevail. Nariantha," he called to me softly, "Adain and I are leaving now. Is there anything we can do for you before we go?"

I shook my head and looked at him with thanks in my eyes

and said, "No Jeon. We'll be fine. Travel safe and may the six gods protect you and bring you back soon."

I stepped forward to hug him and he held me tight for a moment before holding me at arm's length, looking steadily into my eyes with conviction, and said, "Take care and we'll be back by the third day."

I hugged Adain then stood watching them as them walked away.

After they had made their way down the mountain and had disappeared from view, I turned to Serri, who was standing silently beside me looking after the men, as I had been doing, and said, "We need to dig for water and roots and collect tinder for firewood."

She nodded, turned to look over the camp surroundings, glanced at Sella, as she tended to Ronnan, and started to work.

Serri and I worked through two days, seemingly energized by determination. The fuel for the fire was plentiful and soon we realized that we could gather water by collecting frost from the lean-to roofs each morning. We found a patch of mountainside where two white oak trees huddled among the boulders and collected two baskets of acorns some of which we immediately roasted. Some we ground into a paste and others we just ate right down until we were full. I filled our stores with handfuls of raw and roasted acorns pleased that we now had something to count on.

I tended Ronnan after having to shoo Sella from his side. She was reluctant to leave him but she needed time to eat, get some air, and after filling up on roasted acorns, she felt calm enough to sleep, undisturbed for two hours. She looked better when she returned, bleary eyed but better.

On the morning of the third day as we changed Ronnan's bandage, we noted that the red fever of his leg was cooler and we were hopeful that he was mending as we expected. His fever dream subsided as well and his eyes fluttered open as I was tending his leg. His soft, broken voice startled me.

"By the six gods... I'm alive."

Sella was overjoyed. "Oh, Ronnan, you're back! This is good!!" Then turning, she called, "Serri! Ronnan's awake!"

Serri rushed in and we three grouped around Ronnan each with a huge, wide smile across our face. Ronnan grinned weakly as he looked from one to the other and then spoke, "Tell me the news of the living." Then dropped his head back onto the bedroll, looking to me.

I said, "You have been fevered and dreaming for three days. The men are away and will be back tonight. Sella has been taking care of you and all of us are tending to the camp."

I felt his forehead and said, "You're not well yet and you need to rest. Do you feel that you could eat something?"

Ronnan answered, "Maybe broth and a drink of water."

Sella was on her feet before anyone could move. "I'll get it, won't take but a moment."

I leaned closer to Ronnan, "She has barely left your side these last three days." He smiled and I went on, "When you've eaten, please sleep. It will help you heal faster."

"I promise. I'll heal faster." Ronnan touched my hand and said, "Thank you." Then yawned and started to shut his eyes.

I left him in Sella's caring hands and returned to my tasks.

The men returned that evening as anticipated. News about our path forward wasn't that good. They had spied what promised to be an easier route through one part of the mountains although they couldn't tell how far it went. The disappointing news was that there were still more mountains.

I was rather hoping to hear that with little effort we would be free of them. I imagined the mountains ending with fields in spring bloom and my face warmed by the sun.

On a better note though, the men hunted small game and brought back one very thin brown hare and two thin birds that were of a kind I didn't recognize. Jeon also handed me a fat root and some dried leaves, telling me that they were abundant ahead. I knew the root by its twisted shape and pungent smell when I scraped its flesh with my thumbnail.

"You didn't eat any of this, you or Adain?"

"No. Not knowing what it was, we didn't dare. Bad?"

I answered, "Very. This root is from the cytisus bush. It causes sickness in the stomach, sometimes vomiting, sometimes death. The leaves are knotweed. A good sign that a root and seed food source might be available soon."

I crushed the dry leaves and tried to smell the familiar aroma of chestnuts but the leaves were too dry and smelled of nothing.

In spite of a steady downpour of cold rain, everyone slept soundly that night, exhausted from three days of stress and toil. Even Ronnan slept peacefully.

The next morning we struck camp and prepared again for travel. Ronnan had gotten to his feet with the help of Sella and made his way to sit by the fire and take a mug of leftover stew that Serri made from one of the little birds. He swore to the six gods that he could travel and insisted that we should not delay because of him.

Adain fashioned a walking stick out of a manza branch. It was stout and strong and would aid Ronnan greatly.

None of this gave me confidence. Although Ronnan was up and alert and hobbled fairly quickly with the aid of his walking stick, I had doubts that he could keep it up for long stretches at a time and voiced my concern to Jeon. He promised to break up our trek more often to allow Ronnan to rest.

Jeon spoke with Ronnan, "It's so very good to see you up and around, my friend."

Ronnan smiled and lightly patted his manza stick and said, "Nice to be up and around, thanks to the women and their healing knowledge."

Sella blushed.

Jeon looked around him. The camp had been packed and the site cleaned. Everyone stood with their packs on, although Ronnan's was considerably lighter than the others. We had divided his load so as not to tax his leg too much.

Jeon asked, "Are we ready?"

Adain said, "Aye."

Serri and Sella spoke together, "Yes."

And I said, "Yes, Jeon. Lead the way."

We climbed down off of the mountain we had stayed on for three days. It had become somewhat familiar to me during our time there, but I had no regrets about leaving. We stopped every two hours to give Ronnan a rest from his leg and he stayed positive and smiled when we asked how he felt but I could tell he was sore and tiring quickly.

After we ate our mid-day meal, I gave Ronnan a drop of prickly lettuce herb tea, taken from my healing bag, and had him lay down while Sella and I changed his bandages. He fell asleep, which I wanted him to do, and woke in an hour feeling much better.

That day and the ten days that followed it were very hard on Ronnan. He did the best he could to keep pace during the day but fell to sleep almost within seconds of our stopping for meals or night camp.

On the fourth day out, it rained. Well, I called it rain even though it was a freezing combination of rain and snow. Travel became hazardous as the rain-snow had frozen in the frigid night air, turning the ground unsure under our steps.

My feet were stiff with cold and we huddled close to our little fires trying to warm movement back into our limbs.

The days were gray and windy and sometimes brought icy rain. We slogged through, doing the best we could. It was almost two weeks to the day that we had started travelling again after Ronnan broke his leg that a fever came upon him. It came fast, too. At mid-day meal he was fine but by the next rest break, he looked flush and complained of weakness.

Sella motioned for me to touch his forehead. He was burning. With my weather-chilled hand still on Ronnan's fevered brow, I called out to Jeon.

"Jeon." He stepped closer so I needn't shout. "Ronnan is burning with fever. I don't think he can go further today. We need to stop here."

Jeon looked about before he said, "Let's set camp over there," pointing off to the right and just below where we stood. "It looks like it may offer protection from the cold wind and rain."

We hastily set the lean-tos and Sella and I moved Ronnan into the center. We managed to get his wet boots off and I got a look at his leg. It was not good. I changed the bandage and gave Ronnan a small cup of dream herbs and left him only when he had fallen to sleep.

The only merit that came from the weather was that it gave us a source of clean water and it cooled the cloths that Sella and I laid on Ronnan's brow in our efforts to reduce his fever. Beyond that, the cold and the gray and the rain were debilitating.

I dozed on and off during the night and was hovering between dream and wake when a flash of lightning lit the sky followed by a deep rumble of thunder that rolled through the mountains, seemingly straight at us.

The ground shook in response and I shot awake. Serri and Sella inched closer to me and lay there wide eyed but neither said a word.

Jeon and Adain were also awake and Jeon spoke to us, "I think that thunder clap signals a storm and it could be a big one. We shouldn't stay here any longer than we have to. We need to find better protection."

Adain said, "Maybe you and I could scout ahead to see if things are better."

"Yes, that's a good idea. It's still before first light but we'll go as soon as possible."

There was a silence, punctuated by the howl of the rising wind, the Jeon said, "Nariantha, we'll be out a couple of days. Tend to Ronnan and we'll do the best we can to find shelter up ahead."

I nodded then looked at Ronnan. He was a bit fitful in his fever but otherwise quiet. His fever was still high, so I moved to give him a drop or two of water.

We fell silent, all of us awake and listening to the storm starting to brew off in the distance.

I silently counted how many days we had been on this journey… one hundred ninety two. And I prayed to the six gods that we would be given many more with which to complete our goal.

Ronnan died the next night. The fever took him. He put up a good fight but it was too much for him to struggle against and in the end his strength left him and then his spirit followed.

Sella took it the hardest of us all. Serri and I were greatly saddened and moved to tears but Sella shook with a deep grief. I believe she had given her heart to Ronnan and a piece of it had gone with him into eternity.

Sella, Serri and I sat vigil for hours only leaving to make tea or stoke the meager fire.

Adain and Jeon were away when Ronnan passed but they returned as promised. They knew right away what had happened and needed no words spoken. They sat with us for a while and then Jeon started to recite a remembered canto he had learned as a child.

"Surely things must come to pass, so hold your truth to light. There it shines for all to see, and all to know it's right."

Sella started to rock gently as Jeon spoke, her eyes fixed on Ronnan's now peaceful face.

Jeon added, "May the six gods show you the way Ronnan. You were a good friend to me and I will mourn your leaving."

Silent tears ran down my face as I sat, cross-legged, leaning on Jeon for support. Adain moved to sit between Sella and Serri and held them both close. We sat together, in the gathering gloom of night, with our private thoughts, until a cold wind gusted through the lean-to, stirring us to our chores.

The next day we laid Ronnan below a rubble of rocks and stones and any loose soil we could scrape from the hard frozen earth. Adain fashioned a pile of flat rocks into a totem to mark Ronnan's grave and we stood for a long time staring at the place until Jeon called softly, "It's time. We must be away."

His words gave us momentum and we all moved to follow him.

Later that day the storm hit us hard. The sky turned dark and the lightning flashed across the heavens. The icy rain started as a few drops but as the wind came up, it drove it down harder and harder until we could barely see a few feet ahead.

We slogged on until nightfall then huddled together, packs

and all, under blankets and tucked as far into a rocky outcrop as we could get.

The rain let up before the dull gray of the new day appeared. We were almost soaked though and stiff from the cramped night. Jeon and Adain were the first to rise and looked about. Adain stepped a few paces away but returned without prompting.

I had a small loaf of dried seed bread in my pack that I now brought out. There was no hope of a fire and tea so I broke the crust into portions and handed them around.

At first, Sella slowly shook her head, declining the offer, but I tapped her shoulder lightly so that she would look at my face.

"It's not for you to say 'no'. It's for you to do as I bid." I looked at her with concern and a faint smile then said, "Please eat this bread. It's not much but it will get us further."

She tightened her lips into a thin line but nodded her thanks and took the crust from my hand.

It's been seven days since Ronnan's grave. I can barely remember any of them. One gray day into another, one painful step in front of another, and one cold mountain leading to another.

My mind cried to the six gods, *How far to the end? Where is our new home?* And after more steps, *Grandmother, I'm lost and I'm afraid. I don't dream. Oh, I can barely remember your face.* And still I trudged on.

My weary steps slipped on a stone causing me to quickly regain my balance and focus my eyes. I was back in the Here and Now. It was cold and it was windy, but the rain had stopped and it was still light enough to see clearly. I took a deep breath, hoping it would revive my mind and as I lifted my head to exhale, I spied a dark black hole in the side of the mountain, about one hundred paces above us.

"Jeon!" I called out. "Look," I said, pointing to the spot.

We stopped walking and all looked at the black spot that stood out against the dark gray stone and earth.

Adain was the first to climb. Serri, Sella and I took our packs off and sat down, watching Adain and now Jeon, climb up.

They reached the spot, hesitated for a brief moment then disappeared from sight. They were gone and then they were back and waving for us to come up.

As I climbed the side of the mountain, I instinctually picked up bits of branches and sticks that littered the ground. By the time I reached the cave opening, my arms were full of fire tinder.

The men had gone back inside and I could hear them talking.

Adain said, "This is a huge space, see how the light fades further back? I wonder how big it really is."

Jeon said, "Let's be sure there's no danger before we settle, we don't want any surprises to jump out of the dark."

Upon hearing this, I turned to Serri and Sella and said, "We should wait here by the entrance until we know it's safe."

The three of us stood, bone tired, at the entrance watching the men move cautiously into the gloom at the back of the cave. When their eyes adjusted to the dark, they moved further in. I could see that both were moving slowly and both had their knives in hand, and after a slow moment, they faded into the darkness.

Jeon called to us, "Everything's fine. The cave is empty of wild beasts." Then he and Adain strode back to us.

"The cave ends twenty paces beyond the light. I trod upon debris that crunched as I stepped. I think it was loose sticks and dried leaves."

Adain added, "The ground is dry back there, also. We should be able to see it when we've built a fire."

This is when I realized I was clutching the bundle of dead branches I collected on my climb up. I had forgotten about them as I stood at the alert for danger. I said, "I have firewood but it's wet and won't light." I then dropped by bundle where I stood.

Jeon said, "I'll see if I can find tinder in the back of the cave."

Adain added, "We should build the fire further back, away from the opening where it's more dry."

I took my pack off and said, "I'll try to get a fire going." And turning to the girls, said to them, "I know you're tired, but we should gather as much fuel as we can before the storm comes."

As if my words were heard by nature, a low, long rumble of thunder rolled through the valleys just a short way off.

Sella said, "I'll dig for roots while there's still light." And with that, both girls took off their packs. Sella retrieved Adain's digging tool and both stepped out and to work.

I turned to look back at the darkness and heard the men rustling around. I stepped carefully as my eyes adjusted to the dark and soon found myself standing next to Jeon.

"There's sticks and leaves and I've uncovered the dried

waste from an animal. Looks like a small carnivore may have used this cave at one time. Look," he said, turning a pile of dry leaves with his foot, "there are small bones here, too."

Adain stopped his rummaging and said, "That's hopeful. I think I'll go hunt. There may be a chance at finding game in this area and I'll return before dark."

Jeon said, "Be mindful of the coming storm."

"Thank you, I will."

Adain gathered his bow and left.

Jeon and I were alone. I said, "It'll be nice to have a fire, my feet and fingers are nearly frozen."

Jeon straightened his back and looked at me. "The storm may force us to be here a couple of days. We should prepare for that, if we can."

"After I get a fire going and we've rested for awhile, I'll look over our food stores to see how long they will last." I was sorting the dried twigs and thought to build a fire ring from the loose stones that littered the cave floor.

"Jeon. Would you try to find water for us? Maybe a patch of ice caught in the rocks?"

"I can do that, I'll take a cooking pot with me." Before he left, Jeon turned to me and said, "Nariantha, will you be alright?"

I smiled, looked around the darkening cave and said, "I'll be fine."

The next four hours were filled with chores. I got a fire started and moved the wet wood closer so that it might dry out. Serri came and went three times with additional armloads of branches and kindling and Sella found a pot full of roots. She came back from her foraging very excited.

"Look what I found tucked deep into a rock crevice!" She pulled a bunch of greenery out of her trove and held it out to me. "It's stonecrop! And it's alive!"

She chattered on excitedly. "I looked around for more but couldn't find any. We should eat good tonight!"

"Yes, this will fix up our root stew very nicely."

When she had calmed herself, she looked around the cave, and then said, "I'll help here. I'll unroll the blankets and lean-tos so they can dry out if needed, then I'll come and help you."

Eventually, everyone came together around the fire. Adain had brought back one winter-skinny hare and Serri and I prepared it into a root and stonecrop stew. After eating and resting, we all just faded into sleep. It was nice to be warm and fed and seemingly safe.

The next morning felt almost normal. Well, except for the fact we were in a cave, in a mountain, many miles and many months from home.

After tea and a bite of cold stew, we left the cave to spend the day hunting and scavenging to shore up our supplies.

The weather was starting to change again and after two days of very little rain the sky and the clouds were turning darker. It was just a matter of time. This put a level of urgency on all of us and we did the best we could to lay in fuel and food.

Thunder had been rumbling almost continuously since dawn and big, heavy raindrops were starting to fall just before dusk.

Again, as evening came on and we sat resting from the day, one by one, the others dozed and nodded and finally gave in to sleep.

But my mind would not rest. I counted the days... two hundred and one and still we have not found a new home. I wondered how many more days did we need? How many more days will we survive? I stared at the flames before me and thought that tomorrow I should check the food stores again.

I fell into a fitful sleep. I dreamt we were chased from the cave by something fearful. We ran into the night without any of our belongings. Harsh noises followed us, snapping and wild. Then lightning struck. I could hear it crackle and smell its acrid odor in my nostrils and I cried... We're going to die... All of us are going to die!

My eyes shot open and I could feel my heart beating against my chest and just then a bolt of lightning flashed across the cave. It was followed by a rolling boom of thunder that seemed to crack the sky. Then I heard the rain pouring down.

My first thoughts were of my dream. I had the distinct feeling that my dream foretold the future and I believed it. I reminded myself that it was only a dream but that thought did not relieve me. *How can I stop this? I have no power to save us. No one does. What will happen when the food is gone?* I clutched the talisman pouch that hung about my neck and prayed. I prayed to the six gods to take us fast, that we wouldn't be made to linger and suffer pain.

The rain was coming hard and I got up from my bedroll and walked to the cave opening. Water was pouring down the mountainside and sheeting across the opening but was continuing on down the side. *At least we won't drown,* I thought. Then I set my jaw and shook my head in derision at how my mind had been running.

The storm raged for the next three days forcing us to stay inside. We busied ourselves mending our clothes and seeing to our stores. Adain and Jeon took care of their tools and sharpened their blades.

On the fifth day, Sella told Serri that she wasn't feeling well, that her stomach pained her. After Serri and I talked, we decided to give Sella a mug of herb tea and have her lay down.

She dutifully drank the tea but almost immediately she made for the cave opening only seconds before it came back up. We helped her to bed and she slept for an hour before waking. She said the pain was letting up and she would be better after more sleep.

Serri was worried and watched her sister closely. We had no idea what could be wrong with her. She had eaten what we had eaten and drank the same water. We were fine but she was ill. It had to be something else, but what?

Serri and I took turns watching Sella and on the second day, she showed signs of a fever and had started to cough. I gave her a small dram of Willow Bark tea which she took without complaint, then laid down and went back to sleep. I thought, *my remedies have no effect, I'm losing her, I am unable to stop the fever and don't know what else to do.*

Jeon left the cave to hunt and was gone about two hours before he returned, half frozen, but without any game. The next day he went out again, determined. This time he returned with two small rodent-looking creatures that, as I looked at them, made me uneasy. I wasn't sure we should eat them but held my tongue until I could look at them closer.

The storm shifted from rain to sleet during the day and the air inside the cave chilled quickly. This aggravated Sella's cough and in turn, her coughing seemed to make her fever rise. She slept a lot and ate almost nothing. Serri managed to get a few drops of broth into her but otherwise she refused everything else. All we could do was watch her and keep her warm.

Sella got much worse during the next two days. Her fever was burning her up and her sleep was fraught with the thrashings of nightmares. Serri would not leave her and often I would see tears on her face.

I took the stones and crystals from my talisman pouch and searched for answers. I held the labradorite stone tightly in my hand and listened for guidance. *Six gods, help me to help Sella.* I remembered the little clear quartz stone I found on my path weeks ago and retrieved it from my pocket where it stayed all this time. Healing. This I placed under Sella's neck roll along with my hope that it would work. I took the little stone of orange calcite and rolled it between my fingers letting it shine in the firelight.

Taking a seat next to Serri and putting my arm around her shoulder, I leaned close and held up the orange stone for her to see.

Her sad eyes looked at the stone and for a moment I thought some of her worry diminished. She said, "For courage."

I nodded and pressed the stone into her hand. "This is for you. It may help you on this path. Sella would want you to be strong right now."

Serri took the little stone, held it tight and fell into silent tears.

I left her to her prayers and her grief and returned to the fire to sit with Jeon and Adain. Both men looked to me with questions in their eyes but all I could do was slowly shake my head 'no'.

No words were needed. We felt terrible about Sella falling ill but no one felt worse than me.

How can I have studied herbs and healing and now, when I need it the most, I fail? I sat with my elbows resting on my knees holding my head in my hands. *First Ronnan. I managed to set his leg but it didn't heal properly. What could I have done to cure his fever?* I gazed into the flames hoping to find the answer but none came. *And now Sella. Oh, six gods tell me what to do! Show me how to heal my friend.* I wiped a tear from my eye. Then a thought came into my mind that would not leave. *It's me. The six gods are punishing me. Ronnan and Sella suffer because of me. I have no skill to heal. I have only fear and hope and both come to nothing.* These words stuck in my mind and the more I heard them the more depressed I became.

On the eleventh day in this forsaken cave, Sella died. She woke briefly from her fever and spoke to Serri in a hushed, dry voice. I moved to go to her and watched as Serri wrapped her arms around Sella, whisper something into her ear, and then sob uncontrollably as Sella slipped away. It was snowing that day.

We sat vigil, as was custom, and buried Sella under rocks

and snow about five paces outside the cave opening. Jeon and Adain built a totem and Serri did her best to embellish the grave saying that it should be special.

The day was crisp and clear although the clouds were heavy and gray and threatened more storms to come.

Adain and Jeon went hunting; I think they wanted to be quiet with their thoughts. Serri and I sat by Sella's grave for a time, quietly talking about our best memories of her. When the light started to fade, I gently urged Serri to come inside and share tea with me.

Shortly thereafter Adain and Jeon returned with a skinny hare and two more rodent-looking creatures. I think these ugly little things are related to the pocket gophers that are found around our village.

Serri and I quietly set about making a meal as the men sat by the fire.

Later that night the wind came up almost from nowhere. It had started snowing earlier and the wind now whipped the snowflakes about in frenzy. Gusts blew snow through the cave opening but within an hour had made a sort of snow barrier that served to insulate us from the chilled night winds.

This kept up for days, leaving nothing for us to do but wait it out.

As the days wore on my thoughts often returned to our problems, but more specifically, my problems. I wrestled between 'what could I have done" and 'there's nothing I could have done.' Each side winning briefly before the other overtook it. The more my mind fought with itself, the more depressed and disengaged I became. Waking, eating, and sleeping all seemed reflexive and more and more as the gray days continued, seemed pointless.

One night, as I stared up at the cave's dark ceiling, I counted the days... two hundred and fifteen. And what to show for it? Two friends gone and three companions and myself trapped in a cave by a terrible winter storm. *Such a waste,* I thought.

Then a sound I thought at first to be thunder, started a low, distant rumble. Quickly I realized it was not thunder and fear shot through my body. Before I knew what I was doing, I was standing, calling to the others.

"Jeon wake up! *Everyone get up!!*" The noise was building and I stared about, wide-eyed and frantic.

Serri woke and yelled, "What is it?" And reached for me.

Adain was on his feet and Jeon had gotten up on one knee as he tried to stand but at that second, the floor shook, knocking Serri and I off balance. We clutched desperately to each other but I was brought down to my knees, not being able to keep my footing.

The floor jerked violently to one side, knocking us all off our feet onto the ground and then quaked steadily for what seemed to be an eternity. Small rocks fell from the ceiling and a dusting of dry dirt with it. The mountain groaned as if in pain.

I heard Adain call out, "By the six gods, what is this?"

Then all was quiet. We stood up in shock and Jeon said, "Everyone be still until I finish." And moved to build the fire back up so we could see what damage had been done.

We got our first look when Jeon held a burning stick up high over his head to throw light into all the corners.

Right away, I noticed how many rocks and how much earth

had fallen from the ceiling. It frightened me to see how thick it had covered the floor and I felt fortunate that no one was hurt or that the damage was not any worse.

It was then I noticed that the back wall of the cave had slumped down into a mound of large stones and powdery dry earth to reveal a dark space beyond.

The floor shook again slightly. We froze in our steps staring at each other, expecting the worst but it passed.

I took another burning stick from the fire and made my way to the back wall. Carefully kneeling on the mound of rocks, I peered through a small opening into the beyond. It was dark. I lowered the torch to the opening and what I saw took my breath.

There, in the light of the torch, I saw flashes of brilliance like the shimmering of bright stars across the black expanse of a wide sky.

I marveled at the sight for a moment, all my thoughts and worries faded to nothing. I could hear the others moving about behind me and could hear the noises of the storm raging against the front of the cave, but none of that concerned me. It all seemed far away, as in a dream. I could not take my eyes from the sparkling stars.

Then a thought came, *I must get closer.*

"Jeon, something is here. Help me uncover it."

"What is it, Nariantha?"

"I'm not sure. There's a space on the other side of this dirt wall." The burning stick was turning to a red ember but shed enough light to show Jeon what I was talking about.

I said, "I want to go in."

Serri and Adain joined us and Serri was bent down peering

through the small opening. She said, "I think we can safely move this mound of rocks to make the opening big enough to crawl through."

She started tossing the smaller rocks aside and then Adain and Jeon started moving the larger, heavier stones. I retrieved two more burning sticks, carefully wedging them upright where I could and helped scoop dirt aside.

It took some time to clear the pile of rocks from the opening and create a space large enough to get through. We were weary and dirty when we finished but one by one we went through. Jeon and Adain brought torches to help light the room.

It was a beautiful room, like no other I've ever seen. Adain measured off the space, saying it was fifteen paces long and nine paces wide.

The first thing I noticed was that the walls were made of the same jasper stone as the large central boulder in our village square and were carved floor to ceiling with fantastical symbols and images.

I scarcely remembered to breathe as my eyes moved around the room watching as the light danced with sparkling inlaid stones. In one part of the room, a long, crystallized cone extended downward from the ceiling almost meeting another cone that rose up from the floor. Water dripped from the end of one to the top of the other and I put the tip of my finger into the liquid then touched the tip of my tongue. Oh, it tasted very bad and smelled worse. It was clear but it wasn't water.

"Look," said Serri. "I know this symbol for female in an arch of sunflower petals. It means 'light'."

Jeon was looking closely at a carving and said, "I don't

recognize any of these symbols."

Adain added, "Most of them, no, but here's one." He held a torch closer and said, "It's the sign for the constellation Taurus."

Serri was with him, looking closer. "It's marked with bits of amber," and looking at Adain, "see how the torchlight makes them glow?"

The star room presented more questions than answers and after an hour of all of us being in there with torches burning, the air seemed thin and close.

It was still the middle of the night and once our fear of the quaking mountains wore down and the excitement about the star room eased, we started to feel our lack of sleep and slowly made our way back under the lean-tos and to bed.

I didn't think I could sleep with my mind so full of events, but even the howling winds of the ever-present snowstorm couldn't prevent it. As soon as my head was down and my eyes closed, I fell into a black dreamless sleep.

The next morning, after a bite of starchy seed bread and a mug of tea, I talked with Jeon.

"I can't stop thinking about the star room and I feel myself being drawn to it." I sipped my tea adding, "I can't explain it. It's just a feeling that I can't put words to."

Jeon said, "I don't think any of us will stop thinking about that room but I also don't think the rest of us are as compelled as you are."

We sat quietly for a minute.

"It's a mystification that has grabbed my mind and my spirit," I said. "The room holds answers and if I look close enough, I should find them."

Jeon smiled at me and held my eyes for a short moment, then said, "The storm is keeping us here and there's little we can do about that. You're free to spend as much time as you need in the star room."

I handed him my empty tea mug and said, "Thank you," and stretching myself up, scooped up a burning stick from the fire and stepped toward the star room.

"I'll build a small fire for light. Call me when you need me."

I spent all my waking time in the star room. The others came and went with Serri staying with me the longest. She would sit quietly for long periods gazing at the walls.

After three days of looking and studying, I found that the star patterns were not just a bunch of random pictures but indeed, formed a concise map.

I found Ursa Major, a very familiar star pattern that was made out of trigonic quartz, so very beautiful in the firelight. I carefully scanned the area moving around to its right, and among the many symbols, some known to me, I found the constellation Gemini. That made two points in the night sky I knew: North and East. This was exciting and I hurriedly searched for Orion in the South and Taurus in the West.

Slowly a map of the night sky became clear to me. It encompassed the entire room and was made up of the constellations I know and of many that I did not. All of them had been carefully carved into the jasper walls and all stunningly adorned with their power stones and crystals.

I found vanadinite, tourmaline, ruby, and rain forest jasper.

When I found the fire agate, the stone of my grandmother, I put my fingers on it and silently called out to her, telling her I felt she was with me.

The most thrilling symbol I found, among the stars and the gods, was an exact replica of the carved oak talisman I carried in my pouch. At first I couldn't believe it and fetched a stick from my fire to hold close so that I might see details. I took my oak talisman and held it up to compare, and, yes, it was exact. North, South, East, West, Above, and Below, complete with a faceted fire agate situated neatly in the 'E'.

That night as I sat with Serri, Jeon, and Adain, I talked about all I had discovered and what I thought it meant. They asked questions and at one point, we went into the star room so I could point to different symbols or show how the map was drawn.

"I think the most interesting point may be all the symbols that we have in common with what's pictured here on these walls." I held up a torch and pointed to the six gods symbol.

"I am imagining that an ancient tribe of Genii lived near here. A tribe so ancient that it was before our stories had begun."

Serri added, "That would make sense and would help to explain symbols that we don't recognize."

"This is a very intricate and complicated star map," said Jeon. "What would be the point of all this meticulous work?"

Adain said, "History. A record of their history."

"Yes," I said, "but I believe it's more. I can't explain this yet, but I think it's also a 'future'. A possible future."

The little torches were burning low so we filed out, back to the main fire. I put more water on for tea and we made ourselves comfortable.

The next day I took pains to copy the unknown symbols into the bound parchments that grandmother had given to me at the beginning of this journey. As I did, I studied each one for meaning and looked closely at its relation to the symbols carved into the wall around it.

The more time I spent in the star room, the more I came to understand many things. As I discovered the truths that had been carved into those walls, I also came to discover truths about myself.

I did have "courage" because without it I would not have been able to come this far. I was sure I had more within myself so put any questioning thoughts I had about that, aside.

I had "knowledge". It was disrespectful to grandmother's teachings to continually doubt myself. I know there are many things that I have yet to learn but having doubt should never be a block to learning them. I became resolved to turn my doubts into curiosity and to look forward to the knowledge that lay hidden in the unknown.

The star room restored my self-confidence. I had been plagued with doubts and worries for many weeks but came to understand that it was hunger, the cold, the unknown future, and fear that drove doubt. I became determined to think through doubts and to call on my inner determination to help move my companions and myself forward.

Once I understood the star room, understood the pictures and symbols and how they related to each other and to the bigger scene, answers to my questions seemed to flow.

At mid-morning on the fifth day after the Earth shook the star room free from the mountain, over a meal of acorn and hare stew, the excitement I felt about what the star room meant, came tumbling out. My animated chatter seemed to stir my companions.

"The map is of the stars we would see from this point, if the sky were in summer and not the winter it now is. Ancient Genii may have believed this cave, with its jasper stone and crystal tower, to be sacred and were drawn to it, as I am."

I looked into the fire then continued, "The stars and symbols tell a story of what was and what would be."

Adain asked, "You think our ancestors were superstitious?"

I answered, "Not as foretelling the future by any mystic means, but as a way to predict. Their world changed just as ours did. They searched and found answers."

Serri asked, "You think famine and drought forced them to leave their homes?"

"Most likely, yes. The answer is in the stars. I think their sky shone with the constellations that we don't recognize. Maybe together with ours or not, I can't be sure. But now we know from our Masters and teachers that our sky only shows our stars but shifted, as they are now."

I looked around at their faces and continued, "The most significant find, besides the sign of the six gods, is its placement next to the symbol for west. It's found throughout the star map, always in the west. We need to continue west. I think our new home is west."

I think I may have overwhelmed my companions with so

much information because when I finished talking, they were silent.

I moved to heat stones in the fire and made everyone more tea. It tasted particularly good right then, warm on my throat.

Jeon broke the silence, his voice soft, "The storm is not as severe today as it was yesterday. The clouds are not as dark. I think the storm may be passing and we should think about moving on."

Adain said, "The hunting is scarce. Jeon and I spend as much time as we can trying to find game and most time, we find none."

I knew what they said was true. "Serri and I are unable to find more food close by and our stores are so low. We'll need to travel farther away from here to find anything to eat."

Serri nodded and said, "This cave has given us everything it can and for that I'm grateful, but if we stay longer I'm afraid we won't endure. We won't find our new home."

Jeon said, "Then we're agreed. When the storm eases, we continue our journey."

I added, "Our journey west."

That night I had a dream. I was standing in a field of wildflowers and bent to look closer at a flower I did not recognize. Hearing a rustle in the near distance, I looked up. It was grandmother, waving and smiling and saying something I couldn't hear. I strained to listen, my attention on her lips, trying to make out what she said, but she was too far away. I wanted to go to her but my feet would not move. I cried out, "I can't hear you, what are you saying?" It was then that she lifted her arm and pointed at something. I looked and what I saw was the sun in a beautiful sunset, golden and orange and pink. Then the dream faded to nothing, as dreams will do.

I woke with two thoughts: I must copy as much of the star room as I can and we were right in choosing to journey west. My confidence in that decision was strong.

On the two hundredth and twenty-fourth day of our journey, we left the cave and the star room and again, climbed and walked westward through the mountains.

At first, it was rough. We had become soft from our long stay in the cave, but soon we found our rhythm and the distance we travelled seemed, to me, to flow by.

The nights were getting warmer and the days of snow turned to light rain making travel easier. Even the mountains started to ease their way down into rolling hills making the way less troubled.

Food and water were found with effort but did not present a hardship for us. The days blended from one to the next.

After seven days in the hills, we came up to the ridge of one hill and a view of a forest of tall trees extended before us.

That night before falling to sleep, we talked excitedly about what the forest meant to us. Game, herbs, roots, perhaps berries and maybe fruit.

The forest consumed us for twenty-one days. It stretched on and on but we didn't mind that. After so long in the cold hard mountains, the forest was a pleasure.

Game was plentiful, so much in fact, that Jeon and Adain passed many opportunities to hunt because we didn't need more.

Serri and I found herbs and berries and more acorns and routinely baked breads in our mid-day fires. Our stews were rich with roots, herbs and wild meats and our stores of dried goods grew with each passing day.

At times the travel was difficult as we picked our way through brush and over tangled tree roots, but as we became stronger, the troubles lessened.

On the two hundredth and fifty second day of our journey the forest ended.

The weather had been mild for several days and on this day, the sky was clear, a pale blue, decorated with thick rounded light gray clouds moving to the east along with a slight breeze.

I saw, through the dappled sunlight of the trees, that the forest ended about one hundred paces in front of us. The last of the black oaks, cedars, and pines bordered a wide expanse of gently rolling flatland.

The view as we stepped out of the forest into the first buds of new grass, was wondrous.

The flatland rolled away and down and far to the left and farther to the right. The springtime sun sparkled off little pools of water that dotted the landscape and shone on little curls of water that came from the hills in the north, linked the pools to each other, and flowed away to the south.

The fields, while rocky where we stood and studded with manza and ceanothus shrubs, gave way to fields of segde, allium, and wild grasses.

Away to the other side, I could see, through the haze of distance, a huge body of water that stretched far, far into the sunset of the west.

I'm not sure why, but the notion of Gaia came into my mind and I said a silent thank you to grandmother.

I moved closer to Jeon and took his hand. We were smiling and looking at the vista and smiling some more. Adain and Serri were close by and I saw that they were smiling, too. I think we all shared the same thought... this was it. We had found a new home.

Jeon pointed to a spot a short distance away, next to a small pool of water, and I knew, without words, that he thought to make camp there.

We stayed in the incredible landscape for thirty two days. We rested, we restored our health, we explored, and we lived. And on the two hundredth and eighty fourth day of our quest, we started our journey home. Back to family and friends to tell them this tale of challenges and growth. But most important of all, to tell about their new home.

Perceptions

It's early morning along a two-lane back road that traverses a landscape interrupted, here and there, by rolling mounds of living greenery. The sun is only a short distance along its daily arc across the vibrant blue cloudless spring sky and the day is not yet become warm enough to dry the evening dew and it glistens like an ethereal carpet of diamonds across the view. The road is roughly paved with stony shoulders where an occasional weed has found the strength to encroach. There is a footpath fifteen feet from the edge of the road where a woman, dressed in loose and flowing clothes and wearing a wide brimmed hat, is walking.

The woman is in her midyears and she is meandering along stopping now and then to take a detailed look at a rock or a plant, but is mostly making her way forward along the road. She is tall and slender in spite of the signs of comfort that have crept in as little puffs of softness around her waist. She walks straight and sure and when a glimpse of her face is observed one can see that there are the lines of time barely perceptible between her alert eyes. She prefers to call these Dove's Feet as the distasteful alternative, Crow's Feet, suggests that time has been too cruel. Signs of age and years in the sunshine are starting to appear along her body but for the most part, she accepts them and takes no special notice. This woman is at ease and walking without hurry. She is smiling to herself because she is happy, with herself and with the current warm day. She appears to have no worries although her mind turns over different thoughts of her childhood, her life as a young adult, and the years she's entering now as a mature adult.

This woman is Nothocalais. She is the second daughter of a somewhat respected town elder and his reluctant wife. Her parents, and their parents before them, were from a period of history filled with poverty, cunning and unsophisticated survival. There were family stories that told of petty skirmishes against other family groups, some won, and some lost, but all with rumors of lies and deceptions, and the gains that could come from such behavior. These stories were always whispered about in low tones with the last few, hushed words always being... don't tell anyone. There was so much business in keeping appearances that this elder and his wife would forget there were several children to parent and would often relegate this duty to a lesser priority or hand it off to re-emerging technology.

As town elder, her father seemed to be in a constant hypocritical state of mind, practicing deceit and disrespect in private while being affable and conventional in public. There was always a desperate need to appear proper and balanced in public, but even a very young child could perceive these actions as sanctimonious. Nothocalais did not embrace this sordid practice and, in fact, would feel a darkness come over her when seeing her parents move from public proper to private disdain, sometimes within the span of minutes.

Her mother was, for the most part, unavailable, preferring to keep company with her past and her own ideas of how the present should be manipulated. She did her duty, as required, but did not go much beyond. There were rules to be followed but she rarely broke them, as they seemed to be to her benefit. She loved the social edge that being married to her husband brought to her. She often felt superior to those around her, thinking that her lineage gave her height.

Years later, Nothocalais would piece together, from snatched bits of conversations she had heard here and there, that her father's family had broken up after years of infighting over a secret treasure a late ancestor was said to have amassed. Everyone thought it belonged to them and not the others. Her mother's family had dark secrets that the clan never spoke of, except in error. It was from these errors that Nothocalais came to think that the grave secret was a blood feud, three generations back, that disinherited her mother's line. It seems to Nothocalais that her mother was trying to make up for that ever since.

Nothocalais felt distressed and confused at not being able to explain her parents' individual actions to herself and wanted deeply to understand their actions as correct but always there were questions. Wisely, she kept them to herself.

In her quest to be fair, Nothocalais searched her memories for examples to the contrary. She could fine one. There were stories of a figure, years and years in the past that knew medicine. Specifically, midwifery. There were vague rumors about this personage that persisted throughout the years. It was said she dabbled in the dark sciences, that she had the secrets of two plants that were spoken about in hushed words. She knew about Vites angus castus with its beautiful blue flowers and green berries kissed with the blush of pink and she knew about the bright yellow

Silphium flower that had been reported as extinct for over a thousand years.

Nothocalais always felt a kinship with this daring woman. Not that there was any real connection between them. It was simpler than that. It was an affinity built on contraries. Both found themselves interested in life in opposition to authority. Unintentionally. But true.

Nothocalais' childhood was the same as it was for many of the other children born after the great apocalypse. It was filled with doubt and nagging fears, but never quite enough to stop her from testing her surroundings and occasionally exercising her own best judgment. As a small child, she can clearly remember with a smile, that in the times when she was alone, her thoughts and questions about things in her environment would carry her for hours. Being by herself was still a sort of freedom for her and she would allow her thoughts to flow over her with little expectation as to meaning or purpose. Her thoughts would drift back to times of happiness when she would explore even the smallest of creatures crawling in the underbrush or wonder at a tiny flower that managed to bloom amongst the rubble. She was curious and was proud to be a daydreamer without a direction.

Nothocalais has one very lucid memory, that of being shocked to the core by the cold isolation of group learning centers and the cruel brutality done in the name of holy order. She often felt ripped out of the happy life she tried to build by the constant threats and endless rules of convention. Now, she shudders at these impressions.

Other times, her thoughts were slammed with injustice and moments of neglect that would evoke an almost instant anger and that were always followed, moments later, with sadness and tears.

Nothocalais found these highly charged emotions disturbing and would push them aside with disgust, to be dealt with at another time. Not today.

Her older sister, Dasiphora, was first born. As the eldest, Dasiphora held a position of responsibility and stature. After her four younger siblings were born, those responsibilities included setting a good example and helping with their care. There was an expectation that Dasiphora would be intelligent, witty, and sophisticated... someone the parents could parade in front of their friends with pride and make boastful statements about. It was as if the parents dared their friends to produce even one of their own progeny to challenge the claim that Dasiphora was all that they said she was. As a result, Dasiphora was smart. She studied hard and learned well.

As she grew through her early life into a mature adult, Dasiphora became very self-assured and walked with confidence. She never thought of herself as beautiful, but she was and never lacked for friends. She is, to this day, personable, dependable, grounded, and above all, a person who loves deeply and with understanding.

From time to time, Nothocalais recalls her own interactions with Dasiphora where Dasiphora would always claim top spot, or the biggest treat, or the softest chair, all because she was the first-born. And because of the truth of it... she was the eldest, after all, the younger ones always acquiesced. Nothocalais always looked up to Dasiphora, will always love her with a special unbreakable bond.

The sun is rising in the sky and the air is getting warmer. Nothocalais has been walking for some distance but has lost track of time. It feels good to leave the clock behind today. She leaves the path to make her way to a stand of trees and finds there a small creek softly running over rocks and long grasses that sway gently in the current. She perches on a warm granite rock and sits facing the creek. There are soft noises of birds rustling between the branches overhead and the short clipped sounds of something darting among the fallen leaves in the surrounding area. She sits looking down into the creek, seeing there the watery reflection of her own face, starting to crease with lines but still somewhat plump. Her attention is drawn to a small creature swimming in the creek moving from one place of shadows to another and peering closer, sees that it is a small tadpole. Looking more closely she sees several more tadpoles swimming heedlessly along the waters edge and all seemingly unaware of the others so closely bound in their liquid home. She lingers, letting her mind go free of restraints and in an unguarded moment...

Water, water lift my soul and float my heart along,
Let me play along your edge and rest a moment more.
Refresh me I implore you, let me cool my skin
For all too soon my harried steps will away again.

A sharp chirp from an unseen bird, high in the trees above her, brings her drowsy attention, from the creek's soothing sounds, to the world outside. In an instant, she is back. Back to where her thoughts return, unbidden, to her life. These thoughts, like electricity, move quickly up the years past milestones and larger memories to present times and Nothocalais wonders why, when one is actually living the moments, time seems to run at a more or less normal speed but in memories, time is but an instant. Smiling to herself, she thinks, perceptions are solitary at best and false at their worst, but, if unobserved then nothing is learned.

Mitella was born after Nothocalais but was first son. Father was so pleased to have, at last, a son. For three years, father had to bear up when boasting about his family... of two girls. He would get a sad look on his face as he explained, no, no sons, yet. But now a son. Mitella was to grow up strong and manly. He would stand tall next to father, learn father's ways and ultimately, take over the business as father's pride and joy. His eldest... son.

Mitella tried very hard to be like father. He spoke like him and practiced walking like him but there was always a small almost imperceptible disturbance with Mitella. He couldn't quite understand how to think like father and this set him up for a lifetime of conflict and erroneous judgment concerning his associates as well as his siblings.

Father was lost to Mitella when he needed him the most. As a result, Mitella grew into manhood without father's direct influence so he built what was not there. Father became a saint and Mitella became judgmental and unforgiving to those who did not measure up to father. And no one ever did.

Nothocalais has come to understand that behind Mitella's mask of control and authority, there is a frightened boy. Faint and fading with the years, but there just the same.

The afternoon has gotten warmer and the birds have gotten quieter. All that can be heard is the low buzzing noises of insects as they call out their frenzied messages to one another and the occasional chirp of a passing bird. The leaves of the trees surrounding Nothocalais barely move in the slight, warm breezes that manage to pull a single leaf from its petiole and carry it downward to a watery ride upon the creek's surface. It's nice here. But it's time to move on. Nothocalais carefully picks her way from the creeks edge into an open field of spring wildflowers. She stops for a minute, half protected in the shadows, and with her hand shading her eyes, surveys the field. Ahead she sees tall stalks of wildflowers dancing in the breeze and watches a small group of birds silently flitting among the flower tops. Very serious business, she remarks to them and with an amused smile upon her lips, steps into the sun-drenched vista.

It's the shifting of time, again. Uninvited, thoughts of Nothocalais' early womanhood flood her mind and what stands out to her the most is the contrast between her structured life, where it was necessary to work to earn a home and food and be the means of obtaining both – and – the unstructured life she desired, where she was free to study diverse subjects and to express her inner creations.

Nothocalais struggled to stay the course. To maintain the momentum of what she helped to start. She was, for a time, living just to her means and had to live in hope that all would fare well. This caused no end of stress with thoughts of losing all that was worked so hard for. It was only later in her life that Nothocalais could look with understanding. She found that the fear was not in the loss of things, it represented her denial of self.

She escaped her troubles with friends and false fantasy, managing to keep a few of the first but eventually losing the later. She was wild but smart. She didn't fall into the traps of others; she felt in control and made her way into life.

She is certain that her finding a mate was by way of serendipity. It is the one thing in her life that she knows was by destiny and not by chance. Nothocalais enjoys the company of her mate almost as much as she enjoys the company of her own thoughts.

Nothocalais' middle-life was barely indistinguishable from her early-life. She was forced to put her girlhood flights of fancy aside to work in the daily grind of survival. To move in the acceptable normality of every day life among the serious, status driven humanity that dictated social acceptability. It wasn't always easy but there were long stretches of time where Nothocalais wouldn't think of floating free at all. She would walk and would talk and would act... like everyone around her. She was accepted and worked to fit in. She was not always happy in this, but the years wore on.

Her steps are precarious as the field has belonged to nature, not to man, and there are teetering rocks and up heaved earth to be careful of. Moving forward, Nothocalais holds out her hands and brushes the tops of the wildflowers and feels their soft petals and new leaves caress her skin before the harsher more thorny guard leaves remind her that even in a field that is so beautiful and seems so tranquil, survival is just under the surface. Everything has a purpose and there are specific struggles that cannot be escaped. As she observes a small insect crawling along a wide leaf, she wonders, *this little bug doesn't seem to be aware of my presence, but can it sense that danger may loom so close at hand? If it does, it has not varied from its random path, nor is it running for the safety of the underbrush. Most likely, it's just unaware. But maybe, at some level, it knows that it can't beat fate.*

Seemingly unaware, the insect crawls away and Nothocalais straightens up automatically rubbing the small of her back to subside the kink that is almost always there.

Fair-haired Justicia was born soon after. Her hair was golden yellow and her body slight. It was said that she favored her mother's looks when she herself was a child. Justicia took pride in looking like mother and strove to be as much like her as possible. She stayed by her side when she could and always seemed to be happy in mother's shadow. She found love and acceptance in the nearness to mother, in contrast to the role that third daughter offered her. And being the third daughter, she could often be found in the company of her elder sisters, Dasiphora and Nothocalais.

On the surface, childhood fun between sisters was always light and humorous with laughing and make-believe and a general pursuit of children's gaming. But lurking under the surface was a complex set of rules: the eldest was first, the second daughter was next and Justicia was last. A role she didn't much care for but had to accept nonetheless.

As Justicia entered her teen years, she longed for independence. She was a hard worker and a serious woman. She has been injured by life as it tossed tough lessons at her. She became hard-edged to protect the innocent little girl within and learned to use a sort of naivety as a constant shield, which belays Justicia's fierce beliefs, her devotion to family, and a boundless strength to carry on, to do the best she can to live on a self-chosen narrow path.

Nothocalais' journey, on this day, has been one of easy progress and somewhat elliptical in nature. Far flung but complete in that Nothocalais' direction has been slowly turning toward the places she loves best, her home and her daydreams.

Home for Nothocalais is her place of sanctuary. It is her escape, her hiding place, and her freedom. She may speak her mind, she may do as she pleases, and she had no one to answer to except herself.

Now, as she is pulled back to the restraining rigors of her world, she feels a strong pull to stay among the flowers, insects and the beauty that surrounds her in these moments. She wonders what it would be like to stay like this forever. Free in a world that is warm, inviting, soothing and lets her mind wander wherever it may without the shackles of pain and life. But as the breezes turn colder and the sun races toward its shadows, Nothocalais knows all too well that her steps must lead her back. She lingers just a moment more, gazing around and wondering where her journey may truly end and because she knows that she has many, many more steps to take, she takes one more and heads to the familiarity of home with one question on her mind, *we don't really have control over Time, do we? Even when it's our own.*

The last-born was Restio. He was second son but two years younger than Mitella, who enjoyed the responsibility of first son and was not about to share the position.

Restio was a bit of a nuisance. At up to five years younger then his siblings, he could not compete. In childhood, he was never as fast, or as agile, or as clever as the others. Nor did he fully understand all the more grownup games the elder children played. How could he? He was the youngest. This never quite discouraged him from trying but also didn't spare him the subtle cruelties of his siblings. He was forever protected by the parents and as a result, grew up safe. It wasn't until he reached manhood that he emerged into his own.

Restio was fairly pliable. He did not force himself on anyone and, for better or worse, lived outside the focus of the parents. He followed along and was just Restio. When he took an interest in active boy's games, father took an interest in him. It was not clearly understood by others, what this truly meant, other than Restio almost certainly received father's advice in whatever form it came in.

Either in spite of childhood or because of childhood, Restio is a passive, loving, and generous person. Nothocalais has always held a special love for Restio, even in light of differences, this will not fade.

Nothocalais does not wonder if her story would be different under someone else's hand, for surely it would be. Just as her perception is here, from this place, from this time, so it is with another.

As a slight smile crosses her lips, she muses, *I wonder if I would be surprised by the humor and understanding of another's sagacity concerning my life? Or would I shudder to think that observations of another were truer than mine own?*

These thoughts, as inconclusive as they may stand, occupy Nothocalais' mind for some measure of time. Eventually, as they start to fade, she lightly puts them aside for another time, with one last opinion, *no one stands where I stand, it's a matter of physics.*

The flow of time through life and the struggle for survival seemed to move uninterrupted with the exception of a few focused moments occurring at random throughout but lacking the energy to force change. Until…

On the verge of passing out of youth and into comfort, Nothocalais faced a sudden upheaval of her life. A catastrophic event that changed her. Everything changed. Everything. For a time, she was lost, thrashing about as a boat in a storm that had lost its rudder. It unnerved her to no end but forced her to look closely at her life. To assess herself in ways that she had not had to do in the past. She was given an opportunity to seek a new path and took it.

After a period of restlessness, trial, error, and fortitude, she now seeks lost freedoms, knowledge, fame, great fortune, dignity, joy, and personal power while trying to avoid fear, pain, and loss of independence. At times, Nothocalais will wonder how she is going to walk the tightrope that lies before her.

All of Nothocalais' siblings survived their childhoods. All have entered into the world with their problems, their expectations, and their quests. All have come to a post-apocalyptic life. All have become crones and hagspawns. Success and failure have rocked the siblings, sometimes together and sometimes apart, making each and every one of them who they are: survivors.

Nothocalais practices tolerance, not always successfully, for the differences between her siblings and herself. Deep in her heart she knows that a part of them is also a part of her. She knows that through it all and in spite of everything in the past and the differences among them, they shared a bond and stood together.

A sharp snap of a thick twig brought Nothocalais back to herself and taking a quick look down, she quickly realizes that her steps have been unsure, that she is standing on the precipice of a huge crater and has almost tumbled in to the murky poisonous waters that have collected there at the bottom. As she peers over the crater's edge she sees her reflection and it is in contrast to her preferred perception... her face shows the ravages of her post-apocalyptic life under a merciless sun whose rays have burnt spots upon her skin and of tainted water that has twisted her once beautiful features. She looks down at her hands, dried and scarred and wonders whose they are. It's then that she notices her torn and faded trousers, the thick woven top that scratches her skin and the thick leather boots that shod her feet. After a long gaze at herself, the hurtful reality of her existence floods back as the beautiful, warm sunlit landscape around her melts into the everyday environment of waste and destruction that she is so familiar with.

Nothocalais is momentarily dazed by her surroundings. She doesn't recognize anything around her and seems to have lost her way. The soil under her feet is burnt black and smells of charred ruins. It's hard and crackles as she steps. Nothocalais becomes painfully aware that she is standing in the wide open. Unprotected. Worse, her steps send noise out to all that would hear. Panic starts to rise, she can feel her chest tighten and hear her breaths coming in short puffs. Automatically, she squats down, trying to look small, trying to disappear as she scans the terrain hoping to find something familiar about it. Everything is either dead or dying. The bad waters have killed all the fauna and driven all the living creatures from this place. Far to her left, she sees a rocky outcropping and thinks: *if I can make it to there, I'll be able to see further, to recognize where I am.*

Head down and shoulders hunched, Nothocalais steps as gingerly as she can, making for the small outcrop of rocks that cling to the barren side of a low hill. She scans left and right keeping a close watch for danger while choosing her steps to avoid tripping in her haste. Having made the little nest of boulders and rocks, Nothocalais takes a minute to catch her breath and to make sure that she wasn't followed. *That was lucky.* She slowly raises her head to take a look.

The shallow valley is filled with craters, all with little pools of poison glistening in the late haze of the day. There is burnt chaparral and browned thistles from one end of the valley to the other. There is a slight breeze that rattles the dead leaves and dried branches sending up a ghostly sound that makes Nothocalais shudder with the fear of the unknown. She stares for some time, looking for the slightest movement that would give away the presence of anything in the area. Anything alive, that is.

The light is fading now and Nothocalais is concerned about getting home with haste. She decides it's time to leave and thinks to climb the low hill to see what is on the other side. This takes her the better part of an hour but eventually she makes it up and over the top. When she raises her eyes again, she breathes a sigh of relief… there, on the far side of the view, she sees her home, her ruin of a home there among the rubble of long ago destroyed stone buildings. She had not been truly lost, just misplaced for a time.

Her fantasy gone, her eyes now sharp for hidden danger and her ears tilted toward the least of sounds, Nothocalais picks up her pace and heads for the relative safely of home.

But even with her head ducked down and her steps quick and sure, she smiles and reminds herself, *tomorrow I will walk again through my fields of spring wild flowers and kiss the blue sky with my eyes and feel the slight breezes on my skin, because it is mine to have just inside my recollection. It's my own perception.*

Swamp's Edge

Emily stood in the window of her now empty 3ʳᵈ story art studio, looking down at the early morning street. *Five years. Who would have thought it would have gone so fast?* She watched her husband, Matthew, as he gave last minute instructions to the driver of the moving van double-parked in front of their brownstone. *Oh, it's only our brownstone for another six hours.* She heard herself sigh as she raised her eyes from the street up to the gray dawn sky and thought, *we've made some great memories here.*

Emily turned from the window and took a step or two to the center of the studio, hesitated long enough to take a slow look around and tried to choke down her emotions.

Everything will be fine, she kept telling herself. *We've made the right decision.*

Emily Harris. At thirty-one years of age, she has already built a successful career as an artist. She paints landscape scenes, some of famous places like the Forest Recreation in the NYC Botanical Garden and some landscapes she brings forth from her imagination. Part of her reputation sprang from the fact that she uses botanical pigments in her oil paints that she herself processes from flowers and leaves from her own garden. She adds subtle hidden figures and images among the flora, like a pair of eyes gazing out of the shadows, looking right at the viewer. Emily thought to create whimsy and a bit of mystery but really, what it created was a sensation among art collectors and gallery owners. Her art shot her to stardom and she quickly found herself travelling in higher circles among NYC's elite.

It was at one of her new series opening night parties, at the Amirror Gallery on the Lower East Side, when Emily met her soon-to-be husband, Matthew Harris. He was gorgeous and she fell in love with him as soon as he locked his hazel-green eyes on her. He had completed his graduate studies in Biophysics at University of California Berkeley and during his time there, invented a mechanical component that could measure electrical impulses emanating from a resonator down to a fantastically tiny particle. Or, that's how Emily understands it. Matthew built a company around this gadget and moved to NYC five years ago to go international, which it did, under his careful hand.

At the time of the Amirror Gallery showing of her recent collection, both Emily and Matthew's stars were rising and life was exciting.

After they met, they dated for a brief time but it was so obvious that they were meant to be together that they soon wed. That was five years ago and they never looked back.

Until today.

Emily gathered her purse and her day bag and turned the front door handle for the last time. As soon as she closed the door behind her, Matthew was coming up the steps. His face flush with excitement and his smile warm and reassuring.

"All ready to go?" he asked, as he reached to turn the deadbolt key.

"Yes, I think I am." Emily stood on the front stoop and looked up the front of the building at the weathered stone of what had been their home for five years.

At length she spoke, "I'm surprised that I'm feeling sad and excited at the same time."

Matthew took her hand.

Emily smiled and said, "How about you? Are you okay?"

Matthew gave her hand a squeeze and smiled at her. "Yea, I'm fine. I think we're doing the right thing and I'm very excited about this. I feel that we're on an extraordinary adventure!" He wrapped his arm around Emily's shoulder.

Emily smiled and relaxed into Matthew's embrace and listened to the soothing tone of his voice.

"Think of it as starting the next phase of our journey and really, we're not starting over, we're continuing." He took a step down, gently guiding Emily to do the same.

"As president, CEO, owner, and big-shot, I can run the company from my home office and," taking another two steps down, "you have a beautiful new studio waiting for you, and an art agent that loves you."

They reached the sidewalk and Matthew took Emily in his arms and held her close and whispered, "I love you, Em."

Emily squeezed Matthew a bit and said, "Love you, too, sweet man. And thanks for the pep-talk, I needed that."

Taking her hand again, Matthew added, "And Biscuit loves you, too!"

Biscuit, a four year old female Bichon Frise, had been sitting patiently in the front seat of their BMW SUV parked at the curb and when Matthew and Emily turned their heads to look at her, she barked excitedly and wagged her little fluff of a tail with anticipation.

Emily, smiling with appreciation, looked from Biscuit to Matthew and said, "It's time to go, isn't it?"

"Yes," Matthew said, "Let's get out of town and look for a nice lunch stop somewhere."

Leaving NYC felt like waving goodbye to a dear friend you may not see again. It almost brought tears to Emily's eyes but she drew a deep breath and, for Matthew's sake, tried to believe what she had been telling herself... that everything will be fine.

The drive out of the city was fairly uneventful with the daily commute traffic starting to back up just as they broke free onto the highway south.

Matthew, true to his engineering discipline, had plotted their course and planned their stops.

"We'll stop in Hagerstown, Maryland for gas and lunch, maybe run Biscuit around a block or two then drive on to Harrisonburg for dinner."

Emily started to rouse herself from her quiet little funk. She had to admit that she was looking forward to the move, that she wanted, almost craved, the artistic stimuli that changing locations would bring. She was grateful for all that living in the city brought to her: opportunity, fame, fortune, but above all, it brought her Matthew.

At the sound of his voice, Emily turned to look at Matthew and smiled, really smiled at him with warmth and love and said, "Dinner in Virginia. Should be nice."

Matthew was relieved to hear, in Emily's voice, that she was less tense than she seemed earlier. "Why don't you surf the web to see what's happening in Harrisonburg? We may be able to take in a show or something."

"Yea, maybe there's a little park where we could sit and relax and let Biscuit run around for a bit."

It was close to late afternoon when the Harris' SUV pulled into Harrisonburg. It was still early and neither Matthew nor Emily were hungry enough for dinner, so after checking into their hotel, decided that they would take a leisurely stroll through the downtown to stretch their legs. It would also give Biscuit a chance to sniff new things. Emily found an address of an art gallery so that became their walking destination.

The downtown was two blocks wide and several blocks long and had an interesting variety of shops and shoppers. There were lots of little eateries, anything from PB&J to French crepes making dinner decisions no problem.

There were clothing boutiques, nail salons, a card shop, and a cute little florist that was open to the street and emitting all the rich perfumes of flowers in the prime of their beauty.

At the end of the little downtown, on a side street was the art gallery Emily sought.

The owner said they could bring Biscuit in. Bending over and smiling at Biscuit making her twitch with excitement, the owner wagged a finger at the little dog's nose and still smiling said, "As long as you clean up any mishaps."

Matthew and Emily spent the better part of an hour in that gallery. Emily was fascinated. There were several artists' installations to look at. One particularly large one was a collection of ski equipment that had mountain scenes painted in acrylic on them. There were skis, toboggans, snowboards, gloves and a ski boot that had a snowy Christmas scene painted all around it, culminating with a Santa figure that appeared to be hiding from discovery around back by the boot heel.

Another installation that both Emily and Matthew found to be rather charming was a collection of Civil War toys. There were mounted cavalry men with swords raised and battle-ready, foot soldiers down on one knee taking aim with their muskets, little metal cannons with their little piles of cannon-balls, soldiers carrying flags and banners, and, of course, the drum and fife boys ready to lead the way.

It wasn't just the collection of Yankee and Rebel toys that warranted attention, it was that they all had been posed on a large, albeit, miniature ballet production stage.

The stage was curtained and lighted and several panels of scene changes were waiting in their specific order. The play would begin in a pretty little town park, complete with a gazebo band-stand, move through three military situations like training and marching, culminate in a horrific war scene with explosions and bloody battles and end among the tombstones of an old cemetery. Behind the curtains, toy soldiers were posed as gaffers and holding ropes that would lower scene panels into place. Two generals were conferring over a script and on stage, two rearing horsemen appeared to be holding aloft a standing soldier, painted flesh toned with a pink tutu, glittery makeup and waving a peacock feather.

It was titled, "If War Were But A Dance." Emily thought it was a bold risk of a statement considering where they were and intended to sneak a picture of it.

Touching Matthew's arm, she said, "No one is going to

believe this. I almost don't myself."

In jest and with his voice lowered Matthew said, "Maybe your agent would be interested?"

It was getting on toward dinnertime when Matthew and Emily left the gallery. The street was filled with the smells of cooking food and in line with Pavlovian theory, both became ravenous.

The next day's drive was fairly uneventful and the weather was a balmy 70-degrees. Emily picked a cute little outdoor café in downtown Kingsport for lunch and after eating, they gassed up and drove the two hundred ten miles to Chattanooga, getting there around mid-afternoon.

While Matthew was checking them into their hotel, Emily spoke with the Concierge about a local tourist attraction she read about online: Ruby Falls. The Concierge provided all the information Emily needed, telling her that it was a truly stupendous attraction, tours left every fifteen minutes, and it was an eight-minute cab ride from the hotel.

Matthew and Emily had their bags taken up to their room and leashed up Biscuit for a little R&R.

The sun was warm and it felt good to be out of the SUV and walking along the tree-lined street close to their hotel.

Emily became a little animated as she told Matthew that they were about to be tourists.

"Ruby Falls is an underground waterfall inside of Lookout Mountain. Basically, it's a natural formation where water has eroded the limestone and spills out from fissures and crevices into a deep pool. They've got it all lit up with colored lights. It's supposed to be quite spectacular."

"Sounds interesting. Maybe better than General Lee in a

tutu!" said Matthew.

"Nothing is *that* interesting!" Emily added and then remembered, "No dogs, though. Looks like hotel doggie-care for a couple of hours."

The falls were everything they were said to be and were just the diversion that Matthew and Emily needed. The water tumbling down the fall, spilling into a lighted pool, the smooth rocks, and the underlying smell of fungus and moss. For Emily it was exhilarating and for Matthew it was a curious study in hydrodynamics.

The little troupe was on the road early the next morning, destination Slidell Louisiana. Matthew had made arrangements with the property management company to pick up the keys to the old DuFrene place, their new home, before 5PM. They warned him that the office closed promptly at 5PM and if he missed the agent, he would have to wait until 8AM the next morning.

Matthew told Emily that they apologized for any inconvenience this may cause but he had complained to Emily that for all the money, nearly $450,000.00, spent on renovations, upgrades, and one completely new out building, the least they could do was to wait for them to arrive. "How hard could that be?"

There was no fighting it, though. Small towns had their habits and apparently weren't going to change them for anyone.

Emily suggested that Miss June, the property manager, may have to run off to an affair and couldn't be late for that... now could she?

That took the sting out of the situation and made Matthew

laugh a little bit as he pictured Miss June, a very rotund woman who loves her fried foods, running… anywhere. Still, he planned to arrive in Slidell at least an hour early.

They took a fast break for an early lunch and a quick doggie jog and made good time down the interstate and into Slidell about a quarter to four, making Matthew very pleased. He slowly drove around several blocks of downtown to get, what he said was, "the lay of the land."

They drove past the property management office, a nicely appointed storefront, painted white with small fake columns to either side of the front door and sidewalk windows. A block west was a small hardware store, the kind that would be stuffed full of nails, hand tools, screws, and other handyman related items. And two blocks further along the main street was a friendly looking diner called, "Angel's Place" sporting a canvas awning across the front, a painted and neon sign above that and on the sidewalk in front, two wrought iron tea tables, set with heavy cotton tablecloths and a colorful centerpiece of Bachelor Buttons, Snapdragons, and Sweet Peas.

Emily commented that the little sidewalk tables looked so inviting and Matthew agreed.

"How about this Em, you and Biscuit take a table and relax, order an ice tea or a glass of wine. I'll park just over there," pointing to a spot under a large Magnolia tree, "and scoop up the keys from Miss June. I think I want to stop at the hardware store too, maybe pick up a few things before driving out to our new home."

The idea of sitting in the shade and not in a car was really appealing to Emily. She smiled and nodded and said, "Yes, all that sounds great. We could both relax for a short while before driving on."

Matthew said, "This won't take me more than fifteen or twenty minutes."

Emily leaned over, gave Matthew a kiss and said, "Come on Biscuit, it's you and me."

Biscuit was up and wagging her tail and more than ready to go when Emily hooked up the leash and opened the door.

"Okay, see you very quickly," said Matthew and pulled the SUV slowly into the road.

Emily watched as he drove up the street and began edging the SUV into the shady parking spot. She turned and walked back to the diner, slowly towing Biscuit who was occupied with sniffing every single inch of the sidewalk.

When she got to the diner, Emily stuck her head in the front door and asked if it was okay if she sat at one of the tables on the sidewalk out front.

The waitress, a small middle-aged woman with light auburn hair, smiled warmly and said, "Of course you can sit there, honey. You just go ahead, I'll be right out."

"There will be two of us, my husband will be along shortly," said Emily.

"That's fine," smiled the waitress.

Five minutes later, the table was set, menus ready, two small glasses of water, and a fine dark Merlot sat waiting for Emily's first sip.

Biscuit had worn herself out sniffing everything within reach and had taken up a position under Emily's chair, gazing about through sleepy, half-closed eyes.

Emily had been looking up and down the street, not really paying attention to anything in particular when Matthew popped out of a side street and strode toward her. As he got closer she said, "That was quick. Everything okay?"

"Oh yea, I've got the keys and a map on how to find the place. Miss June says hello and if we need anything to call. There was a sign on the hardware store saying they would be back in fifteen, so I thought I'd wait here with you."

"Nice."

"I may have a beer."

"Our waitress, Bea, said she'd watch for you and come out when you got here," said Emily. "Want a sip of Merlot?"

"No thank you," said Matthew with a smile then lifted his glass for a drink of cool water.

They passed the time in amiable chitchat and when Matthew had taken the last sip of his beer and chewed down the orange slice garnish, said, "Think I'll try the hardware store again, then we can go. Might take about thirty minutes to find our way home. Are you getting excited about seeing our new place?"

Emily smiled and nodded, "I am excited! It's like getting a big present!"

"I hope it's a good one!" said Matthew. "I'll be back shortly." Taking a twenty out of his wallet said, "This should cover the bill. Be right back." And strode away.

Emily finished her wine and paid the bill, leaving a generous tip for Bea, thinking, *it won't hurt to start out right and besides, I liked her, she was nice.*

Emily roused Biscuit and got up from the table. She had relaxed so thoroughly that her legs were stiff and thought to stretch them out. She walked a few feet along the street, led Biscuit to the curb and stood waiting for Matthew to pick them up. Momentarily, Emily noticed an old woman coming up the street toward her.

The old woman may have been 5'4" tall at best, but was stooped a little at the shoulders and that belied her true height. She wore a dark brown rough-spun skirt that fell to her ankles and a heavy woven beige cotton blouse that looked two sizes too big for her small frame. A frayed length of rope was cinched about her waist holding the skirt up and the blouse down.

Emily smiled at her own thoughts, *if a big wind were to come up, her blouse would billow out like the sails of a ship and carry her up and away!*

The old woman wore a tattered gardening hat with a wide brim that hid her eyes as well as shading most of her face and wore upon her feet, heavy black leather work boots, scuffed and caked with dried mud. Her steps were short but sure. It seemed that life had not robbed her of her legs.

Fascinated, Emily stood on the sidewalk and watched the old woman slowly coming toward her, head down, watching the sidewalk. This woman was dressed so differently from everyone else Emily had noticed out and about that she had the idea that the woman was probably very poor and fancied that she was from another time.

The old woman walked right up to Emily, stood facing her, and lifted her head, presumably to speak. But she did not speak; she smiled up at Emily, studying her face.

Momentarily she found her voice, "My dear, I thought to meet you on the 'morrow. I knew you would come, I've been waiting."

Emily was taken back by the old woman's statement and immediately replied, "Oh, you must have mistaken me for someone else. I'm new here, just arrived an hour ago."

The old woman stood quietly, looking up at Emily and slightly nodding her head, murmured, "Yes… yes… I know… yes. That's right."

When Emily stopped protesting, the old woman's smile widened, showing a mouthful of yellowed and missing teeth.

"The old DuFrene place out on White Egret Lane. Yes… yes… I know."

Emily's first thought was that half the town might know about her and Matthew buying and renovating the old DuFrene estate east of town. It had been vacant for such a long time before being offered for sale. Something like that was surely to make good town gossip.

The old woman went on, "Everyone calls me Nanan Marie and you will call me Nanan Marie, too." She pulled a worn handkerchief from her skirt pocket and wiped the back of her neck and forehead then turned her gaze down the street in the direction she had come from. She furrowed her brow in thought.

Emily nervously said, "Okay Nanan Marie. My name is Emily."

Nanan Marie set her thoughts and turned back to Emily. "Yes, yes, child. Emily, I know." She put the handkerchief back in her skirt pocket and spoke again, "You come on the 'morrow. I thought to meet you on the 'morrow. You'll come, yes?"

"I suppose I can. Meet here?" Emily said, pointing to the spot she stood on. "What time?"

"Here. When the sun is high. On the 'morrow." And Nanan Marie turned abruptly and walked quickly away, disappearing around the next corner.

Matthew came along less than two minutes later and eased the SUV up to the curb in front of Emily.

"The guy at the hardware store told me there is a small mom

& pop grocery store on the next exit going down Highway 190. He said it's more of a convenience store for the locals who don't need to drive into Slidell to the super store there. Milk, eggs, butter… that sort of thing. He said the owner's wife bakes the best cinnamon bread he's ever had!"

Emily said, "We should get some fruit and cereal and coffee. How are we going to wake up without coffee?" and laughed.

The little store, called appropriately enough "The Little Store", was a nice place, clean, and packed with almost anything you might need for your kitchen and laundry as well as paper goods and a nice assortment of romance novels and westerns.

This seemed a bit funny to Emily and as she pushed her little cart up and down the aisles she started to notice other oddball items like large cans of Hi-C Orange Drink, six packs of Diet Tab and Pabst Blue Ribbon beer tucked among the more modern conveniences, like Pellegrino bottled water and rice crackers.

On their way past the bakery section, both Emily and Matthew spied out two loaves of "Mrs. Barnaby's World Famous Cinnamon Bread" and with eyebrows rained and faces lit with mirth, talked about how could they possibly pass this up? There's no way, how could they live with the embarrassment of not trying this bread? And into the cart it went.

The drive down Highway 190 was fast and the exit for White Egret Lane was well paved and fairly new-looking but that changed nearly a half-mile from the exit when the road abruptly went from smooth asphalt to compressed dirt and gravel. Matthew had to slow down because the tires threw stones that banged along the frame and axles of the SUV and sent huge dust clouds up in their wake.

The SUV crawled along the gravel road. On either side were overgrown Cypress trees with thick and twisted trunks. The underbrush was chocked with swamp grasses and wild iris. Emily was awestruck with the view, thinking, *I've never seen anything like this. So far, my nature has been manicured and managed.* She couldn't take her eyes off the huge trees, adorned with long tendrils of Spanish Moss waving seductively in the slight breeze that moved in the hot afternoon air.

She heard herself say, "It's so primitive."

"Yes, and so is this road. I hope we're still going the right way," Matthew replied as he eased the SUV over a large burrow in the road.

They passed another worn gravel road to the right and Emily read the signs that were nailed up on a tall wooden post.

"180 The Blanchets, 182 the Halcourts, 188 The Hurleys. Looks like there are three houses down that road." And looking at the hastily drawn map that Matthew had gotten from Miss June, added, "As far as we've come on this gravel is as far as we still need to go to our driveway."

"That's another twenty minutes on this road. I knew it would be rough, but not this rough!" said Matthew. "Look for a sign so we won't miss it."

The SUV gently rocked back and forth as they drove over uneven rocks in the gravel road and as the satellite radio jazz station, the volume turned low, flowed across the air, Emily found herself drifting into a state of consciousness somewhere between awake and asleep, between sleep and dream, and her thoughts were slowly pulled back to the old woman, Nanan Marie.

That was such an odd occurrence, that woman. Her way of speaking reminds me of old style English, no, not old style... English learned as a second language, or learned without proper schooling. Emily thought to mention this to Matthew but was mesmerized by her half-dreamy state. *We can talk later... and what did she mean that she knew I would come here? She was very determined that we talk.*

Just then, the SUV thumped down into a small pothole and jolted Emily from her thoughts. Looking out through the windshield, just forty feet ahead, she spotted a drive to the right that was flanked by two great stone monuments. They were at least seven foot tall and three foot wide; both of them made from tumbled smooth rock and fitted seamlessly together, giving the imposing introduction to the property. Each had a large oval of engraved stone embedded toward the top announcing... DuFrene.

"This is it, Matt. Our driveway is that road to the right."

"Okay. Easy enough to find. That's good," and Matthew deftly steered the SUV between the stone wardens.

The thick tufts of wild brush were starting to encroach on the gravel drive and here and there lay matted down into tire tracks.

"We'll have to do something about trimming this back", Matthew said. "Maybe even resurface this drive. Might want to ask the locals why nothing off the highway is paved. Maybe it's not efficient against the weather... or the trees."

Biscuit had made her way up from the back seat into Emily's lap and was sitting at the alert watching everything. She gave out one bark as a Great Blue Heron lifted itself out of the tall grass and floated away.

"That's right," Emily said, scratching Biscuit's chin, "there's lots of new stuff to look at."

The drive seemed to go on and on, bumpy and lumpy, until it took a small curve from left to right and opened up to a breathtaking view of the front of Matt and Emily's newly restored French Country home, the DuFrene estate.

The home is a beautiful two-story stone faced home with a number of large paned windows across the front. The drive, as it swept past the front door was made of tumbled pavers and the front landscaping was neat and trimmed, but planted here and there with lavender and rosemary to add just a touch of wildness to the elegance.

Emily leashed Biscuit and opened her side door. The late afternoon warmth rushed over her, bringing the perfume of grass and wet soil with it.

Matthew called out, "Let's take a look inside and come back for our things later." And came around the SUV jingling the small ring of keys the management company had given to him. "One of these keys will open the front door."

The first thing Emily saw, as she stepped through the front doorway was the view straight through to the back of the house that was framed by large doublewide French doors. Literally, it was a picture of the rear property and just as the Sirens of Anthemoessa called to passing sailors, the wild and magical tangle of plants and trees as viewed out through the doors, called to her. And she could not resist.

Matthew was a step or two ahead of her and making comments as they walked through to the back of the house.

"I was thinking that this room would make a good office and library." And looking left through a large arched doorway, "What a nice sized great room. Christmas will never be the same!"

Emily glanced at the cavernous empty room and almost felt

lost in all the space, then caught her thoughts, "I hope we have enough furniture." But returned her gaze to the back property and let her eyes float across the setting sun glinting off the treetops and the smoky shadows of the underbrush.

Stepping through the wide hallway into the kitchen-dining-living space that sprawled across the back of the house was a real treat.

The kitchen was all she hoped it would be. Wide, large, and beautiful. Emily's dream.

When she found her voice, Emily spoke, "I am so impressed. I love it!" And running her hand across the granite counter said, "We must really thank our designer, maybe a small informal brunch, so we can applaud her skill and show our appreciation for what she has done for us."

Emily stood looking from the formal dining room (it could comfortably seat sixteen) across the spacious kitchen to the living room with its huge centerpiece fireplace and looked out at the views of their property that were framed, tantalizingly, through banks of paned windows and the two huge sets of French doors. Emily felt as if she were home. Truly home.

The moving van wasn't scheduled to arrive for two more days but Emily and Matthew had planned for that. They brought an air mattress and bedding and a few other "camping" items so they didn't have to suffer too much in the meantime. The management company had the utilities turned on and had set up a patio table and chairs so they wouldn't have to eat "over the sink".

Matthew retrieved his work valise and was scouting around for an Internet DSL outlet. He thought to connect to his company and spend an hour sifting through email to catch up.

"Hope my executive officers haven't crashed my company!" he said. Then unfurling a wad of Internet cable said, "Let's meet back here in an hour and relax with a nice glass of wine... maybe setup the bed first."

Matthew stood smiling at Emily, looking at her a little expectantly. She had to laugh. He stood there holding his Internet cable, a small length of it dangling from his closed hand, smiling at her and she smiling at him and Biscuit straining against her leash, eyes glued on the back property. It was funny.

"I'll take Biscuit out for a bit then come back to help set up for the evening."

"Okay. See you in a while." Matthew kissed her and turned his attention back to finding his Internet connection.

The back patio was a large area covered in flagstone that ran the length of the house. The landscaping had not been done, on Emily's request. She wanted to plan the layout based on how they wanted to use the space and had a vested interest in choosing the plants for the gardens. Her supply of flower pigments would last for a while but she needed the time to get a new garden up and blooming.

Matthew had worked with an architect who was experienced in French Country architecture and together they designed a new out building on the estate, Emily's new studio.

Emily picked her footing through the stubbles of recently mown weeds and wild grasses, making her way to the new building, excitement growing.

She let Biscuit's lead way out and the dog was happily sniffing at everything along her trot beside Emily.

The studio door was unlocked and the mechanism turned smoothly in Emily's hand. As she pushed the door open her eyes widened with joy and a smile crept across her face. The space was large, airy, filled with wonderful light and touched a place in her heart. Her mind flooded with possibilities and happiness and she knew the space would be perfect for her creative endeavors. In fact, three new projects leapt into her mind as she stood looking at the space. She thought, *is it possible to get any happier?*

She closed the studio door behind her and slowly walked through the rough so that Biscuit could get a good amount of sniffing time before they went in for the evening.

The rest of the DuFrene estate covered about seventy-five acres and was bounded on the east by the Old Pearl River. Across the river was the Honey Island Swamp, wholly owned and operated by the state of Louisiana, but this didn't stop locals from rowing their boats over the Old Pearl and as Emily discovered, it probably didn't stop the DuFrene's either. She found a small two-man dinghy pulled up onto the riverbank and overgrown with vegetation.

At the end of her quick exploration of the immediate property, Emily decided that Biscuit had sniffed enough and that it was time to see what Matthew was up to.

When she got back, she noted that he found his Internet connection and was having a quick FaceTime conversation with his CEO of operations. Apparently everything was fine but could Matthew be available for a team meeting tomorrow morning about eleven?

Emily took Biscuit off the leash and immediately the dog trotted away to check on Matthew. Emily went out to the SUV and brought a few things in and was shortly joined by Matthew. Between them, they emptied the SUV, stowed the groceries, set up the bed, using the great room as the Master, and set the table for dinner, complete with tablecloth (Emily's idea) and a small desk lamp (Matthew's idea) making the table very intimate.

Dinner was fruit, three kinds of cheese, stone ground crackers, and a simple bruschetta made from cherry tomatoes, basil, white cheese and a simply delicious baguette, made by Mrs. Barnaby of "The Little Store" fame. All of this was paired with a nice California Merlot.

As the daylight slipped into dusk, Matthew and Emily, sipping their wine and unwinding from the day, started to talk about tomorrow and things in general.

Matthew said, "I'm on the hook for a conference call tomorrow, late morning."

"Is everything okay?"

"Yes. We've got a new product we've been working on and operations have a couple of technical questions they need answered before moving forward. Nothing drastic."

Emily said, "Let's set up the patio table for you to work on until your desk and worktables get here." Then added, "I'm thinking about going into town tomorrow to do some general shopping and just look around."

"That might take you a whole thirty minutes," said Matthew as he sat smiling at her.

"That reminds me… I met an old woman today, outside of the diner. I forgot to tell you about that."

Emily told Matthew about talking with Nanan Marie and how she was to meet her at noon tomorrow, "For something important. I don't know, what do you think?"

Matthew put down his glass and said, "If you do see her again, be careful. She may be a little crazy... Alzheimer's or something."

"Yea, maybe."

Matthew added, "I wouldn't put too much credence in her saying that she was destined to find you. She may just be a little addled about who you are."

Emily thought about this for a second and said, "You're probably right." And after another second, "It's nothing."

The next morning started early enough but Emily felt wonderful after a night of sleeping without the typical big city noises and interruptions like the occasional fire truck siren, loud car door slamming, or music from a neighbor's backyard party.

Breakfast was simple: coffee and Mrs. Barnaby's famous cinnamon bread. Toasted it was soooo good, Emily and Matthew almost ate the whole loaf!

After showering and getting dressed, Matthew set up a little work area on the table, including his laptop, a cell phone (landline service was not enabled yet), and a print/scan machine. By the time Emily was ready to drive into town, Matthew was in full swing. He was sending and receiving email, chatting on the phone and generally being ensconced in his business.

Emily kissed him on the forehead, indicated that she was taking Biscuit with her and waved goodbye even as Matthew was talking with a colleague about schedules and costs.

Emily had made up her mind to go ahead and meet Nanan Marie in front of the diner at noon. When she got to Angel's Place, she poked her head in the door and spotted

Bea pouring coffee for a customer sitting at the counter.

Bea looked up and smiled, "Hello darling! What can I do for you today?"

Emily smiled and said hello then tied Biscuit's leash to one of the chairs in front of the diner before stepping inside.

"I'm meeting someone." Then hesitated before continuing, "Bea, let me ask you this."

"Of course, fire away."

Emily tried to form the question so as not to offend anyone. "I've met a woman named Nanan Marie. What can you tell me about her?"

Bea returned the coffee pot to its burner and motioned Emily to have a seat at the end of the counter and joined her there, leaning close with her weight resting on one elbow. When she spoke her voice was low and controlled.

"Nanan Marie is a town regular, if you will. Her family line goes way back, probably further than anyone else who lives here. She's a recluse and has lived alone for many years. She doesn't really talk with anyone, doesn't have any friends. There's hushed talk around here that she went a little mad."

Emily asked, "Do you think that's true? That she might be a touch insane?"

"Oh, I don't know, she manages to keep herself going. I imagine you couldn't do that if you were crazy." Bea put together and iced glass of water and set it in front of Emily and continued.

"Stories tell that Marie started spending more and more of her time in the swamp until several years ago, she just stopped living in her house altogether. They shut the gas and electricity off years before. Apparently Marie had been living close to nature for years, if you get my meaning."

Emily listened intently and absentmindedly twirled the water glass in the little pool of condensation that had formed at its base.

"Is Nanan Marie dangerous?"

Bea laughed and said, "Oh no, darlin'. She's not dangerous. But people around here will tell you this: when you see Nanan Marie, trouble usually follows."

Emily could feel her spine stiffen at those words. Her thoughts were immediately put on alert and she asked, "What kind of trouble?"

Bea patted her hand and said, "No, no, not the big trouble... nobody dies, if that's what you're thinking."

"I don't know what to think," said Emily.

"Well, the best way I can explain it is like this." Bea took a small breath in and let it out while she searched for the words. "Nanan Marie would never hurt anyone, but she's a little off, paranoid, if you will. Invents all kinds of wild stories about what goes on in the swamp. When she starts her crazy talking, things happen. Some say she has the second sight, knows things will happen before they do. I think most of the stories about Nanan Marie are made up, some might be true, but I think people let their imaginations get away from them, once in a while."

Biscuit gave a little yip and was standing, eagerly tapping her little paws, looking at Emily.

Emily said, "Oh, I'd better go, looks like Biscuit's had enough of waiting." Turning back to Bea, she said, "Thank you for taking the time to talk with me."

"No problem! Stop by any time!"

"Yes, I will," said Emily, "next time I'll bring my husband!"

Emily stood outside the diner resting her back against the clapboard siding, trying to find shade from the noon sun and glancing up and down the street. She looked at the face of her watch to note the time, and when she looked up, she was startled because Nanan Marie was standing not four feet away, staring at her. And biscuit hadn't made a sound. Odd.

"Oh! You surprised me, I didn't see you coming!"

Nanan Marie took her hand and said, "Come. There's a nice bench under the trees where we can sit."

Emily let herself be led a few steps down the street and around the corner where she saw, further on, a stand of Large Leaf Maple and tall Elder trees shimmering in the hot sunlight.

Nanan Marie indicated that they should step off the road into the little park-like setting among the trees and led Emily a few dozen paces to an ornate wrought iron bench beneath the shady canopy of an ancient, twisted Alder.

As they sat down, Nanan Marie took out her handkerchief and wiped her brow and said, "My old bones don't tolerate the heat any better than my young bones did."

Emily was listening to the locust singing in the treetops and thinking that the heat and humidity really seemed to slow time down. At Nanan Marie's voice, Emily turned to look at the old woman sitting beside her.

She seemed to be wearing the same clothes she wore yesterday, certainly those were the same boots. Emily could see Nanan Marie's face clearly now and noted the deep creases that etched their way around her eyes and mouth. Her eyes were pale blue, so pale that they almost disappeared into the whites yet somehow, they carried knowledge and sharpened intensely when focused.

Emily said, "I've been so curious about why you wanted to see me."

"Yes... yes. I have something for you." Nanan Marie rummaged through a skirt pocket and finally brought out what she had sought. She looked at it for a moment and then pressed the object into Emily's hand.

"For your protection. You must wear it. It will help to keep you safe."

Emily was a bit stunned at what Nanan Marie had just said and looked at the object in her hand. It was an old penny with a hole through its outer edge and it hung from a thick beaded gold chain. She looked closer. The penny was ornate, unlike any Emily had seen before. The date was 1858. Emily was holding a United States Flying Eagle penny that hung from a tarnished gold chain.

Finding her tongue, Emily asked, "Did you say it would keep me safe? From what?" Holding the chain in her fingertips, watching it dangle, added, "I'm not sure that a penny can keep me safe from anything."

Nanan Marie was closely watching Emily, as if to study her face. She raised her eyebrows and nodded as she spoke, "You're on the old DuFrene property now. You listen to this and then you will believe." She wiped at her neck with her handkerchief and pulled at the rope that belted her waist.

Emily's mind raced, *I hope I haven't gotten myself into trouble by talking with this woman. She may be a little crazy, maybe addled with age. Be careful. Stay alert.*

Nanan Marie stuffed her handkerchief back into her pocket and began. "Wear this gree-gree, always. Go on, girl," Nanan Marie said, wagging a finger at Emily. "Go ahead." Nodding.

Emily slipped the chain over her head, the penny fell in front of her breastbone and as she looked down at it thought, *what could it hurt to wear an old penny?*

Nanan Marie smiled and touched the penny with one finger. "Over your heart. Good."

"This is an old story. Starts over two hundred years ago… There are dark and mysterious things that go on in the swamp."

Nanan Marie slowly turned her gaze across the park and seemed to be listening to something. Emily could only hear a lone locust, hidden up in the Alder's canopy, buzzing, buzzing. Momentarily, Marie spoke.

"An old story. Not like the swamp. The swamp is before time, before DuFrene, before you." She smiled her near toothless smile and continued, "There are things in the swamp that we'll never know. Should 'naught to know. But I know." Nanan Marie's voice trailed off. She had dug her kerchief back out of her pocket and mopped at her neck.

Emily shifted in her place to better face Marie and was regarding her closely. She watched as Marie picked at her kerchief, trying to smooth it down and fold it up, only to pick at it some more, unfolding it with the effort. She seemed to be struggling with her thoughts and the struggle reflected on her face as she knitted her brows together, then let out a little snort of laughter.

"Oh," Nanan Marie said, nodding in acknowledgement, "the new moon will tell, it will show." Then gazed away again.

"Will show what? Marie. What will the new moon show?"

Nanan Marie didn't answer Emily's question but forged ahead. "Swamp tells me things, sometimes shows me the 'morrow. Told me about you, child. Told me how you needed to be here."

The heat of the day was taking its toll on Emily. She was not used to the stillness of the air, the humidity that seemed to cling to her skin. She was wishing that she had brought a bottle of water with her and thought of poor little Biscuit who had stopped foraging and now sat at her feet, panting with the effort.

Nanan Marie had stopped talking and Emily became aware that Marie was looking at her with a mixture of curiosity and skepticism.

Before Emily could speak, Nanan Marie had hauled herself up, grunting with the effort and hobbled as she straightened her legs. "Yes... yes... you know. The swamp says so. Then it is so." And started to walk away.

Emily stood but before she could think what to say, Nanan Marie was fifteen steps away and walking with purpose. She made it to the street and veered her path to the right, away from town and in another two steps was out of view.

Emily and Biscuit made the street a few seconds later but Nanan Marie was nowhere in sight, seemingly vanished into the steamy afternoon air.

Emily went over and over the things Nanan Marie had said trying to make sense of it all. She tempered some of it with what Bea told her earlier. That Nanan Marie was rumored to be a bit touched but harmless. That she lived in the swamp. *How can she possibly be living in the swamp? It seems almost unheard of.* Emily's mind started to reel with the stimulus of her thoughts so she figured to settle down to the task of getting the groceries and maybe looking around the large retail mall in Slidell before driving home.

With the groceries stashed and the afternoon wearing on, Emily put several tea bags into a water-filled pitcher and was headed for the back patio. Biscuit had drank a lot of water and found a cool dark area by the great-room fireplace and was uninterested in accompanying Emily any further.

Emily made a tsk-tsk sound causing Biscuit to barely raise her head to look.

"You're such a city dog." At which, Biscuit stretched, yawned, and closed her eyes in total disregard.

Matthew looked up from his laptop and said, "What'cha got there?"

"I'm going to make a pitcher of solar-tea, the sun is going to bake the tea right out of these bags. Probably take an hour or so... well, maybe faster this afternoon, though. How's it with you?"

"I think this is going to work out. All my work connections are up and I'm able to monitor and communicate just fine. May need to fly out every couple of weeks for face-to-face meetings but otherwise, I think I can manage from here."

Emily was standing near Matthew watching his face as he spoke. He looked very pleased with his new set-up and he had a genuine happiness in his eyes. This was going to be good for him, for both of them.

She lifted the pitcher and said, "Care to join me while I watch tea being made?"

Matthew smiled and said, "I have a few more things to do, but then I'll come out. Give me a few minutes?"

"Absolutely. Take your time." Emily gave him a quick peck on the forehead and left him to his email and screens and quietly let herself out into the back patio.

With the pitcher placed in the center of the patio where it should soak up a lot of afternoon heat just fine, Emily thought to look around a bit. She stood listening to the afternoon sounds and looking objectively at the grounds immediately surrounding the house, the garage, and her new studio. She started to imagine how Matthew and she would move through the space, where gardens should be and if she were ready to start growing her own tomatoes. *Anything is possible,* she thought with humor.

Then her mind moved forward. *The moving truck will be here tomorrow, it'll be a busy day, but then I'll have my drawing books and worktables and can be more serious about design and other projects. I think I'll try to enjoy what's left of my "vacation" and not worry about all of that right now.*

Emily's gaze went to the thicket of woods along the back of the property and momentarily wondered if they should have need of a private boat dock on the river. One thought led to another and shortly, Emily found herself picking her way down to the river's edge.

The property was fairly flat up to the last fifteen feet when it sloped quickly away and down to the muddy water. Emily stood, holding on to the trunk of a small maple tree, watching the muddy water flow by. Here, The Old Pearl River was as wide as an eight-lane highway but didn't appear to be moving too fast. She scooted down the slope and stood in the wet gravel that had collected along the sides, looking up and down the river.

There was not much to the North. The river took a bend about thirty yards up, disappearing to the right. The view to the south was a bit more interesting. The Old Pearl ran straight for what may have been half a mile, although bending slightly to the left, allowing Emily to see along the back property lines of other privately owned acres along the river. Some distance down, Emily did see what might have been a small boat dock, although from this distance, it could have been a pile of abandoned lumber. Too far away to tell for sure what it was.

Emily found a large boulder and presently perched herself upon it. The air was a bit cooler here by the water and it seemed to her that some of the tension in her muscles started to relax as she sat. It relaxed her to sit here, on a boulder, and stare at the river moving by. She tossed a dried leaf into the water and watched as it bobbed and turned until the current caught it and moved it away.

In the solitude of the moment, Nanan Marie sprang to mind with all the questions and concerns that meeting her brought with it. Emily's thoughts were a jumble, everything swirling and making no sense but mesmerizing her into a kind of daze, neither here nor there.

Emily was roused from her lethargy by Matthew's voice.

"Hey Em! Emily!"

"I'm here, Matt. Down by the river."

Matthew popped out up on the ridge and stood with his hands on his waist looking up and down the river. "This is really something. Shall I come down?"

Emily stood up, "No, don't bother, I'll come up."

When she got to the top, she took Matthew's hand and they stood for a moment before she spoke, "What do you think? A boat dock right there with guided tours for our friends?"

Matthew slapped at his forearm then absentmindedly scratched at it. "Not without a bug repellant dispenser." Then, "You know, this could be pretty nice. Wonder if fish live in there," eyeing the muddy water suspiciously.

"Wonder if alligators live in there," added Emily.

Matthew turned and started his careful gait through the stubby vegetation with Emily following. After a few steps, a small tingling along the back of her neck prompted Emily to turn around. As her eyes swung out across the river to the thick flora of the swamp, she was sure she glimpsed Nanan Marie standing in the shadows watching her. As Emily strained to see across the river and through the dark gray light under the trees, the apparition deliberately turned and disappeared.

Matthew's voice broke Emily's concentration. "Are you coming?"

And Emily called back to him, "Coming right now."

Emily and Matthew walked back to the house, collected the pitcher of nice dark solar-tea and headed indoors while continuing their animated conversations about this and that.

"Dinner will take about an hour, when would you feel like eating?" asked Emily.

"Oh, I don't know. Let's sit for awhile then I'll help you."

Emily said, "Okay. Want to take chairs out on the patio, have a glass of wine, then start dinner?"

"Yes, let's do that." Matthew took both chairs from his ad hoc work desk and headed for the patio.

They found a bit of shade along the back of the house and were sitting, chatting idly, when a series of musical chimes startled them both.

"Is that the door bell?" asked Matthew. And they both laughed at themselves for jumping at the unfamiliar sound.

Both Emily and Matthew went to see who was there, putting their glasses down in the kitchen as they went through to the front door.

Opening the door revealed a man and a woman, both nicely dressed and smiling. The woman was holding a large casserole in both her oven-mitted hands and excitedly sang out, "Welcome new neighbors!"

And the man said, "I'm Brad Halcourt and this is my wife Christine. We're your neighbors. Our place runs along side yours, just over that way," pointing off into the woods to the south. "Probably a mile through there, although shorter if you drive. We're one road back down White Egret, toward the highway."

Emily stepped back from the doorway and motioned for them to… "Come in, come in!" and heard Matthew's introductions.

"I'm Matthew Harris," shaking hands with Brad, "and my wife, Emily."

Smiling, Emily said hello and then indicated to Christine that the kitchen was through the wide hallway. "What'cha got there?"

Christine, smiling and clearly proud about the huge La Cruset she was carrying, said, "This is Jambalaya. Made from an old family recipe. You're going to love it!"

Brad said, "We wanted to welcome you to this neck of the woods, just say hi, let you know that you can call if you need anything."

Emily had gotten two more wine glasses out and was busy pulling the cork on a 2004 Dancing Vines Pinot Noir from Napa Valley.

Everyone was talking excitedly and after Emily gave their guests their wine, heard Brad ask Matthew to show him the garages and watched as they went out the patio doors.

Meanwhile, she stood with Christine in the kitchen. "I'm sorry we don't have anywhere for you to sit, the moving van isn't due 'till tomorrow. We're sort of roughing it."

Biscuit had joined them and Christine was bent down scratching her neck and patting her affectionately. Biscuit was showing her appreciation by leaning against Christine's leg, soaking it up.

Christine said, "Don't you worry for one minute about it. We won't stay more then a few minutes anyway. Just wanted to welcome you and make sure you had a good home cooked meal."

"This is so nice of you, we truly appreciate all the work that must have gone into it."

"Nonsense!" Christine waved her hand to lightly dismiss the thought, "It was not work at all! I love to cook, almost as much as I love to meet interesting new people!"

Smiling, Christine took a sip of her wine and then asked, "How do you like it here so far?"

Emily nodded and said, "We both like it a lot. I think we'll be happy here." Her gaze slid slowly to the back windows that framed the wonderful view of her new, exciting property.

Christine continued, "I'm so glad that you bought the old DuFrene estate and have fixed it up so nicely." Raising her glass to indicate her appreciation for the renovations.

Emily smiled her thanks, "We didn't know much about the DuFrene's when we started." Sipping her wine. "I'm afraid we still don't know much more."

"Oh, there's such a rich history connected with this land. It started with Captain DuFrene somewhere around the early 1800's."

Emily poured more wine and said, "Let's sit outside, I want to hear all the stories," and led the way to the back patio.

After settling down, Christine started.

"I'll give you the highlights. Our local library is a good source for details but like all histories, may be a little dry."

Emily asked, "You said it started with Captain DuFrene?"

"Yes. Captain DuFrene was a sea captain. He made his fortune building trade routes along the Southwest Pacific Basin. Some say part of his fortune come from pirating French shipments of gold, although that was never proven. Captain DuFrene successfully brought many exotic goods from unknown places and traded up and up until he was filthy rich.

"In early 1800, he bought over a thousand acres, here along the Pearl River. This house is standing where the original French Country farmhouse once stood. There were many other buildings at that time, too. Mainly a large barn and a few workers quarters.

"In 1824 there was a huge fire. Destroyed everything but the main house. Captain DuFrene was at sea when it happened and didn't return for another four years. But when he did return, he brought back a wife. She was a dark beauty, as exotic as some of the spices he traded. Her name was Freitah and must have been about twenty years old. DuFrene was fifty-eight at the time so their marriage was a bit scandalous.

"They had three children together. One son died very young. Their only daughter never married. There's lots of stories about why that was but none ever made it into history books."

Christine took a moment and sipped her wine. "The oldest boy, Henri DuFrene, followed the Captain into ship sailing and at the age of sixteen, was the first mate on a clipper ship that ran from New York to Hong Kong.

"After their youngest son died, Freitah became a recluse and rumors spread that she was involved with dark practices... the kind only whispered about.

"The eldest son, Henri, ended up the Captain of his clipper ship at the age of twenty-three. Quite an accomplishment."

Emily sat in rapt attention. "This is so fascinating. Sea Captains, exotic women. Interesting stuff."

"And it gets better!" Christine raised her glass for a toast, "To the DuFrene's!"

"To the DuFrene's," repeated Emily, and the two women took sips from their glasses.

Christine swirled the wine around her glass and took a dainty sniff. Encouraged by the fruity notes of the red wine, she continued.

"Henri stayed at sea until he was forty-nine, then returned to Slidell to retire. His daddy had long since passed and the DuFrene estate was his. He also had the pick of the eligible daughters of local predominant bankers and landowners. So. In 1878, Henri DuFrene married Thema Baudin… eighteen years old, another little scandal."

Looking over at Emily, Christine bobbed her head a little and said, "I'm lovin' that part of it!"

Emily laughed, mostly at how far into the story she was. She was a bit embarrassed. It felt like she was gossiping, it was almost shameful.

Christine must have seen this on Emily's face and quickly added, "It isn't gossip if they're all dead, is it?" and smiled.

Emily felt her face flush red and said, "I hope not, but I'm kind of hooked. You've got to tell me the rest of the story."

"It's a good one." Christine sat for a moment, thinking, then said, "Where was I? Oh, yes. Henri got married." Then went on, "Henri's mother, Freitah, and his new bride, Thema, became inseparable. They would disappear into the swamp during new moons. There were rumors that Freitah taught Thema the black arts… casting spells, making charms. Very dangerous things for the time.

"Twelve years after the wedding, Thema gave birth to a daughter, Manette. Pretty little girl. When Manette was young, Thema would take her into the swamp. Thema maintained that she was teaching the girl how to find special plants and roots, but rumors sprang up, as they will do, telling tales of potions and charms and unholy things.

"Now they say that Thema and Manette can be heard calling softly to anyone in the swamp after dark."

This sent a chill up Emily's spine. "Is that true? Have you heard them?"

Christine's eyes widened an her breath shortened, "Honey, there's no possible way I would be in that swamp after dark!"

Both women laughed and while Emily didn't completely dismiss that statement, she tried to act as if she had.

Christine continued her story, "Manette had a son… out of wedlock, when she was sixteen. No one knew who the father was. She named him Reynauld and Henri gave him the last name of DuFrene. Most everyone thought that Henri wanted rumors about his daughter to stop and thought that by giving the bastard-boy a legitimate name would somehow… legitimize him. Don't know if that worked, though."

Emily asked, "Would you like some more wine? Let's get some more wine," and stood up, reaching for Christine's glass.

Christine said, "I'll come with you," and stood up, too.

When they got to the kitchen, Emily pulled a plate from the cabinet and crackers from the pantry. She added slices of cheese, a few grapes, and found a couple of napkins. Christine poured a bit more wine and then joined Emily, as she returned to the patio.

Emily looked around and caught sight of Matthew and Brad sauntering around the outside of the garages. Matthew was pointing up to the roof and Emily guessed that the men were deep in architectural discussions and construction evaluations.

The ladies returned to the patio but moved their chairs a little way from the house so as to catch a pleasant early evening breeze coming up from the river.

"The story is coming to the good part... hold on now." Christine continued, "In 1941 Reynauld, now twenty-five years old, marries a local gal, Marie Agness Winton, daughter of a prominent landowner. She's a scandalous fourteen years old at the time!

"Two years into the marriage, Reynauld dies. His body is found in the swamp but the funeral is rushed and the death certificate is never made public."

Emily asked, "What happened to his young wife?"

Christine said, "Oh, she's still around. She's about eighty-seven or eighty-eight years old now. Wanders around muttering. We call her Nanan Marie."

Emily froze at the mention of Nanan Marie's name. A small chill ran through her spine and time seemed to stop. "Are you serious? The last of the DuFrene's is Nanan Marie?"

Christine smiled, "Oh, I see you've heard of her!"

Before Emily could reply, Brad and Matthew came across the patio. Brad was saying, "Ok, it's dinner at our place two weeks from now. I'll invite the Blanchets and the Hurleys. Just a small affair. You've got to see my brewery!"

Christine got up from her chair and added, "It's two steps up from a bathtub operation but makes pretty good beer!"

Matthew gave a chuckle and said, "Looking forward to it!"

Brad slipped an arm around Christine's shoulder and asked, "You about ready? We should get."

Smiling, Christine turned to Emily and Matthew and said, "Congratulations on your beautiful new home and welcome again to the neighborhood."

Brad added, "Call if you need anything." And with that, they took their leave.

Twenty minutes later, over a wonderful jambalaya meal, Emily and Matthew swapped Brad and Christine stories. Emily broad-brushed the DuFrene story that Christine told, instead leaving out all the rumors and the part about Nanan Marie. She wasn't sure why she left all of that unsaid. But she did.

The moving truck arrived early the next day and the entire morning was spent managing the seemingly endless influx of boxes and furniture. The chaos was barely contained and at its peak came close to impossible.

One of the moving company men, Jim, asked Emily where she wanted the master bed placed and after a brief consideration, Emily asked that it be centered on one of the walls. The mover took a few moments to assemble the frame and set up the box springs and mattress for them saying that they would be pretty tired later to do it themselves.

At about eleven-thirty, Emily scooped four generous portions of jambalaya from Christine's large La Cruset into a smaller oven dish and started heating it up. She pulled together some crackers and grated some cheese and set the now present dining room table for herself, Matthew and the two moving company men, Jim and Chuck.

Just past noon, she called the men to wash up and come to the table for lunch.

After everyone was seated and the Pellegrino poured, Emily kicked off a bit of light conversation, "So Jim, how long have you worked for Green Leaf Movers?"

"Almost five years now. Chuck and I have partnered this route for about a year and a half."

Emily asked, "Do you like it?"

Jim said, "Yea, it's a good route, busy enough to stay interesting."

Chuck added, "But not so busy that it becomes all stress. Nice and steady."

The conversation fell a bit quiet as everyone forked the jambalaya with hunger.

After a minute Matthew asked, "Does Green Leaf move things other than residential persons?"

Jim answered, "Yes. Every once in awhile a business will change locations and we'll do that. Green Leaf has a couple of carriers that specialize in moving delicate things like computers or hospital equipment, things like that."

There was a short pause in the conversation and Emily considered asking the movers a question and before she could check herself, she blurted it out, "Have you, in your travels, ever heard facts or legends about the DuFrene family or the Honey Island Swamp?"

The suddenness of the question stunned Emily, she could feel her face redden with embarrassment for her abruptness and with a quiet, almost hushed, voice added, "I'm just a little curious about our new home."

Chuck looked up from his plate, smiled as he looked from

Matthew, over to Emily, and then at Jim, who spooned another bite of jambalaya into his mouth.

Still smiling Chuck said, "I've heard that most people here about believe that the swamp is full of monsters and indescribable phantoms and that evil spirits stalk the night looking for victims. That all of the people who lost their lives in the swamp are a large population of walking dead brought back in payment for their unspeakable sins."

Energized by his enthusiasm for the subject, Chuck's voice quickened as he continued, "There's one tale that I've heard at least three times from different folk, that tells about the DuFrene ancestors casting voodoo spells and talking to demons to ensure that their lands and goods stayed out of the hands of unbelievers, and—."

Jim noticed that Matthew was listening and starting to laugh at what Chuck was saying but that Emily was staring wide-eyed and her face starting to go pale. He thought to interrupt Chuck's tall tale.

"A lot of the people that live around here are from French Creole descent and have heard these kinds of tales their whole lives. They're superstitious and there's no real fact to verify the folk stories or to rationalize their fears. It's all talk and better left unsaid, like bad gossip."

Jim glanced over at Chuck and nodded, "Don't you agree?"

Chuck smiled and said, "Yes, I kind of do, although you've got to admit that the rumors and tall tales do make good stories. And these, in particular have survived for several generations. Makes me wonder if there isn't a small shred of truth in 'em after all."

After a minute Chuck said, "Well," as he finished his lunch

and cleared his plate to the sink and addressing himself to Emily and Matthew, said, "Thank you so much for lunch," and to Jim, "I'm going to get back to work."

Jim finished his last bite and wiped his mouth before saying, "What a nice meal, thank you."

Smiling, Emily said, "Our neighbors brought a huge pot of it last night."

Jim said, "Be sure to thank them and thank you for sharing your table with us." He nodded to them and left to rejoin Chuck and continued moving boxes and other items to their respective rooms.

Emily laid her hand gently on Matthew's arm and smiled at him. "I'll take care of the clean-up. You go do what you need to do and when I'm done, I think I'll walk Biscuit."

Matthew pushed out his chair and got up. He leaned down and kissed Emily softly on her lips and said, "Okay, thanks. I think I'll start putting my office together, see if I can't get it wired up before dinnertime."

Emily smiled to herself as she watched Matthew stride down the hallway, through the stacks of boxes, to his new office. However, the second he was out of sight, her mind filled with strange pictures of voodoo rituals and other images that she decisively pushed from her thoughts with a clearing shake of her head.

Emily and Biscuit were enjoying their exploration of the riverbank. The early afternoon sun was warm but not yet hot enough to force them back inside.

Biscuit was taking it all in stride, thoroughly sniffing at this thistle and that rock. As she sniffed along the tide's edge, she frightened a large toad that made one long hop before splashing into the river. Biscuit almost jumped in after it and if not for the taut leash-line, probably would have.

"Steady little huntress. That guy didn't look that tasty, anyway."

Biscuit was staring steadily at the spot where the toad had hit the water and disappeared. She gave out a little huff, turned herself around and kicked a small scattering of pebbles with her hind leg.

Emily laughed out loud, she had never seen Biscuit do such a thing. It was almost as if Biscuit had dismissed the toad and declared that she had "won that round."

Emily said, "Oh, Biscuit, you're becoming so primal, aren't you?"

At which, Biscuit looked up at Emily and sort of huffed-sneezed her consent before putting her nose to the ground and moving off again.

Emily was looking at the wild grasses and little weed flowers with interest. She picked a tiny orange flower and brought it close to look at it in detail. It had five petals that were veined with red, three anthers and a fuzzy blue stigma. Looking at the little flower filled Emily with wonder. *Even a weed has beauty.*

As she stood, breathing in the fragrances of the river, feeling that the stresses of moving were melting away, she happened to look up the bank and noticed, hidden in the tall grasses, the little dinghy she had seen the day before. It was overgrown with tall grasses and, Emily thought, probably rotted and full of holes.

She tugged at the leash and said, "Biscuit. Let's go look at this. Come on." And started the short climb up the riverbank into the tall scrub, Biscuit bounding effortlessly past her.

Emily reached the dinghy and stood looking at it. She bent down and tugged at a board that presumably was a seat. It was solid enough. Emily twisted biscuit's leash around it so that the dog wouldn't get away from her. Then she got busy pulling on the weeds and freeing the boat from its land-locked mooring.

Forty-five minutes later, and thoroughly drenched in sweat, Emily had freed the boat and stood looking critically at the wear and tear that the years had imposed upon it.

The sides were intact and there weren't any visible holes in the bottom. The seat was solid and the oarlocks were solid, although the metal was pitted from salt air and river use, they were securely bolted to the sides, giving only a little under Emily's hand. She gently rocked the boat to one side and saw that the keel was straight and true even if there were little nicks in the wood along its line.

Rocking the dinghy over on its other side revealed two oars laying on the ground. Emily picked one up and had to tug a bit to free it from the little bindweeds that tried to hold it steady.

They were caked with dried mud and had bits of weed stems stuck to them but otherwise looked in good shape.

The mid-day sun had become very warm and Emily started to realize that maybe she had gotten a little carried away with her preoccupation with the dinghy. Exhausted, she climbed into the boat and sat down. *I should have worn a hat and brought a bottle of water.* And looking around, *poor Biscuit. She's panting.*

As Emily sat in the dinghy she became aware that the air was still and the birds were quiet. Faintly came the sound of a lone insect's buzzing and in a moment, even that quieted.

It was eerie. Emily's skin started to crawl. Rubbing her arms to smooth down the goose bumps, she thought, *Come on Em. Get it together. There's nothing to be afraid of.*

Just then a loud snap and then a kerplunk sound of something hitting the water made Emily jump and caused Biscuit to come to her feet and emit a low growling sound from the base of her throat.

Emily was out of the boat in a heartbeat. She snapped up the leash and in a voice, edged with nerves said, "Time to go home, girl."

In a short twenty minutes, Emily and Biscuit were letting themselves in through the patio doors. Both had calmed down from the little incident earlier.

"Matt, we're back! Emily sang out.

Matthew answered, "Hello! I'm in the office."

"It's so quiet in here."

"The men finished up and said they wanted to make Baton Rouge by dinner. They left about ten minutes ago. Said that if anything is broken, they apologized, or if we had any questions, we could contact Green Leaf."

Emily said, "I'm sure everything is fine but it may be weeks before we know for sure." She was standing in front of Matthew's desk, looking at his set-up. "Looks nice. Do you like it?"

"Yes. I think it'll do nicely. Hey, I hooked up your laptop to the Internet for you. I used the connection in the kitchen, at that small workspace. We can move it later but I wanted to get you up and running."

Emily smiled, "That's great! I'll check in with New York, see how they're doing." After a short pause, Emily asked, "Dinner at seven?" And raising her eyebrows in mock surprise, "We're having jambalaya."

Lighting up his face in mock happiness, Matthew said, "My favorite!"

"Okay, see you later." Emily blew him a kiss and left him to his work.

Biscuit had already lapped up a bunch of water and made her way into the great room to flop down on the cool stones of the fireplace hearth. She was already asleep with her feet twitching in dreams of running through tall grass and after flying toads.

Emily strolled slowly past boxes and hastily placed furniture and almost froze with the enormity of unpacking all of them. Her very next thought was to let it go until tomorrow. Right now, she thought to bring her laptop up and check her email.

After clearing the junk and making note of who had emailed her, Emily clicked the Safari icon on her dashboard and typed in "Honey Island Swamp."

The next day, armed with a few local fauna fact sheets Emily printed off the web, she and Biscuit headed out for a morning of discovery. She had promised Matthew to be back by mid-afternoon, in time for them to clean up and go into town for dinner.

The fact sheets promised swamp grasses and wild iris and although the iris may already have bloomed, the grasses and sedge might still have lots of delicate flower stalks tall and ready in the bright sunshine.

Emily was amazed at the number and types of trees that thrived in the muggy heat of the area. There were Cypress and Willow, Alder and Gum, and River Birch. She couldn't wait to see how many grew around their property. This was very exciting. They actually owned trees!

As she led Biscuit down toward the river's edge, the fright of the previous day was almost forgotten. Her steps were sure and the direction true. She headed straight for the little dinghy.

Emily wrestled the little dinghy half way into the water and after a moment of fiddling around with the oarlocks, figured out how to mount them and lock them into place.

So far so good. No leaks. Now let's see if I can aim this thing across the river.

Biscuit was in the bow, looking a little worried but otherwise holding her own.

Emily managed to get the back half of the dinghy into the water and jump on-board. She sat for a minute inspecting all the joints and fasteners and when she was satisfied that the little craft was going to float, slung the oars over the side and started to row.

The slow current took the dinghy quickly out to the middle of the river and Emily knew that she had better work those oars or she would soon find herself miles down river.

It took some time but she did it. She managed to hit the opposite shore only a dozen or so yards down river from where she pushed off. Emily decided to drag the dinghy back upstream so that her return trip might be more accurate and having accomplished that, drug the dinghy up onto the riverbank to make sure it didn't drift away without her.

Emily stood for a minute on the riverbank sipping a bit of water from her bottle and staring into the darkness of the overgrown trees and shrubs before her. Biscuit stood by her side, silently waiting for her mistress' command.

I'll walk straight in and straight back, that way I won't get lost. Emily pulled her little sheaf of papers out of her back pocket and using it as a field guide, stepped into the dank underbrush.

The ground under her step felt spongy from seasons of undisturbed leaf-drop, and the air seemed to close in on her, making her breathing a bit labored. As her eyes adjusted to the dim light that filtered through the thick tree canopies, a marvelous new world appeared.

Amid the pungent and all encompassing leaf litter sprang little bright green plantlets some of which were adorned with unopened flower buds. Emily recognized the Carex that dotted the immediate view, with their long slender leaves and saw tall stalks of what she thought to be cattails grouped in one spot off to her left. Must be a little marshy area there. *Better watch my footing and keep Biscuit on a short leash. Maybe I should have left her home…*

As Emily slowly moved forward she noticed the proliferation of vines that seemed to dominate the landscape. They were tangled across the ground and twisted up most of the tree trunks, climbing up and up to the light. *That doesn't look like a symbiotic relationship. The vines appear hostile, just using the trees as ladders, not caring that the tree might eventually die.*

She looked at her guide pages that had become wrinkled with the perspiration of her hand and were quickly wicking up moisture from the thick oppressive air. The tree was a Gum tree. Encouraged by her new-found knowledge, Emily continued on.

Straight in and straight back. Thirty minutes… tops.

It was slow going for another sixty or seventy feet but Emily was determined to move forward. There was a break in the dense canopy just ahead and possibly the air would be less humid there.

Breaking out of the forest into a small more open area was easier going. The vines thinned out and were closer to the sun-dried ground making her footing more sure. Biscuit was surely relieved and relaxed her vigilance enough to check her steps with curious sniffing.

Emily was trying to catch her breath and steady her pulse. It had been more of a struggle to "walk" through the thick jumble of green brush that she had anticipated. It was going to take a minute to settle down.

The wide brim of her hat shaded her eyes from the now glaring sunshine and a slight warm breeze brushed her face. Emily stood looking at the trees that enclosed the little clearing periodically checking her battered field guide papers against the surroundings.

As she looked up from the papers, Emily thought she saw something shiny, wink in the moving shadows, off to her right. She turned her head to look at the spot more closely and yes... the small shiny thing appeared again.

Her curiosity piqued, Emily walked toward the object that was visibly affixed to a tree trunk at about eye level. And getting close enough to focus on the object, Emily stared in disbelief. It was a copper penny. An 1858 United States Flying Eagle penny. Emily fished the chained penny that Nanan Marie had given to her, out from underneath her sweat-soaked blouse and looked closely at both. They were identical.

As Emily stood in disbelief with fragmented questions flooding her mind, Biscuit tugged at the leash as she dug at the ground.

Her attention now on Biscuit, Emily said, "What's that?" and stepped closer. "Did you find a lizard?"

Biscuit's digging uncovered part of a clay object and Emily watched as the dog pawed and worked at the ground. Eventually Biscuit dug away most of the hard-pack and Emily thought to help by jabbing at it with a stick. In time, the two of them freed the object. It was a clay figure of a human, crudely done. It had arms, and legs, and a torso but didn't resemble male or female. There were no real facial features, just suggestions of eyes, a nose, and the mouth. The head was poked full of holes where hair might be and Emily thought, as she studied the figure, that real hair might, at one time, have been stuck into them. *Is this some kind of child's doll? What would it be doing out here?*

Suddenly, a noise Emily couldn't quite identify brought her to attention and as adrenalin shot through her, her mind screamed, *what was that?* She kept still and listened. She then became aware that there were no insect sounds, no birds chirping. The small clearing was silent.

Biscuit had heard the sound, too, and stood rigid, staring at the spot across from them, a small rumbling growl building in her throat.

Emily touched her lightly and whispered softly, "It's okay, it's okay," in an effort to diffuse her growing protective stance.

Her thoughts ran wild, *who knows what kind of creatures are living here. Dangerous ones. Alligators!* Emily stood and tugged Biscuit's leash, "Come," and stepped quickly across the clearing back to where she thought they had entered.

Her fear started to rise. She quickened her pace and plunged into the dark shadow of the forest. Biscuit worked hard to keep up, yipping with the fear she sensed from Emily, but was getting caught in some of the tangle so Emily scooped her up into her arms and forged on.

The going was rough. Emily tripped as her foot was caught in a mass of vines and she fell to her knees. Her breathing was labored and as she tried to pull in enough air, took a moment to listen to her surroundings. *Is it following us?* All she could hear was her blood rushing in her ears and Biscuit's panting.

Move!

She stood up and came face-to-face with an object that was just inches from her eyes. It was dangling on a thin piece of twine rope that was tied to a branch just above her head. Focusing, Emily saw that it was about five inches around, made from willow stems fashioned into a hoop, and had what might have been a net woven from the same twine stretched across it. The hair on the back of Emily's neck prickled when she saw a little figure of a woman caught in the net. But what really frightened her was that the figure of the woman, clearly tangled in the net and without hope for escape, was wearing an old tarnished penny around her neck.

Snatching at the woven likeness and yanking it free of its thin twine, Emily, fueled by fear, plunged ahead hoping that she was going in the right direction.

After an eternity of pushing through overgrown shrubs and having branches and thistles scratching at her face and arms, Emily broke out of the forest and fell with exhaustion into a weakened heap at the river's edge.

Relief filled her body, so much so that she broke out into tears and trembling, hugged Biscuit so close that the little dog whimpered in her concern.

Emily recovered herself. She wiped her eyes on the sleeves of her blouse then noticed that her arms were scratched, muddy, and somewhat bloody. The left knee of her pants was torn and through the ragged hole she could see a bruise starting to form around a red lump just above her shin.

I'm a mess. Oh, poor Biscuit. "Biscuit come." Biscuit went to Emily and looked up at her. "Look at your beautiful coat," and stroking Biscuit's head, bade her to sit still as she pulled bits of greenery and dried leaves out of her matted hair. Emily wondered again why she would have taken Biscuit into the swamp.

What's the matter with me?   Of course the swamp is dangerous. Such a little sweet dog. I shouldn't have done it.

Emily groomed Biscuit as well as she could, rinsing her paws in the river and checking her over for cuts. When she had finished she sat back on her heals and looked over the river. She spotted the dinghy some one hundred yards down river, *so much for straight in and straight back. Next time I'll mark my path, oh, listen to me talking about "next time"… well… I don't know… maybe.*

It took a great deal of effort but Emily's tired muscles pulled them back across to their side of the river.

She brushed at her clothes hoping not to look so disheveled when she got back home but it was a futile effort. There was no hiding her scratches and bruises not to mention her embarrassment.

After explaining why she and Biscuit were in such a state of disorder, Matthew "ordered" Emily into a hot bath and brought her a couple of aspirin. He sat with her and listened as she told her tale of mysterious things and pennies nailed to trees. The hooped figure, Emily felt, would really make her case but as Matthew looked at it, couldn't agree as to what it really was. He certainly didn't agree that it was a facsimile of Emily and basically dismissed her theory.

"You've let your imagination run away with you, Emily."

"I don't think so. What about all the things Nanan Marie said to me? Or finding the same penny as she gave to me nailed to that tree?"

Matthew knelt beside the large claw-footed tub. He fished the loofah out of the water, briefly turned the hot water on to warm the bath again and gently dabbed at Emily's bruised arms. "Nanan Marie is not in her right mind and the whole penny 'thing' is circumstantial at best. You yourself admit that you were frightened, and Emily, you must know that fears build upon themselves, for no solid reason."

Emily wanted to believe Matthew. But in the back of her mind she knew that she was right.

Matthew continued, "You were alone in a strange place with unfamiliar sounds. It's natural when you can't explain something to try to make sense of the situation. In this case, fear got the better of you. I'm just glad you didn't hurt yourself any worse than these scratches."

He got up and brought a bath-towel closer to the tub so Emily could easily reach it and said, "I'm going to make you some hot broth and bring it up to you. I'll see to Biscuit and be back in a few minutes." He smiled at her, "Are you ok?"

Emily looked at Matthew and let some of her doubt go with a little exhale and a smile and said, "Yes. I'm fine and thank you for taking care of me."

Matthew stood for a brief second smiling and then turned to leave.

She heard his soft steps retreat through the bedroom and out into the hallway.

Emily sat low in the tub feeling the hot water against her sore muscles, lost in thought. After a moment, she lifted the chain that she still wore around her neck and dangled the penny just inches in front of her eyes. *It all makes sense. Right from the beginning.*

Emily rinsed off and towel-dried her hair before wrapping herself up in her thick warm robe. She was brushing her hair when

Matthew appeared with a bowl of soup, a few crackers, and a bite of cheddar cheese.

"I'll sit with you for a few minutes but then you should get into bed and relax, take a nap. I'll check on you in a couple of hours. OK?"

"I think I will lay down. I'm feeling very exhausted, probably the hot bath."

Emily sipped her broth and nibbled half the cheese and a cracker.

Matthew cleared the tray and drew the curtains a bit to dim the room then quietly left.

Biscuit trotted in and jumped up onto the bed. Emily embraced the little dog and cooed, "There you are, sweet dog." Encouraged, Biscuit snuggled down next to Emily and rested her head against Emily's legs and closed her eyes.

Moments later, Emily drifted off to sleep, too.

Night had fallen and through the fog of her semi-wakefulness, Emily heard the beat of a far-away drum carried to her across the still, humid, heavy air. It was deep and rhythmical and lulled Emily into a state of drowsy awareness yet she could focus on nothing else.

The darkness around her seemed to move like a gentle fog and she thought to look out the window. She slipped out from beneath the covers, checking to make sure she did not wake Matthew, who, lying next to her, breathed quietly in his sleep.

Standing at the window, Emily was confused, yet curiosity would not let her look away.

The trees appeared to be undulating to the insistent rhythm of the drum. Their branches moving like tendrils, swaying seductively, beckoning to Emily to come, come.

She next found herself walking across the patio and as she stepped off the cool stone into the thicket of wild weeds, Emily reached up to touch the leaflets along the branch of the Willow that grew there. Its wispy branches responded to her touch, wrapping lightly around her wrist and forearm, gently pulling her forward. She did not resist.

Presently she found herself at the river's edge, the drum still beating but now joined by another. Their music provoked something in the pit of Emily's stomach, it tingled her nerve endings and sharpened her focus. She stepped into the river, the cool refreshing water, and started to swim. Her arms pulled hard, her legs kicked, and her breath came easy. She reached the opposite shore and hauled herself out, still focused on the transcendent beat of the drums that she now thought sounded slightly louder.

The full moon, briefly glimpsed through the slow rippling movement of the forest canopy, could only dimly light the landscape but Emily found her steps to be sure as she moved toward the sound of the drums.

Every step took her deeper and deeper into the swamp. Her foot tangled and she reached down to pull at the vines that had momentarily halted her progress. She freed her foot and noticed with mild interest that she had lost her slipper, then thought, *did I even have slippers on?* But before she could think back, the hypnotic and insistent drums pulled her attention and she lifted her gaze up and into the darkness.

Hesitating, against her will, Emily tried to hear through the dark forest for the point from which the drum beats originated. She reached out her left hand to lean against a tree and felt an odd sensation press into her palm. Lifting her hand, Emily saw that the object that poked her skin was a penny that had been nailed into the trunk.

Turning her head to better catch the rhythm of the beating drums, Emily's eyes landed upon another copper dot on a tree trunk five or six feet further on and moved toward it. From there she saw another and another leading the way into the dark, leading further into the swamp.

And Emily followed.

Heartbeats leading to minutes leading to more minutes later, Emily stopped to shake the lethargy from her mind that the drums had created. She wiped her forehead on the sleeve of her garment and tried to pull more air into her lungs. *Wonder where I am? What time is it?* And looking up, tried to see the night sky through the tree tops but only saw the interrupted view of the full moon above swaying branches of the ancient Alder and River Birch standing all around her in the pale midnight light.

What is that? Emily strained her eyes to peer ahead, past the trees and tangle, her breathing nearly stopped. It was the yellow light from three torches slowly snaking across her view before they turned to recede into the gloom away from her.

Emily did not call out but thought to follow until she could determine who carried the torchlights and if they were friendly.

Now, with torchlight to focus on, Emily's path became clear. With her resolution fixed, her awareness expanded outward. Suddenly the sounds of the swamp flooded her ears. The constant buzz and low hum of insects was punctuated by the low two-tone croak of a toad or the occasional dull-splashing sound of something disturbing the surface of an unseen pond somewhere... nearby... in the dark.

Emily closed the distance between herself and the torchbearers to a few yards but no closer. When the little group had moved another dozen paces, Emily thought she heard voices and her heart leapt to her throat. Her ears keen to hear, picked up on a murmuring sound and Emily's reaction was to lower herself down into the foliage in an attempt to hide.

The torchbearers split their direction and appeared to be moving around in a circle. Soon, several more torches were lit in addition to a small fire located in the center of what evidently was a clearing. The murmurs turned to rhythmic chanting, the words foreign but lilting.

From her hiding place, Emily watched as the area slowly became lighted. She was now aware that the trees around her were adorned with talisman and symbols all suspended from thin twine from branches or nailed into trunks. *Is that a goat bleating?*

Emily's eyes, nearly adjusted to her surroundings that were now dimly lit in the firelight, could make out the objects closest to her.

There was a small, hooped net holding an exotic flower resembling an orchid. Another was a grouping of twigs, leaves, and feathers, tied with twine and securing a Flying Eagle penny. Yet another, a fairly large six-sided figure surrounding a six-pointed star and as it gently turned in the night air, Emily could see it had writing on it that traced the outline of the star. *Is that Latin? French?* A fourth symbol dangled a few feet away and as Emily stared through the dim light, she twitched with recognition. It was made from three twigs, crossed at their centers and strung like a spider's web. Caught in the web was the woven figure of a woman, who was wearing a copper penny around her neck.

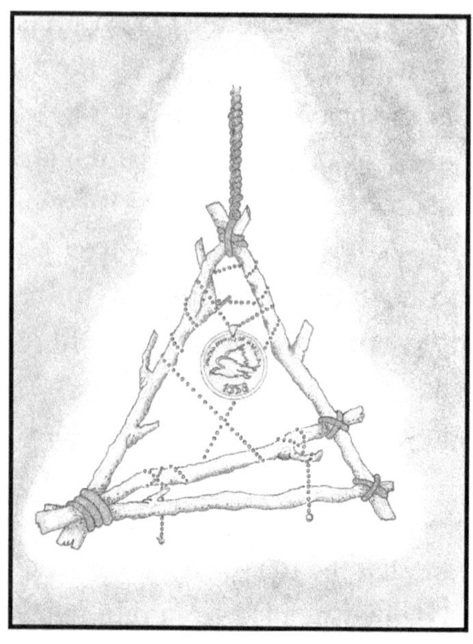

Emily leaned closer to see if she could make out more details of the clearing, straining to see faces and hear words.

Suddenly everything stopped. The drums, the night noises, the chanting, even the air around her became dead quiet.

Emily caught and held her breath in fear, her eyes opened wide, vividly seeing the undulating flames of the fires in the clearing ahead of her.

Without a sound, as Emily's mind raced to tell her what to do, a face burst out of the darkness inches from her. Its eyes glowing like the full moon above, its mouth agape in a silent scream.

Frozen to her spot, fear chocking her, Emily managed to fill her lungs and, feeling her heart thumping wildly against her chest, shattered the silence with a bloodcurdling scream.

And then she woke up.

Aware of her still pounding heart, Emily knew she had been dreaming, had experienced a nightmare the likes of which have never happened to her before. She untangled herself from her sweat-soaked sheets and slipped out of bed. It was then she noticed it was daylight and momentarily felt confused about what time it was. Matthew was not in bed with her so Emily thought to go look for him.

The smell of coffee took Emily down the stairs. She turned to walk past Matthew's office and found him tapping away on his keyboard and when he looked up at her, he smiled and said, "Good morning. How are you feeling? Sleep well?"

"Yea. My head is a little fuzzy. Maybe too much sleep. I had the strangest dream." Emily's thoughts drifted off to the dream, she couldn't decide if it was real or not and if she should say anything to Matthew. She decided that she needed more time to sort it out so quickly changed the subject.

"Where's Biscuit?"

Matthew said, "I don't know. Haven't seen her for a while. I'm sure she's around here somewhere."

Emily nodded. "I'm going to get a cup of coffee and get dressed. I'll fix us some lunch a little later. Ok?"

"Yea. That would be good."

Emily made her way to the kitchen by way of the great-room to see if Biscuit was in her favorite napping place by the hearth. Which she wasn't. Calling softly, "Biscuit," and making kissing sounds did not bring the dog out from her hiding place.

Down the hallway and through the dining room, Emily continued to call. Rounding into the kitchen, still no biscuit, Emily had a sudden fright. The two French doors leading out to the patio stood wide open.

She immediately stepped out onto the patio and called out, "Biscuit! Come Biscuit!!" and listened. Taking steps to the edge of the patio, by the large Willow tree, Emily called again and waited to hear Biscuit's bark in reply.

She heard nothing.

Emily ran back to the house and rushed through the doors. In her panic she yelled out, "Biscuit's gone!"

Together, Matthew and Emily searched the house and grounds but to no avail. Biscuit was not to be found. They had, at Matthew's insistence, methodically looked through the wild brush that surrounded their home. He calmly explained that Biscuit might be hurt and unable to answer their call. May be laying in the brush unconscious. Such talk, while meaning to calm Emily's rising emotional turmoil, only succeeded in making her more determined to find little Biscuit. It did nothing to compose her fears.

"Look, Emily," said Matthew, "we need to stay calm and do this right. It wouldn't help if we did a careless search and felt we needed to do it again."

Emily's face was pale with worry. "I know, but I keep thinking Biscuit is hurt and in pain and we must hurry."

They searched in front, around the drive and garage and all around Emily's studio. No Biscuit.

In an orderly fashion, they quickly but thoroughly searched the property starting from the back patio and soon found themselves at the river's edge.

"Biscuit, Biscuit!" Emily called, her voice raised in fear.

Matthew cupped his hands to his mouth and called, "Biscuit! Come girl," first along the river's edge to the south and then again to the north.

Both Emily and Matthew stood still, straining to hear Biscuit's bark. Emily actually had a little hopeful thought. That she would see Biscuit bounding along the shore toward them, tongue lolling and feet muddy with her adventure but happy to see them and barking in her little way of saying hello.

Emily's weak rally of hope was interrupted when Matthew

called out again.

Emily sharpened her hearing, picking out the familiar sounds of the wind in the trees, the water moving along the shore, buzzing bugs, birds calling, and strained to hear beyond them.

Matthew called again.

"Did you hear that?" asked Emily. "Listen."

Matthew stood silently, head cocked. "No. I didn't hear anything."

Emily pointed across the river into the swamp. "From there. Call again."

"Biscuit! Come!"

There was, off in the distance, a little bark in response.

Emily grabbed at Matthew's arm, "Biscuit's in the swamp! We have to go over there and get her. Now!" Her voice was rising and her thoughts started to race and then splinter. She felt her heart thumping and gulped at the air. "How did she get over there?"

Matthew took hold of her sleeve and lightly shook her arm to force Emily to look at him. "We can't just charge into the swamp. Take one minute to calmly think it through. We need better clothing, not these shorts, and we should wear our hiking boots. And we'll need water. Emily, look at me."

Emily had been trying to calm herself but now she was looking intently at the swamp and actually leaning her body toward it. At Matthew's command, she looked back at him and saw his calm leadership taking over and knew he was right.

"We'll change, gather a few supplies and row over. We'll be fine. Biscuit will be fine. Ok?"

"Ok."

Less then a half an hour later, Emily and Matthew were in the little dinghy with Matthew pulling steadily at the oars. He was wearing a daypack that he had hastily thrown four pints of water, a dozen power bars, and towel rags and adhesive tape into.

Emily sat facing the swamp, her hands clutching the rocking sides of the small boat, her brow furrowed in worry.

They reached the other side and together they pulled the dinghy up into the brush so it would not accidentally drift away.

"Matthew, call Biscuit again, I think she hears your voice better than mine."

"Biscuit! Biscuit! Come girl!"

Nothing.

"Biiissscuit!" called Matthew, a bit louder.

Emily stood still listening, concentrating. Then came two barks in reply but they sounded farther away this time.

Both Emily and Matthew stepped into the forest in the direction of Biscuit's barking. Every few minutes, Matthew called Biscuit's name and almost every time, he was answered with short barks.

After twenty minutes of struggling through the underbrush, Matthew said, "I don't understand it. Biscuit answers my call but every time it sounds like she's the same distance away. We don't seem to be getting any closer."

They stopped walking and Emily fished a pint of water out of the daypack. "Maybe she's disoriented. Who knows what's happened to her." And turning to look in the direction they were moving, called out, "Bissscuiiit!"

"Bark-bark," came the reply.

Stowing the water pint, Mathew and Emily continued on. Several minutes later, as Matthew was pulling free from a tangle of ivy that had almost tripped him, he noticed something dangling from a tree about thirty feet away. With curiosity, he made for the tree and halfway there saw that the object appeared to be a bundle of twelve-inch long sticks tied together at one end. It was twisting slowly back and forth and as he got closer, Matthew could clearly see, bound to the sticks by a rusted chain, a dried chicken head, feathers brown with old dried blood and eyes desiccated in death. And if that wasn't strange enough, someone had pushed little red painted stones into the sockets. It made the chicken head appear to be demonic.

Matthew was looking at it with calm curiosity when Emily spoke, "It makes my skin crawl and that's not all, there's a lot of those things hanging all over. And look!"

Emily was pointing at an old penny nailed to the tree trunk.

Matthew looked at the penny and back at the chicken head and steeling his resolve said, "Ready to move on?"

Emily nodded and Matthew called out, "Biscuit!"

"Bark-bark," came from ahead and the two continued forward.

The sun was high overhead. The air had become oppressive and both Matthew and Emily were drenched in sweat from their efforts.

Emily spoke, "Matt, I have to sit down, I have to catch my breath."

"Ok. There's a tree stump ahead where we can take a break."

"How far do you think we've come?" Emily asked.

Matthew took a swig of water and ran his shirtsleeve across his forehead and the back of his neck. "I don't know, but we've been out here for hours. We should eat a power bar while we're sitting here, rest for a bit and go again." And handed the water to Emily.

Emily looked drained but stood up for a second and called out, "Biscuit!" then plopped back down.

The swamp was still. Only the low sound of buzzing locust could be heard.

As they sat, silently chewing on power bars, Emily looked at Matthew and when he turned to her, she pointed upward and off to the right. Without saying a word, Matthew looked in that direction and saw another voodoo-like charm suspended at the end of a thin line from a tree. It was square and bound up in twine, hung from one of its corners with a circular disk of white feathers in the center.

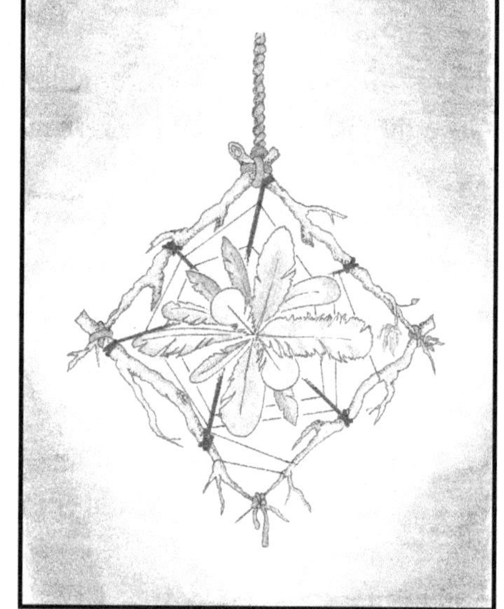

Matthew huffed his breath and slowly shook his head. "Looks like the rest of that poor chicken."

Emily had no reply but took another small bite of her power bar.

When they were rested well enough, they agreed to continue.

Matthew called, "Biscuit!"

"Bark-bark" came the reply and they followed.

When what seemed like an eternity had passed, Matthew said, "There's more light ahead. Looks like a clearing."

"Be careful, Matt, there could be trouble."

Matthew stopped about five feet from the clearing and motioned to Emily to squat down and brushing his lips with a finger, asked that she be quiet. He then knelt in the decaying earth and leaned slightly to his left thinking to hide himself behind a tree trunk while he observed the clearing.

It was a lot to take in.

The clearing was roughly thirty feet long and wide and looked to have been recently cleared. There was a torn and dirty oil-cloth lean-to off to the right with a filthy blanket tossed over a pile of dried leaves and green ivy vines that may have been a bed hastily shoved beneath the lean-to.

A few yards into the clearing just to the left of Matthew's position was a Dutch oven tripod positioned over an open fire pit that was circular and constructed from large river rocks and piled high with firewood. Beyond that, Matthew saw a large tree stump with a chopping axe imbedded in it.

The entire area was a mess. Whoever was using it did not believe too hardily in cleanliness.

Matthew quietly surveyed the camp. He had been silent for minutes upon minutes when he finally turned to Emily and whispered, "I'm going to check it out."

"I'm coming with you," Emily quickly added, her fear almost palpable.

"Ok, but stay quiet, stay close, and be ready to bolt back into the trees."

Emily gravely nodded and pulled in a breath meant to steady herself but it did little to ease her tense muscles. She felt tightly wound and the pit of her stomach was in a terrible knot.

They moved into the clearing and slowly walked to its center.

Matthew's mind was racing with everything he looked at. Beyond the cooking pot, heaped and strewn about were rusted and broken hand tools. There was an ancient two-man crosscut saw with missing teeth that was also starting to rust.

Matthew moved toward the pile. Hastily tossed on the ground were a hammer and a handful of rusted ill-matched nails, chipped screwdrivers and little bits of metal – who knows for what purpose.

Emily, just a step behind, couldn't take her eyes off of the chopping stump. It was discolored, *is that dried blood?* and there were moldy bits of something viscous, along with feathers, stuck to places all around its base.

Matthew turned slightly to walk past the lean-to tarp around to the area beyond it where he spied another pile of debris, topped by a makeshift cage made from sticks and twine. There were about ten little cages, none bigger than would hold a small dog, and to Matthew's relief, all were empty. He noticed a long length of steel chain lay strewn next to them with little tufts of grass and weeds growing through the chain links.

Emily was trembling with fear, almost unable to speak. She reached out and clung to Matthew's arm to get his attention.

Matthew turned to look at her but Emily was wild-eyed and looking around, from left to right, through the encampment into the dark, dank swamp beyond.

The words, "We should leave," came from her parched dry throat and Matthew readily agreed, nodded, took her hand and led her to the clearing's edge.

Once back inside the humid shadows of the swamp forest, Matthew surprised himself by thinking that they were now safe. They were not safe. They were far from safe. He stopped and faced Emily.

"We should wait here and watch. I want to know whose camp this is. Maybe they can help us find Biscuit. But I don't want them to know we're here until I can tell if they're friendly or not."

Emily looked to be in a state of mild shock. Her face was losing its color and her eyes had a far-away look in them. She rallied enough to say, "What if there's trouble?"

Matthew, a sly smile starting to form, held up an old boning knife for her to see, "I picked this up off the ground by the tools. It's not much but it's something."

Emily wiped the sweat and grime from her face and said, "I have to sit down, Matt, I'm feeling woozy."

Matthew led her a few more yards deeper into the shadows and helped Emily to sit down with her back resting against a tree trunk.

"Oh look," said Matthew, pointing.

Emily looked and saw an old penny nailed to the trunk. Smiling a wan smile, she said, as she eased herself down, "Maybe they're good luck."

Time seemed to pass slowly or so it appeared to Matthew. When sitting quietly in a swamp, limiting your movements, not talking, and waiting for the unknown... time will move slowly.

The sun was starting to fade, turning the bright yellow sky an inky blue. The air became still but less dense.

Matthew whispered, "It's too late to try to find our way back to the river. Are you ok?"

Emily shifted her leg, stretching it out and rubbing her knee. "I'm fine, a little stiff but fine. What are you thinking?"

"I'm thinking that we should stay here, we're relatively safe, not too many crawlers or biters so I think we'll be fine," continuing, "whoever owns this camp may be back any time then we'll play it by ear."

Emily nodded and reached for a bottle of water. "We should pace out our water so we have some for the struggle home."

The sounds of the swamp at dusk rose to a frenzy. To Emily, everything seemed angry. The insects were buzzing. Birds sounded frantic, squawking and calling loudly as they darted from tree to tree. Even the landscape made noises. Creaking and snapping. It was all a bit overwhelming and all Matthew and Emily could do was to huddle together and ride it out.

After the sunlight disappeared and the inky sky turned black, another set of sounds started up. The insects and birds settled down into silence but a chorus of toads and snapping twigs took their place.

The night sky sported a sliver of a moon but none of its light reached through the tree canopy to where Matthew and Emily were ensconced.

From his vantage point, Matthew could just make out the camp. Once he thought he saw movement. A small dark shadow inched its was across his view, hesitating before moving on. Matthew thought it might be the size of a raccoon but was not sure since it was really just an indistinguishable shadow among shadows.

Emily was exhausted. She rested her head back against the tree and felt her eyes droop and her mind slow, her thoughts retreated into dreams.

Matthew heard Emily's slow soft breathing through the darkness. He was glad that she nodded off, the day has been a strain and he had been worried about her.

He listened to the sounds around him in the pitch black of the night and thought to fight off sleep by trying to identify them. *The toads are obvious. I almost wish they'd knock it off, it's too much. The plopping noises could be anything. Toads hopping. Fish jumping. Could be turtles, wonder if turtles move around at night?* A twig snapped off to Matthew's left. *Hope there aren't any wild cats here about.* And tightening his grip on the boning knife, *hopefully they're more scared of me than I am of them.*

Somewhere in his litany of identifying or trying to identify the sounds of the night swamp, Matthew fell asleep.

A restless dream filled his mind. A smoky swirling mass of shadows moved about him. He called out Emily's name and she answered, "Here I am." Matthew tried to see into the darkness to find her. As he strained to focus, a set of white glowing eyes came into view, then another and another and dozens more… all staring at him, coming closer, closer. Voices, all saying, "Here I am," whispered to him. "Here I am." He was standing, facing the floating eyes, anxiety gripping his chest, when he was jerked back into consciousness.

Emily's face was inches from his and her hand was over his mouth. She shook her head then nodded toward the camp.

Matthew came to heed and shifted his focus. Emily removed her hand from his mouth but remained still and tense. Both stared through the darkness to the camp, but strangely, Matthew noticed that the night noises around them had stopped. *That's odd.*

Then a whack! broke the silence followed by a low guttural growling and a throaty warning roar. The sounds of thumping, grunting, and growling were pierced by painful shrieks and the sounds of breaking twigs and the crisp sound of dried leaves being trod upon.

Eyes wide in terror, Emily was frozen to her spot. Matthew leaned closer and tried to make out what was going on but the moon had retreated and the camp was blanketed in almost total darkness. *Is that two animals fighting? A man fighting an animal? I'm not getting it, I can't make it out.*

Almost as fast as it started, it was over. Dead silence all about them. They dared not move.

Matthew could hear his breaths coming in short puffs and thought to calm himself by bringing his breathing down to regular movements. His thoughts were scattered but he forced them into a semblance of normalcy, thinking, *we need to stay quiet, don't bring attention to ourselves.* Looking at Emily, he knew she was thinking the same thing.

As the night noises gradually resumed, Matthew and Emily rearranged themselves into a tight huddle, down among the vines and weeds and grasses that surrounded them, hoping it was enough to hide them from... that.

It was a long time until dawn came. It was a long time to stay silent. To stay hidden among the ferns, the iris, and the tall marsh grasses that tangled and fought for light and nutrients below the forest canopy.

Matthew dared to steal a peek at the campsite and what he saw caught his breath in his throat.

There was bloody viscera strewn about the site. Some of the tools had been moved about, the lean-to was half down, and the cast iron cauldron was simmering away over a bed of red glowing wood-coals left over from a large bonfire, its lid lifting with the thick bubbles of something rapidly simmering over the heat.

Matthew stared for a minute longer, looking for the camp's

inhabitant but no one was present. Nothing moved but the steam roiling from the cook pot. He strained to hear anything that would give away a human presence but could detect nothing.

Turning to Emily, Matthew hand gestured that it was time to slip away. They were to leave now. Quietly and with as much stealth as they could manage.

It took them four hours of hard labor to make the river. When they emerged from the swamp they were disoriented. They had no idea where they were. After a minute, Matthew elected to turn south and within a couple of hundred yards, spotted the little dinghy, still clinging to the brush just where they left it.

With a smile, Emily said, "Look! We're almost home. We're almost home."

Matthew said, "We've got to call the local sheriff's department. We've got to tell them what we saw, tell them about the bloody awful mess back there. Tell them that Biscuit is missing and could have been killed by a maniac!"

"Do you think they'll believe us?" asked Emily, only half caring if they did or not. "Really, I just want Biscuit back."

Matthew pulled a reserve strength from deep within and rowed the dinghy straight across the river to their shore. Both he and Emily stepped as lively as they could up the bank and across their property, heading for their back patio, making snippets of conversation as they went.

Emily said, "You call the police, I'll make a pot of coffee."

"I'll ask how long it might take them to arrive," said Matthew, "We might be able to clean up a bit before they get here."

Step after exhausted step.

"What a nightmare."

"It may not be over yet," said Matthew.

Just as they emerged from their forest of trees, Emily was saying, "Poor little Biscuit."

And as if to answer... "Bark! Bark!"

Emily, a huge smile wide across her face, cried out. "Biscuit!" And the little dog, who had been curled up at the door waiting for them, sprang up and raced to them, barking and yipping with joy.

Matthew bent down and scooped the puppy up into his arms and together, he and Emily, hugged and patted and kissed their little Biscuit dog.

The nightmare was over.

The Midnight Sky

For three days rain brushed down the windows of Daniel Dwyer's flat without hardly a notice, giving pause only when occasional gusts of the cold northerly wind drove it against the panes, rattling them in their casings.

Daniel lives in a one bedroom flat in Regent Terrace, Cambridge UK, with a big red tabby cat named George. George is a well-disposed, friendly and loving cat. He is content to spend his time watching the world as it moves past the windows from high atop his one meter tall cat "tree", suitably built with a carpeted observation platform that more than comfortably accommodates the one stone eight pounds of his solid cat-self. The rest of his days are spent perched on a corner of Daniel's desk watching him work or sitting drowsy-eyed on the couch while Daniel reads. George is a happy cat.

The flat is well appointed with a leather couch and brocade chairs given to Daniel by his mother. His father always insisted on sturdy oak wood tables and shelving and upon Daniel's graduation, gave him a large oak desk that had belonged to his great-great grandfather. It sported the Dwyer coat of arms deeply carved into the drawer front with a translation of the Dwyer family motto, "Virtue Alone Enables", ornately carved into the desktop's leading edge.

Daniel has, since moving in five years ago, managed to fill all the shelves with books, books, and more books. His desk usually appears in disarray but Daniel affectionately calls it his "controlled chaos experiment." The desk evokes sentimental feelings for Daniel when he thinks of the study, research, and writing he has accomplished while sitting at the family heirloom.

Daniel graduated at the top of his class in astrophysics. The weeks leading up to his finals were stressed beyond imagination but the ceremony itself, the cap and gown, the enlightened speeches, and the huge campus party following the event, filled Daniel with so much promise and expectation for his future. He was more than ready and very excited about taking his place among the scholars who went before him. He would solve solar mysteries and lend his name to discoveries at the outer reaches of the cosmos. Daniel spent days refining his CV before mailing it out to a couple of dozen prestigious and highly recommended institutions, and further weeks waiting for the requests for his services to return. Gradually it started to dawn on Daniel that he would not be able to pick from among a myriad of generous offers, because none came.

Eventually, Daniel had to admit to himself that the mysteries and discoveries of the universe weren't his to find. Reluctantly, he took a job in the university's Astronomy Department and for the past five years thoroughly immersed himself in his work on the department's "Spectral Ruler" project. But lately, as the work turned from an exciting new frontier to cataloguing and filing, Daniel's mind started to wander again. He thought back to his graduation and asked himself what it was that he had hoped to gain but had somehow lost sight of.

Over a year ago, Daniel started writing a book. He was sure it was the first of many. Daniel thought he could offer excitement to curious non-scientific types by sharing all the fun stuff about astronomy and titled his book, "How To Stargaze." He was sure it would become a best seller and had made a good start completing the first two chapters. His best friend, Madaline "Maddy" Ryan had agreed to be his unofficial proofreader and editor thinking that her master's in English Literature could use a good wake-up, and that having a book credit wouldn't hurt her professional CV. Maddy was impressed with Daniel's first two chapters and told him so. She looked forward to reading the follow-up chapters but Daniel had lost his spark, his writing suffered over several months and then virtually stopped. Maddy tried to encourage him but Daniel couldn't seem to rally himself to the task. As of late, Daniel hadn't written two sentences and started to worry that he wouldn't be able to finish.

Six months ago, Daniel typed a letter of resignation addressed to the Cambridge Chancellor. He hadn't a clue as to what he was going to do but felt that a change was desperately needed. He taped the letter to his bathroom mirror and every morning for a month, he stared at it while doing his washing up. Daniel was concerned that resigning from the Astronomy Department might not be advantageous to his career so he carefully reworded the letter into a request for a sabbatical. The university had such a program and adding his accrued leave to the time, Daniel figured he would have a total of a year and one half off to work on his book. Thinking about this prospect brought back the excitement missing from Daniel's life. It gave meaning to his days and added a spring to his step. Daniel was excited enough to start making plans.

Two weeks ago, he submitted his sabbatical letter and had received a reply in yesterday's post...his leave had been approved!

Daniel invited Maddy to join him for dinner tonight. He purchased two nice filets of whitefish, planned to roast vegetables to go with it, and splurged a bit for a 2012 Artisan Chardonnay from the Dionysus Family Vineyards all the way from California.

Tonight Daniel would tell Maddy the news.

"Dinner was really nice, Daniel, thank you," said Maddy as she helped clear the dishes to the kitchen.

Daniel said, "Oh, you're welcome. I wanted something special for tonight."

After stacking the plates in the sink, Daniel said, "I'll get those tomorrow. Let's take our glasses to the couch and relax. I have something to tell you."

Daniel retrieved the open bottle of Chardonnay from the refrigerator and nodded at Maddy, gently ushering her to the sitting area.

There was a nice fire gently burning in the fireplace and Maddy arranged herself on the couch cushions nearest to it, tucking one leg up under so she could sit facing Daniel, who sat down at the other end.

"What do you have to tell me, Daniel?" Maddy was getting excited, like a kid about to receive a big present. "What's your news?"

Maddy could hardly contain herself and sat nervously watching Daniel as he smiled a Cheshire cat smile and teased for a time by slowly adding wine to their glasses.

"What is it, Daniel, tell me!"

Daniel handed Maddy her glass and sat back into the cushions.

"Maddy, I'm about to embark on a wonderful adventure. Last week I submitted a request for sabbatical to the Chancellor and he approved it. I've got a year and a half off. I start in two weeks."

Daniel sat smiling at Maddy. He thought the news would please her, that she would be happy for him. But as he spoke, her smile faded and her face became a mix of confusion and concern.

Maddy sat listening in disbelief, her brow knitted, her jaw starting to tighten.

"What are you saying, Daniel, why do you need a year and a half off?"

Daniel put his glass down and got up. "Just a minute. I've got some things here to show you."

Daniel retrieved a stack of papers and three books from his desktop and brought them back, laying them on the couch between he and Maddy.

"I've been thinking about this for months, Maddy. Work has turned into a drudge, a monotonous march to my end. It has bored me stiff and after a point, I just couldn't take it anymore." Daniel reached for his glass, took a sip and gently set it back down before continuing, "I've started getting restless and at first I thought to log some time on the department's observatory telescope looking for undiscovered objects that would make me famous, something I could include in my book. But there were too many obstacles in the way. Rules about using university property for personal gain, and all of that."

Daniel absent-mindedly fingered the papers between them and thinking to himself, offered a weak smile before going on, "I thought I would go mad if I didn't get out, but then it came to me, if I had a nice long sabbatical, I could finish my book and maybe the department will have concluded their infernal paperwork and have started a new and exciting project by the time I return."

There was that Cheshire cat smile, again.

Maddy watched Daniel as he spoke. His face seemed to light up with excitement and she couldn't help but smile at him.

"So, you're starting your time away in two weeks?"

"Yes, I have until then to finish my current task and brief a co-worker to my other duties, then I'm my own man!" Shuffling the papers around and picking one page out, Daniel said, "Maddy, I've been thinking about this and planning the details for six months."

"But you've never mentioned this to me in all that time."

"I know. I'm sorry. Up until yesterday it was all just a dream so I kept it private. I didn't want to look foolish in case it didn't work out."

Maddy smiled and said, "So. Tell me about your plans."

Daniel became very animated as he spoke but after a few minutes managed to settle down into the rhythm of a storyteller.

"When my attitude soured at work I lost interest in my book, although I knew the book to be a good idea, I just couldn't make progress. I then thought that if I had the time to write, not just in the evenings or on the weekends, but to write full-time, what would I need to finish? That's when I came up with this..."

Daniel held out a copy of his sabbatical request letter to Maddy who took it and carefully read it through. With great detail, it explained the premise of Daniel's book, "How to Stargaze," and proposed adding a chapter that would enumerate any astronomical subject the University wished him to add as well as including a very enthusiastically worded endorsement of the University Astronomy Department.

The Chancellor's letter of response was stapled to the request and Maddy read that page as well.

Daniel's leave was approved and the "extra chapter" subject named: a publishable paper on the Northern Constellation, Pegasus, worthy enough to be lifted out of a book for amateurs and published by the Royal Astronomical Society. This alone was the basis for the Chancellor's decision to approve Daniel's leave.

Maddy looked at Daniel, who was expectantly looking back at her. "Pretty impressive. Do you think you can do it? I mean, write a R.A.S. level paper?"

"I've been training my whole life for it!"

Excitedly, Daniel pulled at the pages in the world atlas he had dropped on the couch with the other papers, and opened the book to page thirty-nine, the Northern Canadian Territories. Here he pointed to a spot and tilted the book so Maddy could see.

"Ellesmere Island," breathed Maddy, "Haven't heard of it."

"I hadn't either until six months ago when I started fantasizing about a forced seclusion that would compel me to finish my book and think about a career change, if need be.

"Having roots in astronomy, I wanted someplace dark, like up in the mountains, away from towns and people. It didn't take me long to find just what I needed. Alert, Nunavut, on Ellesmere Island. Look, it's right here," Daniel said, indicating a tiny dot on a most northern-looking point on the atlas page.

"There's a small four-man weather station and semi-regular transport planes bringing supplies and what-not...I can be the 'what-not'...as long as the weather holds."

Maddy absentmindedly picked up one of the loose papers that were strewn on the cushion between them and now lifted it to her eyes. It was a schematic of what appeared to be a house of some sort.

"What's this?"

Daniel leaned in to see what she was looking at and said, "Yes, that. It's a yurt, my yurt to be exact." He took the page from Maddy and continued, "Finding Alert sort of led me to thinking about living there. I would either have to 'hope' there was an available cabin or provide my own living situation. Also, I need to have a telescope, nothing too big after all, the book is for amateurs, but big enough for me to get some real use out of it. Can't expect to write convincingly using only a 38cm brass telescope and viewing celestial objects with a 50mm lens."

Maddy said, "May I see that again?" Gently taking the page from Daniel's proffered hand, she looked at it more closely and this time became aware of the level of detail that the drawing contained.

"Oh, Daniel, I'm impressed, although this doesn't surprise me. I wouldn't expect anything less. You've always been so good at drawing what you imagine and also so very skilled with technical aspects. This is amazing, really."

"Well...," Daniel said, "I found a company that manufactures yurts and while the basic style is static, they will work with you to customize it to your specifications. I spent many nights thinking about what I would need for a long-term stay in the northern Canadian outback. When I thought I was done, I spent more nights studying my drawings, refining them until I was satisfied that everything was as it should be."

After taking a small sip of his wine, Daniel added, "And isn't it fortuitous that the Chancellor named the constellation, Pegasus as a requirement? It's a northern constellation, very prevalent in the sky of the northern hemisphere. This adventure, my quest for my muse was meant to be."

Straightening the messy pile of papers and scooting closer to

Maddy, Daniel took one edge of the diagram between his fingers so that both he and Maddy held the page steady and said, "Here, let me show you…"

Pointing to this and that, Daniel explained what they were looking at. "The yurt is twelve meters in diameter and wrapped in a heavy winter liner, rated to stand up to many degrees below Celsius. It has a thermopane plexiglass skylight…for those days with a sun. I've had to modify the center ring to accommodate my two-meter reflector telescope. See how there is a circular mount for the scope? That's so I can slide the scope around in a circle to track stars without interruption. Also there's a closure to keep the rain and snow out. And if that wasn't enough, there's an advanced digital camera that fits on the scope. I'll be able to take wonderful pictures for the book!"

Maddy pointed and said, "This is your bed and a sitting area with a table, and this looks like a desk and storage cases, but…what's this?"

"Oh, that's the stove and here," pointing, "is the stove stack that vents the gasses out. The stove would be my only source of heat, well, that and my snow boots! And I would also use it for cooking. I've included all the comforts of home, minus two things."

Daniel looked at Maddy and when Maddy looked up at Daniel, she thought she saw sadness in his eyes.

"What, Daniel. What two things are missing?"

"George for one. I won't be able to take George with me." Glancing at the cat, "Would you consider taking care of him for me?"

Some minutes before, George had jumped up next to Maddy and snuggled down next to her. She had been so absorbed in the conversation and unaware that she had been gently stroking George's head with her fingertips. He reciprocated by purring softly and resting his head on her leg.

"Absolutely and without hesitation. George is a wonderful cat. No problem."

Maddy waited for Daniel to go on but felt the need to prompt him. "What's the other thing, Daniel, you said two things."

"You, Maddy. I'll miss you, your company, and your companionship. I'll miss you, Maddy."

T he next week flew past. Daniel was extremely busy trying to complete everything on his to-do list. He multi-tasked between his work and making plans to leave. After less than a moment's thought, Daniel decided to pack up and make the move to Ellesmere Island as soon as his sabbatical started, or as close to that date as he could manage. He reasoned that the weather there might hold out long enough for him to effect his relocation.

First, Daniel made a formal request to the Canadian government asking that they grant him permission to take up residence in their country for up to a year. He sent an explanation of what he wished to accomplish and provided the appropriate longitude and latitude of where he would construct his yurt. The coordinates, as it turned out, were about eleven kilometers north east of Alert, closer to Cape Sheridan. Daniel thought the midnight sky would be perfect there.

The Canadian government replied by wiring a letter of acceptance that included a temporary work permit. They also authorized Daniel's plans for the yurt and the workers needed for its construction, asking only that the manufacturing company provide an overview of the necessary activities and an estimated timeline for completion. This was fabulous news and took a load of stress off of Daniel.

Packing up his personal items should have been easy but it hit a bit of a snag as Daniel considered which of his books to take and which to store. He kept second-guessing his "take" pile and the titles had changed three times already. Daniel smiled to himself every time he passed the box as it accumulated more and more books. *If this goes on much longer…I'll need a bigger box!*

Maddy stopped by often, helping to pack kitchen items and other breakables being extra careful with packing bubbles and listing most of the items on the outside of the boxes.

When she noticed Daniel starting to become overwhelmed with the number of things he was trying to accomplish, she would put the kettle to boil and make tea, forcing Daniel to sit quietly for five minutes and collect his thoughts.

It was during these brief moments that she heard more and more of the details surrounding Daniel's new journey.

"Hey, Maddy, look at this rucksack I'm taking. It converts from a frame to a frameless and will hold a ton of essentials. And look at this," unzipping a side pouch and tipping the bag so Maddy could see. "It's a 'hydration system'…for water! Pretty interesting addition, don't you think?"

Maddy looked dubious then said, "Wonder what kind of bacteria will grow in there?"

Daniel lifted his eyebrows up into a look of stumped surprise, "I hadn't thought of that. Maybe I'll just fill it with a bottle of Jameson Rarest Vintage Reserve Whisky…you know…to clear it out first."

"That should do it…and you!" Maddy laughed and Daniel

joined in.

When they had settled down, Daniel spoke again, "I've borrowed two steamer trunks from my parents. One is a large wardrobe trunk, perfect for my clothes and the other is a wooden barrel stave trunk, quite large, that should do for my incidentals like my cast iron pot and the tea kettle."

And as if on cue, the kettle whistled making Daniel laugh and say, "See! Can't leave that behind now could I?"

"Of course not," said Maddy as she got up to tend to the tea.

Daniel rummaged around the icebox for a second and came up with an apple that he then washed and cut up to share.

He and Maddy sat quietly for a minute and sipped their tea. Daniel let his eyes wander over the mess the flat had become since packing had started.

Maddy spoke, "I know, looks hopeless doesn't it?"

"Yea, wish it was done. I had no idea I'd accumulated so much 'stuff'."

"You've arranged for storage, right?"

"Oh yes. They'll come next week with a big truck to move anything that's ready to go. My mother wouldn't hear of my storing the furniture. She told me that father had a fit thinking about great-great grandfather's desk in a storage bin for a year."

"That's right," said Maddy, "the conditions may be damp, may cause the joins to pop and who knows what else. Oh, Daniel it would be a shame if bugs got at it!"

"Father would have a coronary!"

They relaxed in their chairs for a moment before Daniel said, "Mother and father are coming this weekend to retrieve the desk, couch and chairs. They'll be saying their good-byes to me then, too. Would you like to join us for supper Saturday night? Nothing fancy. Probably at father's club."

"Sure, I'd love to see your parents again." Maddy took in a good breath of air and let it back out again before asking, "Speaking of good-bye, when do you plan to fly out?"

"I'm thinking that all plans would be final in just over two weeks from now. I've wound up things at work and only need to turn in my keys and sign a couple of forms. Then I can concentrate on finishing up the packing and winding down here."

Maddy cleared the cups and saucers to the sink and ran hot water on them intending to wash them and let them sit in the rack to air dry.

"Maddy, will you take George to your place this week? I can come by several times to see him before I leave to make sure he knows I haven't abandoned him."

Maddy looked at Daniel as he looked at George and she felt a pang of sorrow. George was well positioned up on his "tree" and lazily watching the activities through half-closed eyes. "George will be fine, Daniel. Don't worry about him at all."

"Thanks, Maddy, I will miss him, though."

"I know," said Maddy. "Shall we get back to packing?"

"No. Let's take a walk around the neighborhood. Get some fresh air, stretch our legs out a bit."

Daniel kicked off his slippers and went to get his walking shoes. He called back from the bedroom, "We've done enough work today. I'll finish up another time."

Later that evening Daniel sat comfortably on the couch, with George tucked up next to him, using his laptop to plot the route between Cambridge and Cape Sheridan on Ellesmere Island that would be his home for the next year. Getting himself there wasn't turning out to be an easy task and getting his possessions there was proving a bit of a challenge as well.

It was the logistics of the move that was the most problematic and Daniel spent a considerable amount of time trying to fine-tune the details.

Getting from London to Montreal was an easy seven-hour flight, sitting comfortably aboard a large aircraft. After a three-day layover in Montreal, which Daniel knew he would be grateful for as he thought it would be his last Internet connection for several days, if not longer, he would board a significantly smaller craft, along with a few other brave souls and bump along through four stops and seven hours to land in Ivujivik along the northern border of Quebec. From there it looked a bit tricky. The convention was to use a series of cargo and charter flights to piece together the remaining two thousand kilometers but Daniel was confident that he and his telescope would arrive, eventually, in Alert.

After two hours and numerous note erasures, Daniel had had enough. He closed his laptop, rested his head against the couch cushion, and rubbed his eyes. It felt good. So good, in fact, Daniel dozed off.

Usually, Daniel's dreams are filed with galaxies hanging precariously among the stars, slowly spinning around their central stars, tranquil and inviting. In a dream moment, the star might expand, pulsating in an orange glow, larger and larger until it exploded in a wild fury, flinging new stars outward in all directions. Sometimes in these dreams, a star would travel straight to Daniel, whose corporeal self was, surprisingly, effortlessly suspended in space. The star would lose speed and drop softly into Daniel's outstretched hand.

He would wake up from these dreams happy and assured.

This time, Daniel's dream was not about stars and happiness.

He was alone in darkness, he felt weightless and singular. He looked this way and that but could not determine what was up or what was down and after a while, Daniel's fears started to rise. He started to move, slowly at first, then faster and faster until gradually, moving dots of light appeared far out in front of him. These dots came closer and closer yet, picking up speed as they moved toward him. Daniel felt they would crash into him and struggled to move out of the way but his body would not respond to his will. He stared, wide-eyed and with rising fear, as the dots grew larger. At this point, Daniel became curious and thought to watch the scene unfold as if he was sitting in a darkened movie house. Some of the tension left his muscles and he relaxed until he floated free. As the dots of light came closer, they expanded and appeared to be figures and symbols that writhed and twisted as a desert mirage would move in the heat of a summer's day. As the lit figures came close, Daniel noted that they were giants, or at least, extraordinarily large persons, lean and glowing with otherworldly phosphorescence. They moved around Daniel, jabbing at him with their fingers and thrusting their war-painted and scarred masks into his face. He thought he heard taunting laughter and became very afraid. The symbols were ancient stylistic renderings that flung themselves onto his body, burning as would fire. Daniel wanted to scream, to call for help but his words caught in his throat. The scene moved faster and faster, Daniel's fear at a fever pitch, and then all at once the giant figures stopped their movements and were still until they slowly turned to face Daniel. One among them shot straight at Daniel, mouth agape, pointed teeth aglow, eyes fierce with intent. Daniel threw his arms up across his face in a defensive gesture, to ward off the blows he could almost feel.

There was a crashing sound and Daniel jerked awake, his heart pounding in his ears, his eyes on the fireplace, witnessing without thought, the spent logs collapsing into a rush of dying red embers. He clutched at his chest, fingers searching for the touchstone he wore around his neck, the one given him by his grandmother. The green-veined Connemara marble was warm to his touch. As he fingered the relief on each side, his heart calmed 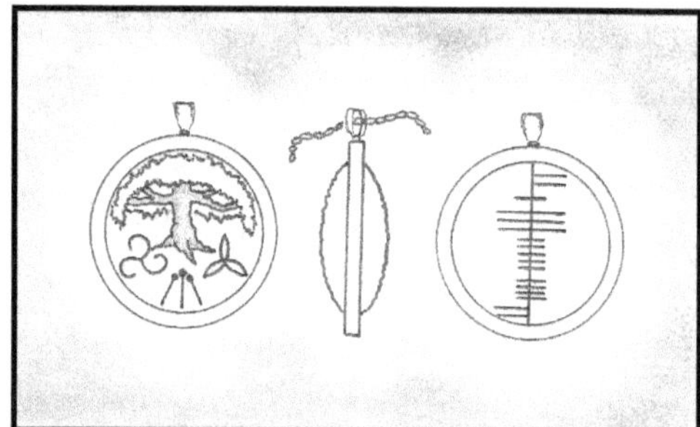 and in his mind he heard his grandmother's voice, "This marble is only found in western Ireland and is over six hundred million years old. That's very old, Daniel. Connemara marble symbolizes luck and serenity. You'll have to make your own luck in this world, Daniel, but serenity can always be found in this stone."

Daniel's fingertips moved lightly across the face of the stone and made out the familiar carving of the oak tree with its roots in the shape of ancient symbols thrust deep into the soil. On the back was his name engraved in an ancient Celtic tongue.

His grandmother believed in the energies of stones and taught Daniel that even stones were living things, capable of emotion and providing support. Daniel never doubted his grandmother because he had always felt that this little piece of west Ireland, this marble that hung from a chain around his neck, had always been his protector. And as it had done so many times in the past, as it was doing just this minute, Daniel felt protected.

Daniel roused himself and looked at the clock on the mantelpiece. 3:40AM. He had been asleep for almost four hours.

George had since moved to the bed and Daniel thought to join him.

It took a creative imagination and more than a middling of engineering force but Daniel, after six days and numerous phone calls, managed to arrange transport for himself and his cargo…all the way to Alert. The yurt company turned out to be the most cooperative of all. They posted the final plans for Daniel's yurt online so he could give one last verifying ok that the customizations were correct. Two hours after Daniel hit the "send" button, he was notified that the crates were in transit and that the crew would meet him in Alert five days after his estimated time of arrival. They required the time lag to ensure Daniel was there before them. Something to do with not having to pay them to sit around waiting.

His parents had retrieved the family furniture and agreed to store several boxes of his books for him. This alleviated so much stress for Daniel. He had started to fear for his small collection of first editions and many of his older books that were surely out of print by this time.

Dinner with his parents went well. They seemed genuinely happy for Daniel. His father thought it would broaden his worldly experience and while his mother voiced, several times during the meal, her concerns for Daniel's well being and safety, she managed a smile and told him she understood why he felt he must undertake such a drastic venture and hoped he would come back with many tall tales.

Now, all Daniel's hard work and planning brought him to his last night in Cambridge. Tomorrow he would take the train to London Heathrow, board for Montreal, and fly away.

Tonight, however, Daniel would spend with Maddy. She had

invited him to dinner and he accepted the offer of sleeping the night on her couch, seeing that he had vacated his flat just that morning.

Maddy put together a special meal of baked salmon with a quinoa salad for supper followed by a plain frozen yogurt topped with a blueberry sauce made from her mother's family recipe and sprinkled with crushed almond bits. She thought to finish the evening with a nice pot of chamomile tea.

Daniel arrived, rucksack and all, in the late afternoon. He immediately sought out George, and upon finding him, picked him up for a hug, burying his face into the soft fur of his neck. George responded by placing one paw on Daniel's cheek and purring.

"Oh my big tabby cat, I'm going to miss you so much," said Daniel before gently letting him down. George sat, looking up at Daniel, who immediately bent down, stroked his head, and smiled.

A soft rain started to fall, turning the light from the windows a dull gray.

Maddy iced up two glasses of Pellegrino, added a slice of lemon to each, and brought them from the kitchen.

"Supper in about an hour, Daniel. We have time to get comfortable before I set the table and check on things."

"Thanks," said Daniel as he reached for the glass Maddy offered, "Let me know how I can help, but I'm doing the washing up! No argument."

"Weeelll...ok! No argument," Maddy smiled.

Maddy sat down on the edge of her favorite overstuffed chair facing the small fireplace and Daniel flopped down on one end of the couch.

Maddy said, "So, this is it. You're on your way. How are you feeling?"

"Pretty good," said Daniel, "almost relieved. It's been a tough haul to this point, a lot of work. I'm glad to have everything here sorted out." Daniel took a sip of his water and set the glass down on the table in front of him, careful to use one of the drink coasters first.

Maddy was squeezing the lemon slice into her water, then used the rind to twirl the ice cubes around before pushing the lemon rind down into the drink with her finger.

"Thank you for helping me along the way, Maddy. You helped smooth out a lot of the rough parts. I appreciate it."

Maddy smiled, "It's what friends do and I was glad to help."

They sat quietly for a few minutes, watching the fire burn and listening to it pop and crackle before Maddy said, "I've got a 'going away' gift for you. I think you're going to like it. Wait here." And getting up, disappeared into her bedroom.

Daniel was surprised and felt his excitement start to increase as the seconds ticked by.

"You needn't have done that, Maddy," Daniel called out.

As Maddy returned, she said, "Oh, yes I did. Couldn't resist." And handed Daniel a beautifully wrapped bundle. Smiling, she returned to her chair.

"Open it, Daniel, I can't wait for you to see it."

Daniel took a brief moment to look at the wrapping and the ribbon that hid the gift. "Oh my dear friend…there's little pictures of planets and stars on this paper. Priceless!" Daniel removed the ribbon and paper and as he did, his fingers touched leather.

Daniel soon learned that the gift Maddy had given him was a beautiful leather-bound journal. The thick, tooled leather cover was adorned with an oak tree, whose tiny acorns were inlayed with gold leaf that glittered in the firelight. The tree roots were tangled around the initials of Daniel's name and the edges of the pages were decorated in gold, green and brown, depicting the continuation of the oak tree on the front.

"This is exquisite, Maddy."

Maddy sat holding her breath watching Daniel as he reverently turned the book over to see the back cover. There he found an elaborately tooled Celtic symbol of a horse in the center of a circular knot design, and gazed at it as he ran his fingertips over the ridges and valleys that were the drawing.

"How appropriate, the horse. Emblematic of the sun and now, Pegasus."

"Open it up, Daniel," said Maddy, smiling with anticipation.

Daniel worked the platinum closure and it fell open. He then gently folded back the front cover and turned one blank page to reveal a portrait of George, looking straight through the camera, directly into Daniel's eyes.

Daniel's heart burst with joy at the picture and with love for his best friend, Maddy. "I don't know what to say. The words 'thank you' are so inadequate. I'm overwhelmed."

Maddy got up from her chair and came to Daniel who then stood up to meet her. She hugged him and as she held him she said, "It's a journal for your dreams, Daniel. And a place to write about all the extraordinary adventures you're about to experience."

She let him go, smiled and added, "And if it's not too personal..." arching her eyebrows in a half-joking, half-mocking manner, "I'd like to read it when you get back."

"You're a good friend, Maddy."

Daniel stood looking at the journal while Maddy collected their glasses and stepped toward the kitchen.

"Are you hungry? Let's have supper."

aniel was about to collapse as he stepped from the passenger/cargo plane onto the thickly oiled tar and gravel that was Alert's only airport runway.

As he trudged, and there was no other way to accurately describe Daniel's labored steps, he thought, *I'm near done in. Thirty hours of travel, I should have known it was going to be difficult...maybe could have broken it up with more breaks...I've got to get some sleep.*

Daniel had spoken with the co-pilot, just now, and was told how to find his way to the only hostelry in Alert. There was no airport terminal, per se, but one of the truckers would certainly give him a ride if he enquired at hanger two. So Daniel was walking along, willing each tired step across the tarmac to the hanger office.

It was a short five-minute ride but Daniel was ever so grateful. His feet had started to tingle and he didn't know how much longer he would last.

Daniel booked into the Atsanik Inn, taking their largest room since his stay was sure to be at least one week long. After climbing the stairs and gaining entry to his room, it was all he could do to muster enough strength to strip down to his thermals and crawl under heavy, warm coverings before falling into an exhausted, deep sleep.

As the gray mist slowly cleared, like a fog moving back to the sea, Daniel found himself at the gates to his family's country estate that had been home to generations of Dwyers, as it would be his home and home to his children, too.

He looked up at the family crest on the huge iron gates and marveled at the intricate details contained within. The lordly helm and the ornate shield, both adorned with red and white. Daniel knew what those colors stood for...strength and sincerity. He had been taught those virtues since he was a child. The shield upon the crest, pictured a fierce lion, the king of beasts, up on its hind legs, all claws unsheathed...the lion rampant in charge of heraldry...bravery, valor, strength, and above all, royalty. "Must never forget that, Daniel," his grandmother would remind him.

As Daniel stood looking at the crest, the great ostrich wing plumes and ornate ribbons and leaves slowly undulating in the breeze, the gates swung open and he gently floated onward, propelled by his thoughts.

He remembered the long drive through the woods and happily thought of the childhood days he would spend in these woods looking for wild rabbits to chase and dandelions that he would pick for his grandmother.

As he moved along, Daniel felt a sense of foreboding start to come over him. He looked around, noticing that the daylight was starting to dim and large, ominous black clouds were moving overhead.

Daniel tried to run for home but his feet would not respond, seemingly stuck to the earth. He managed, with a great concentration of his will, to wrap his arms around a huge oak tree just as a bolt of lightning loosed from the sky and struck the branch above him, tearing it from the trunk with a loud and horrid sound...that of a scream of pain, filling Daniel with a fright he had never known.

On an impulse, Daniel reached for the Connemara touchstone he wore around his neck, and grasping tightly to the stone, knew he would be fine, that the storm would pass, that the sun would shine again.

Daniel slowly opened his sleep-filled eyes and as his mind started to wake up, tried to focus on his room through the dusky evening?...the pre-dawn morning? He couldn't tell which. The bluish, smoky gray light filtering through the window curtains could have been either one or the other, so Daniel decided to lie still, under the warm comforter, and wait.

After dozing off and waking up several times, sure enough, the answer came two-fold. It was getting lighter and as the minutes clicked forward, the aroma of fresh coffee and warm bread wafted through his room and permeated his still half-asleep senses.

Daniel roused himself and sat up, his legs dangling over the side of the bed, barley touching the chilly floor. It was cold in his room and instinctively, Daniel looked around for a fireplace or a stove and finding none, figured he had better dig his snow boots out and put them on before his toes froze.

Daniel's room was nice and had a homey feel to it. It was a large room with a good-sized single bed, a desk, a chest of drawers, a large leather chair and a wash-up sink with a crisp clean towel hanging on the rack. He felt he would be quite comfortable here, even with the lack of a heater and the shared bathroom down the hall.

Daniel hurriedly dressed and washed and made for the lobby in quest of a cup of that coffee.

The owner was standing at the entry door looking out the small window, watching the street, when Daniel came down the stairs.

"Good morning! I trust you slept well...everyone does on their first night here!" and stood smiling at Daniel.

Daniel answered, "I went out like a light."

"You must be hungry. I have oatmeal and a large pot of

coffee on the stove in the kitchen. There's no dining room, turned that into my den years ago. Everyone eats in the kitchen. Down this way," and led Daniel through a hallway to the back of the inn.

It was nice and toasty warm in the kitchen. So much so that Daniel pulled his sweater off and placed it over the back of one of the chairs.

The owner was pouring a cup of coffee and waved for Daniel to take a seat and placed the cup down in front of him.

"I'm Touk Amaneotuha but you are to call me Touk. And you are Mr. Dwyer from England, U.K., yes?"

Daniel smiled, offered his hand and said, "Yes, please call me Daniel. I'm fresh off the cargo plane as of yesterday." Daniel wrapped his hands around the mug and inhaled the steam rising from the hot black liquid that was coffee and tasted a hot drop before making up his mind…it was good.

Touk was standing at the stove with his back to Daniel and said over his shoulder, "What brings you to Alert, Daniel?"

"I'm here from the University at Cambridge doing research. I'm an Astronomer. I'm also writing a book for amateur astronomers. I've come to study the northern skies."

Daniel waited for a response but got none. Touk was stirring the big pot and coming up with spoonfuls of oatmeal that he then glopped into a bowl. He brought the bowl and coffee pot to the table and filled Daniel's cup as he set the bowl in front of him. Touk then went over to the ancient refrigerator and retrieved a small bowl of butter and a creamer that he brought and placed within Daniel's reach.

Daniel watched with mild interest as Touk went to the stove and tipped open the oven door, reached in and pulled out a small loaf of bread, golden brown all around its crust, placed it on a plate, grabbed a knife from beside the stove and returned to the table.

Having then sat down at one end of the table, Touk picked up his own coffee mug, a terribly dark stained affair with a round, chipped yellow smiley face on it, that looked to be winking, and took a drink before saying, "That's nice."

They sat together like that as Daniel ate a spoonful of oatmeal and broke into the bread loaf. It was a brown bread rich with seeds and nuts and had the faintest taste of cinnamon.

Touk broke their silent revelry, "How long will you be here studying the sky?"

Daniel wiped his mouth before speaking, "Until October, when the winter storms will probably prevent my viewing. Then I'll pack up and head back home."

Touk turned his mug around a few times before saying, "Flights during winter always depend on the weather."

"I imagine they do."

"Will you be staying here?"

"No. I've arranged for a temporary living shelter to be built out by Cape Sheridan. Do you know the area?"

"Yes. When I was young, my father and I would go out there to hunt and fish. We would stay for many weeks before returning. We had to stop when the game moved away." A pause while Touk looked wistfully into his coffee. "It's a very wild, primitive area. Very beautiful."

By now, Daniel had finished his meal and was clearing his dishes to the sink.

Touk said, "Just put them with the others, I'll get everything at the same time. Saves water."

Daniel nodded. "I may go upstairs and read for awhile. May I come find you later, ask you about Alert, maybe just talk for awhile?"

"Absolutely. My pleasure. Look for me either here or in my den, just off the hallway, on the right."

Daniel thanked Touk for the meal, complimenting him on the mini-seed loaf and said he would see him later.

Back in his room, Daniel organized his things. His travel books and a tablet of paper on the desk, his shaving kit by the sink, and his alarm clock by the bed. He hung up his shirts and refolded his cotton and wool tops and soon found he had run out of domestic chores so stepped to one of the windows to look out at the town of Alert.

Daniel gazed down on the street that ran in front of the inn. There wasn't much to see. A few weathered buildings stood on either side of the road, looking dejected and gray in the late morning light. The clock ticked its time: 10:52AM. As Daniel stood watching, two dog sleds, pulled by teams of eight dogs, came silently gliding up the street. *Now there's something I've never seen in person!*

The sleds stopped in the middle of the street and Daniel could see that the drivers were talking together. Some of the dogs started yipping while others sat quietly. Then one driver yelled a command and gave his sled a push while his dogs leapt against their harnesses and smoothly pulled the sled away, down the street.

The second team, guided by their driver, slowly edged their sled into an alley between two buildings across the street. The driver hopped off the skids and tended to his dogs before rounding the corner and disappearing through the building's front door.

As the door opened, Daniel saw only the bright yellow glow from the lights inside and nothing more. He stood at the window for a moment more before turning back to his thoughts, *I should arrange my schedule, it'll help me to organize my time…for work and for play.*

Daniel sat at the desk and wrote on his tablet…"Questions to ask," underlined it twice and wrote, "One: is there heat in the rooms?"

Daniel worked through lunch and into the mid afternoon, organizing his travel notes and reviewing, for the third time, the schedule for the arrival of the yurt crew, as he had taken to calling them. He needed to be on hand when they landed and to have as many of the details of his expedition to Cape Sheridan settled before that time…four days from now.

Daniel went in search of Touk and a cup of tea and found them both in the kitchen.

Daniel knocked lightly on the door before gently opening it and stepping in.

Touk was at the stove dropping slices of carrot and chunks of potato into a huge black cast iron cauldron that sat simmering on a back burner and slowly stirring the contents with a long-handled wooden spoon. He turned to glance at the visitor and seeing that it was Daniel, smiled and said, "Well, hello. Dinner's not for another few hours. If you're hungry, there's canned sardines and beans in the pantry."

"Ok, no, I'm not hungry. But I could use a pot of tea if it isn't too much trouble. Show me where everything is and I'll get it, no need to interrupt what you're doing."

"Good," Touk said and turning, used the big spoon to point at a cupboard. "The tea is there along with a cast iron pot. You'll have to fill the kettle to boil, though. It'll take a few minutes."

Daniel thanked him and asked, "Will you have a cup with me?"

Touk nodded and said, "Yes, could use a break right about now." And dumped the rest of the chopped vegetables into the pot, adding a generous amount of black pepper ahead of putting the lid on and quickly wiping his work space.

As the two men moved around the kitchen preparing tea and setting mugs and sugar on the table, they conversed about small matters. How did Daniel like his room? Quite nice. Did he sleep well? Yes, comfortably. Is he getting settled in? Rather easily, to Daniel's mild surprise.

When the kettle started to whistle, Daniel brought it to the table and filled the teapot, checking the time to clock a three-minute steep. When both men were seated, Touk spoke first.

"So, what are your plans from this point forward?"

"Well," Daniel started, almost lost in the myriad of small details that crowded his mind, "My yurt and the four company men who will build it for me, arrive on Friday. I have to arrange provisions and transportation out to the setup location."

Touk nodded and sipped his tea, waiting for Daniel to continue.

"I think the crew will need to stay overnight, to rest up. Then we may start out the next morning, if possible."

Touk went to stir the dinner pot and Daniel went on.

"I've arranged for several flatbed trucks to take everything as far as they can...all the way to the setup point if the weather holds. The truckers seem to think it will. The crew needs two days to construct the yurt and assemble the stove and my telescope hardware then they'll return to Alert and fly out early the following Wednesday. If the weather holds."

Touk said, "Sounds like you've thought of everything."

Daniel twirled the hot brew around the mug the sipped at his tea before speaking again, "Just about." And furrowing his brow, "I do need to make sure I have enough supplies. Several crates of food and fuel will come with the crew but I'll need to check that and make up the difference. Is there a general store, here?"

"Yes, there's the 'Old Post' at the end of the street, run by Wise Willem. He can get almost anything you need."

"Good. I'll go tomorrow." Daniel then asked, "Would it be possible to arrange delivery of supplies to my camp in, let's say, six or eight weeks from now?"

"Hmmm," said Touk and thought for a moment. "Wise Willem's son, Ray-Sivullik runs a team of sled dogs, huskies, bred for the task. His lead dog is one of the best I've seen. Smart. Strong. You can usually find Ray at 'The Ptarmigan's Nest', across the street and then you can ask him about it."

Daniel queried, "The Ptarmigan's Nest?"

Touk gave a short laugh then said, "Yea, it's a café bar. Funny story about that name. Years ago, when Old Natik was building the place, seems a bunch of Ptarmigan decided to nest in the chimney, blocking the flue and causing the place to smoke out. Chased everyone out into the worst storm that season. Old Natik was really angry. Took his ice spear up onto the roof in order to skewer those birds. He was so angry!" Touk snorted with mirth. "Old Natik slipped on the roof and fell into the street, right in front of his friends. He lay there, embarrassed, the ice spear sticking out of his left rump with everyone laughing at his folly. It was then he raised his eyes to the roof and declared, 'The tundra bird is stronger than fire. I will name my house in its honor,' and that was that."

Daniel was slowly starting to realize that Alert was more wild than a deep blanket of snow. That people did more than "live" here, they toughened up to the survival of it. While the population was small, everyone needed everyone else to make it work. Daniel felt small in comparison, and, in spite of his high degree with honors...he felt uneducated. The awe he felt for the land was growing into respect for its people.

After dinner, Daniel decided to visit The Ptarmigan's Nest and ask about Ray-Sivullik, maybe grab a pint and meet the locals.

Touk declined Daniel's offer to join him, saying that he had lots to do before bedtime and said he'd see Daniel in the morning.

The Ptarmigan's Nest was warm and well lit. There was a bar along the right and several oddly matched tables scattered about the left. The "café" part of the business was nothing more than cold cuts and bread and as Daniel spied that out, gave a silent "thank you" to Touk for his culinary expertise.

There were two men in the café, in addition to Old Natik who was tending bar. When Daniel stepped through the door from the mudroom at the entry, the three men all turned to look at him.

Old Natik waved at him and called out, "Come. Come. Sit here with us." And pointed to a stool next to the two men already seated.

As Daniel took the stool and made himself comfortable, Old Natik plunked down a wooden tankard of ale in front of him.

"It's all we have until the delivery next week, so there was no point in asking you what you wanted. My name's Natik and this is Illik and Nataii."

Both men smiled and raised their tankards in greeting.

Daniel said, "Yes, thank you and hello, my name is Daniel Dwyer."

Old Natik said, "We know. You're the star watcher from England."

Smiling, Daniel said, "Yes, I am. Will be around a few months before going home, again."

Daniel was only mildly surprised that the townspeople had already heard of him. There couldn't be that many new things happening here and the arrival of such an oddity as an astronomer was surly a cause to sit up and take notice.

"I was wondering if Ray-Sivullik might come in tonight. I'd like to talk with him about possibly hiring him to transport some supplies for me." Daniel looked at Old Natik and waited for a reply.

Natik said, "Ray usually comes in around eight," and checking the clock behind the bar, continued, "about an hour from now."

"Oh, good. I'll wait then." Daniel took a mouthful of the lager and noticed the bitter tang against his tongue, but it was cold and went down fairly smooth.

The four men filled the next fifteen minutes with banter about "Where are you from," "What do you do for a living," and other sorts of banality right up to the point where Daniel explained what it was he was doing in Alert and what he hoped to accomplish before he went back home.

The three men looked at him like he had just lost his mind. None of them spoke. Natik turned to some bar task and Nataii, who was sitting two seats down, hung his head a bit and looked into the bottom of his tankard.

After a slow silence, Illik turned his head to look at Daniel. "I am Inuit. My family goes way, way back in time. We've lived here for many generations. Seen many things."

Daniel placed several coins on the bar and signaled to Natik to pour pints for everyone, including himself, if he so desired.

Natik accepted and freshened everyone's tankards.

After Daniel graciously accepted their thanks and the men settled back down, Illik said to Daniel, "Would you like to hear a very old story? One from my family's clan?"

"I'd love to, please tell."

Illik sipped his draft and steadied his thoughts and in a brief moment, began…

"Many generations ago, before time, before iron and clay, when there was only the Tiinu people and the ice and the ice animals, there lived a powerful magical leader named Thualt. He had many great powers. It was said that Thualt could calm storms, he could call the animals, see into the beyond, to foretell the future.

"This great chief fell in love with and wed the most beautiful maid in his clan, Moett. She was gifted in art, having received that gift in a dream of Aptol when he smiled at her and gave her a white feather. She also received the gift of healing. It was said that the embodiment of Eh'Iaso attended her birth and when she drew first breath, Eh'Iaso touched her forehead thereby bestowing the gift of healing. The mark of Eh'Iaso's touch left a small white star on her brow.

"Thualt and Moett married and held sway over their clan. He with wisdom and she with kindness and the Tiinu people prospered.

"Soon after, Moett gave birth to a son and they named him Boreas. The clan was overjoyed and celebrated for one turn of the moon. Gifts and blessings were given in excess and Thualt and Moett were bursting with happiness. But the time of joy was short.

Boreas fell ill on his first year. Moett tried with all her healing knowledge to cure Boreas. She worked tirelessly and as the days turned to more and many, Moett's heart filled with sorrow. Night after night, Thualt sat in worry staring into the night sky waiting for a message from tomorrow to relieve the illness that was upon Boreas. But none came.

"After a long, sad time, Boreas died and Thualt and Moett fell into a deep melancholy from which they could not be reconciled. Both retreated to their silence and to their dreams. As a result, the storms became more severe than ever before, the ice animals vanished and the Tiinu people suffered pain and hardship and soon were scattered far and wide never to come together again.

"Legend tells that Thualt and Moett's sorrow never ended. Before both were lost to time, it was said that Thualt gathered up the dust and bones of his son, Boreas, and flung them with great power up into the night sky. Seventeen bones pierced the heavens and where they touched, points of light shone. The dust caught in the sky and moved in the night. It can be seen to this day, and is now known as Aurora Borealis.

"It is told that Thualt and Moett went mad with grief and walked the land in search of Boreas. They disappeared into legend. Some say they never died but walk the earth still. Many believe that they can hear Thualt and Moett calling, their voices carried on the night wind."

Daniel sat spellbound. He didn't know what to make of the story. It was the story of a great love that ended in an unfathomable tragedy. What could the lesson of that story be, or was there a lesson in it at all? Daniel was fascinated and turned the particulars over in his mind, determined to record them in his journal.

A minute later, the front door opened and in stepped Ray-Sivullik, blustering with the cold and knocking snow from the treads of his boots.

"Hello! Hello you old snow dogs! What's new?"

The weather did hold, just as the truck drivers had said, but the journey was slow and not without its perils.

The first setback happened when one of the four flatbed trucks in the convoy threw a tire. Daniel was riding in the truck following it and had seen the tread literally rip itself from the wheel in a gust of blue smoke. It came off like a giant orange peel. Immediately, the truck halted and the driver hopped out to look at it, slowly joined by several of the other men.

After two minutes of conversation, there was a flurry of activity as men loosed the wheel bolts as others unbound the spare and jacked up the truck.

The spare was on and bolted and the small caravan moving again within a total of fifteen minutes.

Daniel had hopped out of the cab to help but found he was spare hands and there wasn't anything he could really do except watch.

By the time it was over, the icy cold air had turned his fingers stiff and Daniel was glad to be back in the warm cab, moving again in the direction of "home."

The second setback was a little more insistent.

As Daniel sat staring out the door window, bouncing along as the truck picked its way across the flat plateau toward the jagged mountains beyond, the radio crackled to life. It was the driver of the truck behind them reporting that he was stuck.

Immediately, all the trucks halted and the men swarmed out to assess the situation.

The driver explained that he felt his right rear wheel violently react to a deep depression in the snow covered terrain and then the entire truck jerk to a sudden halt.

Everyone gathered around the wheel and Daniel, for one, was surprised at the result. The right rear "dually" was sunk into a hole up to its lug nuts. So much of the wheels were buried in the snow-hole that the opposite side of the truck, the front left, was raised up off of the ground.

Daniel didn't think this looked like a simple task. In fact, he thought it would take hours of toil and some sort of huge mechanical apparatus to free the truck from its icy bonds. His mind almost shut down against the number of thoughts that sped through his brain as he tried to figure out how the problem would be solved.

Daniel's driver, Mel, explained what had happened.

"The roads through here are not real," said Mel as he swept his arm across the vista. "The snow and ice that cover the land hide it from our view so we drive in the direction we need and pick the most likely path. Essentially, we make out own road as we travel."

Daniel said, "That makes sense. Roads made from asphalt would never survive the damaging freeze-thaw of the seasons."

Mel nodded in agreement and continued, "KT's truck wheels just found a buried ice hole. It's not uncommon. This might happen to anyone's truck and at least twice a winter."

Daniel was relieved to hear this, that it wasn't too much of a big deal, that the drivers had experienced this before.

It did take a small amount of finesse to set the jacks just right, move another truck into correct position to winch KT's truck upright, and use another truck to pull it out of the hole.

All of this took about an hour of fussing with details but eventually the truck and its cargo were safely back in business and the four trucks moving again.

Travel time was estimated to be between two and three hours but with the hold-ups, the group arrived at the approximate coordinates in a little over five.

As Daniel jumped from the truck cab to group up with the others, he noticed that his leg muscles were getting stiff from sitting so long.

He joined Mel and KT and the others in a small ring that had formed up by the lead truck. The driver, Puinik, a robust red-cheeked man of about forty-five, was saying, "This is the designated place. Cape Sheridan is over those mountains, about thirty more kilometers.

Mel, addressing himself to Daniel, said, "We should determine the best place to build your yurt and at least unpack the trucks before we lose the light."

Daniel spoke, "I'll need the widest expanse of sky available without placing myself in any danger from high winds or snow slides. With that in mind, I would ask the yurt crew members what their opinions are."

After five minutes of discussion among the company men and the local men, an appropriate spot was chosen and Daniel concurred…it would be perfect.

Journal Day One.

Yesterday, after three days of construction and furniture assembly, the crew packed up their tools and gear and drove away, returning to Alert. I can't say I was altogether happy to see them leave. I had gotten accustomed to their jocularity and how, with good nature, they teased each other and told stories from their experiences.

As I stood and watched the trucks drive away and listened to the engine noises fade, I realized how desolate this place is and how alone I really am.

Was glad to watch the yurt being built, it gave me confidence that my seemingly meager living quarters will withstand the winds and weather coming off of the North pole. The yurt crew gave every assurance that everything would function "as advertised", more so since they were the ones who built it. I'm sure their statements were a bit clouded with bravado but nonetheless, I feel secure in my new home.

As I sit here writing, I feel a sense of expectation, an excitement about this phase of my life and about the things yet to come.

Ideas for my book crowd my thoughts with one conception showing promise until another replaces it that is equally as good. I am being carried away with excitement...something I have felt lacking in my life...and am determined to ride on this wave of passion for as long as possible!

I must add though, for my future reference, that a small percent of my elation about the book, my close study of the northern stars, exploring the contents of who I really am and where I feel I should direct my life, is rooted in fear. Fear of failure, of embarrassment, of looking the fool to my family, Maddy, myself.

But if I were to be totally honest, I'm in fear of...the unknown."

Daniel sat for a moment rereading that last sentence, then added…

"There is such a rich almost living folklore among the locals here. Wonder how much of it is real?

Daniel closed the door behind him and secured the additional solar flat across its frame to prevent cold air from seeping though. He turned and surveyed his new kingdom. It was a shambles. Crates were stacked in odd places, the wardrobe trunk was trapped under a crate of wood, and everything else was shoved anywhere there had been room.

On the bright side, the thermal plexiglass pane in the center of the yurt's roof was letting natural light flood the space with a rich white light, the furniture, Daniel's bed and desk, stood where they should, and his telescope boxes were within easy reach. Daniel had opened each one and inspected the contents for any irregularities…no use staying if the telescope was damaged.

The remaining daylight hours were spent like this: the area around the stove was cleared, a portion of the fuel stacked neatly at the ready, the bed made up with linens, wool blankets and comforters, the food stowed according to its needs, kitchen utensils stacked onto shelves and into drawers of a makeshift sideboard, a fire built, and a kettle set to boil.

As Daniel sat with a brisk cup of tea, he marveled at what he had accomplished so far. His home was starting to look organized and almost livable. He was pleased with his progress and thought it would only take a few more attempts to completely finish.

That night, after a meal of jerky, dried apricots, and an oatmeal bar, Daniel sat at his desk and tried to put together a list of the work still needed in order to put the yurt to rights. He thought to get his living space very organized before he started to assemble the telescope atop its mount. His reasoning was this: he was sure that once the scope was up and calibrated, he would get lost among the stars and it was likely that from that point forward, the living space would be ignored.

It took two more days to unpack and stow just about everything Daniel brought with him. But his pace was simple and contained reading breaks and tea breaks that Daniel enjoyed so well. He was starting to think of himself as the sole owner of a new business. Each day he was eager to rise and "go to work" and each evening he felt he had made progress.

On the third day, Daniel woke up and said to himself, "Today's the day I work on the telescope. From beginning to end. Tonight I'll see my stars," and a smile came across Daniel's face that even minutes couldn't relax.

By dinnertime, Daniel had finished working and cleared the crates to a small lean-to annex the yurt crew built outside the front door, on the south side, out of direct wind.

Daniel found that by stacking empty crates inside empty crates in the fashion of a Matryoshka doll, he economized on the space, leaving room to store wood fuel and a crate of canned food provisions that he would bring in as needed.

As he stood looking at his living space he thought it to be perfect. Then it occurred to him to take a picture for his book, to show how he lived as he gathered data and information to share with his future readers.

Dusk was settling in along with a slight wind and a few ominous dark clouds rolling across the western foothills.

Daniel was confident that the sky would remain mostly clear and thought to have a bite to eat and catch a nap before his first full night on the telescope.

At precisely 10:45PM the shrill piercing sound of the alarm signal of Daniel's bedside clock jarred him back to consciousness but it took him a few seconds to understand where he was. He had been so deep in dream that when Daniel woke, he momentarily thought he was still asleep.

Shaking off his drowsiness, Daniel quickly dressed and, burning with curiosity about the weather conditions, climbed the two-step ladder on his telescope mount to get a closer look out through the yurt's center ring.

The sky was pitch black, blacker than Daniel had ever seen in England and the stars shone like the bright facets of a diamond glinting in the sun. He...was...elated! Quickly he opened the plexiglass window and got into position on the padded seat affixed in front of the telescope and twisted knobs and levers until the starry sky of the northern territories became clear as crystals.

Daniel stayed in position at the telescope, transfixed by his wonder, until 4:30AM and would have stayed longer if not for the stiffness in his back that clearly told him that he had sat for too long.

Daniel retracted his scope, closed the window and climbed down from the apparatus. He thought to have a hot cup of tea, write in his journal, maybe take some notes, and go to bed.

It was time to start shifting his wake/sleep cycle. It was time to get serious.

Journal Day Five.

I can hardly describe the elation I feel right now. I'm exhausted and enlivened and the two things together have combined into a sort of calm joy. There's no other way to adequately summarize what I'm feeling. I'm calmly joyful.

My telescope and the mechanics of the custom mount work exactly as expected. No worries there.

Oh, the midnight sky. It took my breath away. The night is so dark and against that, the stars ripple in bright splendor.

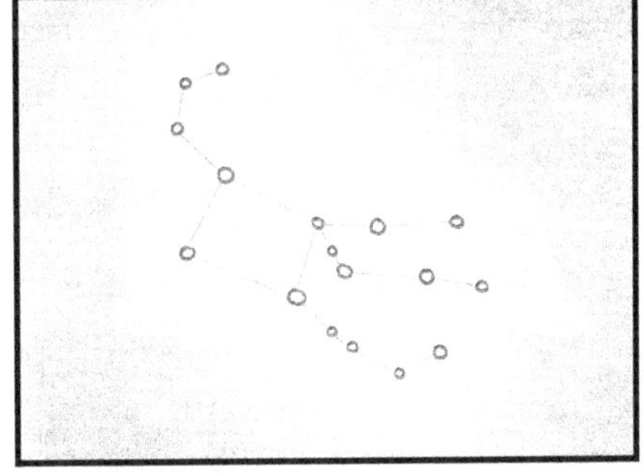

It took me awhile to locate the Cassiopeia cluster of stars and when I finally did, I realized that it appears in these skies much larger than in the skies above Cambridge. After I adjusted my preconceived reckonings, other stars became measurably more evident.

I've mapped the square of Pegasus and from there, located Capella, Polaris, and Deneb, but it was so hard to focus my attention anywhere for more than a few minutes at a time. It was good to gain a footing but I couldn't concentrate, and eventually gave up and let my eyes and mind wander where they would. Plenty of time for seriousness later.

During the following week, Daniel established a routine of sleeping from noon to about 7:00PM, taking an hour to wake up, dress, have a meal, and "go to work" at his desk, reviewing his notes from the previous night and setting at task or two to accomplish before "calling it a day", that is to say, finishing a good night's work before going to bed again.

With his sleep/work cycle in place, Daniel worked in the time to write his book. He decided to set specific times dedicated to the endeavor which turned out to be three times a week for two hours each sitting.

Daniel would start his "book writing" time by consulting his growing list of "must have" subjects and reread the last few pages of the chapter he was currently working on. For those times when composing seemed forced or he found he was uninspired, Daniel would sift through the myriad of digital pictures that he collected to date or simply outline ideas on how to organize information on the book page.

Toward the beginning of week two, Daniel figured out how to wash his clothes in the snow and dry them by the stove. One of his big maintenance lessons was that it was easier to do many small batches and not wait until his entire wardrobe was in the hamper at the same time.

Kitchen chores were easy and preparing food was quickly falling into routine, too. Once a week, maybe twice, Daniel would put the cast iron pot on the stove, fill it with canned tomatoes and beans, drop in a handful of jerky, an onion, and part of a potato, put the lid on and climb onto his observation gear for a couple of hours.

Midway through his star gazing, Daniel would have a nice hot bowl of stew, wash up, and return to the stars.

When his nightly viewing ended due to the lightening sky or hadn't happened at all due to clouds or the occasional snowfall, Daniel spent his time recording his observation notes and clearing up any data he had noted during previous sessions.

Daniel's life fell into a routine, interrupted only by the occasional change in the weather pattern.

By week four a repeatable, but not unsatisfactory daily pattern had been set. Daniel moved through his days on a schedule.

Journal Day Twenty Six.

What a relief it is to have the maintenance part of life in a yurt fully established. Now, I don't have to think too much about it or discover that I've forgotten to do some chore. It's a good routine not worth too much further thought.

My time is spent on my work.

I've made an awfully good start on my book. I've completely revised the chapters I wrote months ago. I now see where I was writing more of a college level thesis instead of writing for those who love looking at the stars and may have a real curiosity to look further. Along the way I have developed very strong notes, putting together an outline to progress the book chapters.

First, I'll start with a little background, mythology, maybe progress to a discussion on telescopes and other technology, and include folklore that endures to this day. I'll bring in basic star constellations and show how to find them...gradually building the reader's knowledge and confidence. Finally, every chapter will culminate and move the reader to the main point of interest...Pegasus. The book's crowning glory.

Speaking of Pegasus. Last night I observed something peculiar. Pegasus star, Enif, seemed to be pulsating, and while that's not out of the ordinary for that star, it appeared, to me, too rhythmic. I'll have to check that later.

However, I have so much information, data, and pictures, for the book that it is almost assured. I'll spend my time at home, back in Cambridge, writing it and finalizing the look and feel.

From this point forward, I'll spend my work time studying and collecting additional information about Pegasus. It'll be a chapter worthy of being published all on its own.

One morning, as Daniel lay in his bed, waiting to fall asleep after a particularly long night of star gazing, his mind restless and awake, it occurred to him that he really hadn't been outside the yurt in weeks. The more he thought about it, the more he was sure of it: he hadn't been further than the lean-to outside the front entrance.

This really started to annoy Daniel and played on his thoughts. He imagined himself on a book tour and having to answer the question, "Was the terrain around your yurt pretty?" He would flush red in the cheeks and be forced to answer, "I don't know. I never went outside." Daniel could almost hear the snickering.

After that night's work, when it became daylight hours, Daniel put on his parka, snow pants, and thick boots and made for the great outside.

It was a fairly clear day. Thin white clouds, high up, were being blown down from the north and moved toward the east. The sun was evident but not warm and last night's snow crunched under Daniel's boots as he took a few tentative steps away from his yurt.

Daniel stopped and looked around.

Far to the north were tall jagged mountaintops with Cape Sheridan just beyond. To the west lay a large expanse of flat plateau followed by more mountains. He had travelled here from the south...there wasn't anything too interesting in that direction. That left east. It was settled. He would walk east for a short distance. Straight out and straight back, never losing sight of the yurt.

Fastening his snow goggles to his face, Daniel started to walk. It wasn't as easy as he thought. Within minutes he was winded and had to stop frequently to catch his breath. But the effort was worth it.

Great tracks of snow ran to the east interrupted, here and there, by patches of bare ground that is covered in low, dry scrub and rocks. Beyond Daniel's yurt, where the ground slowly rises to the foothills, snow clings to the valleys and pools around large boulders to form scenery that is both surreal and hostile at the same time.

It took Daniel an hour and a half to make the base of the foothills. More than once he had told himself it was foolish to push so hard on his first brief visit out of doors. But he pushed on, wishing to make it partway up the first set of hills, for the view, before making his way back.

That afternoon, after he returned to the yurt, and climbed into bed to warm up, Daniel was very proud of himself. He managed to gain the foothills, climb up a hundred feet, snap a lot of digital pics and get back without incident. He made up his mind to do it again.

And indeed he did. Daniel made it part of his routine to take walks almost daily, during which he would think about how to solve a problem or think of a creative way to progress his Pegasus paper or just think about nothing.

His walks weren't without incident. Once his foot slipped on a rock and he twisted his ankle. It was bruised and bothered him for several days. Another time he slipped on a patch of ice and his feet flew out from underneath him and he went down with a thud, banging his shoulder and elbow hard on a rock. That really hurt. Daniel was afraid he might have dislocated his shoulder or broke a bone but no, he survived the mishap with what amounted to a bad sprain. However, it gave Daniel reason to be more careful with where he was about to step.

Journal Day Thirty Nine.

Work on my book is slow but my Pegasus paper is coming along nicely. Last night I tracked the constellation steadily for five hours, taking time-lapsed pictures the entire time. What a thrilling composite picture that will be, it should impress the Chancellor to no end.

I've been walking almost daily two to three hours, sometimes more and I can feel my body getting firmer and my breathing steadier as the days roll past.

Lately, as I walk, I do not think of work, I let my mind go and my thoughts roam as they will. In the beginning, random thoughts would stream past, but now, my mind is quiet and I've become attuned to my surroundings.

Today, I listened to the wind and watched it move over the ground, blowing loose snow from the rocks and quaking through the low, dry brush. What an odd sound the wind makes as it builds in speed and rushes past my ears. At one point I thought I heard voices and turned to look. I actually expected to meet another human out there in the desolation of the foothills.

I'm sure it was my imagination running wild because there was no one there.

Journal Day Forty Two.

A snowstorm blew in from the north three nights ago. I've been trapped indoors and honestly, I'm surprised at this: it nearly killed me not going out for that short amount of time.

It wasn't that long ago that it wouldn't have bothered me one whit to stay indoors for days and days. I was perfectly contented to do so.

But now.

I'm compelled.

It beckons me.

The storm left a fresh blanket of snow across the landscape.

Everything looked new and changed. The foothills dazzled in the distant sun.

It took Daniel a few minutes to work the plexiglass window open and clear the snow from the opening and another few minutes to dislodge the door. Apparently it had frozen into a little ice seal around the edges during the night. Daniel was careful not to harm the frame as he worked to free the door. Once he cleared the ice, he stepped outside into the chilly, northern sun-lit day.

This is fantastic! The snow has covered everything, it all looks new, almost a different vista altogether. Feels good to be out!

Back inside, Daniel grabbed a bowl of cold chili, hurriedly spooning it in, stuffed two dried fruit bars into his parka pocket, donned his boots, grabbed a water, his ice pick, and struck out into the blinding white snowscape…headed straight for the foothills.

Daniel gained the foothills and started climbing, paying attention to his footing but unaware of the time. He picked his way up and up and when he had exhausted himself, thought to rest and enjoy the picture-perfect scenery. As Daniel made himself as comfortable as he could, perched upon an icy cold boulder and facing the expansive valley before him, he slowly realized that he could not see his yurt from his position.

It should be just there. I'm sure I came straight up. The new snow has changed everything. I don't recognize anything.

Daniel stood up and put his hands over his eyes to shade them from the almost blinding glare of the snow and to focus down along the hills, trying to locate his camp.

I can't believe I did this! Bloody hell!

Immediately, Daniel started down, following his uphill footsteps in the snow but having to pick his way down icy slopes proved to be precarious and soon he lost the trail.

Daniel tried to suppress the rising panic that gripped his chest. *I'll just get to the valley floor and be ok.*

But Daniel's fear told him he wouldn't be ok, that he should smarten up, he was in trouble.

The sun was fading as hazy thin wisps of clouds began to fill the sky as Daniel finally reached the valley floor. He was winded and his legs were starting to cramp, his toes were frozen and his nose was running.

Daniel looked up the valley and then down the valley but could not see the yurt. He panicked.

As he stood, fear still rising, asking himself what he should do, then cussing himself out for losing his head, Daniel's hand instinctively moved to grasp his touchstone. As his fingers touched the area above his breastbone, Daniel felt the marble press against his chest and he knew...*Walk down valley. Home is there.* And took the first of many steps that finally brought Daniel to his yurt.

Journal Day Forty Three.

What a crazy, horrible, foolish, stupid, astounding day yesterday was.

I will endeavor never to repeat my recklessness.

Enough said about that.

The panic and fear I felt as I clamored and slipped my way down the mountainside made me feel like a wild creature. It blinded my thoughts and completely overshadowed my reason. Even as I gained step after step, my thoughts were frayed, I imagined horrors...wolves running me down like a wounded caribou, me wandering aimlessly until I dropped in the snow, perishing without a trace never to be heard from again.

Of course, sitting here, safe and warm, fed and sleepy, it all seems laughable, but I assure you, dear journal, it was all so very real.

And I heard the wind-voices, again. They came just as I felt for my touchstone. A sharp gust of wind blew past me almost knocking me down. As I stood, terrified, with no thought other than the question, 'which way?', the wind, its sharp biting chill, turned me in one direction and the voices I heard, I plainly heard, said, 'That way. Go that way.'

Daniel buried himself in his work. He resumed his routines and soon found he had written a solid outline for his Pegasus paper and that several days had clicked by.

One morning, around noon, Daniel was awakened by the sounds of dogs barking. It took a moment but then he remembered he arranged with Ray-Sivullik to deliver more supplies.

Daniel jumped up and quickly dressed and stoked his stove with additional fuel before grabbing his parka and going to the door.

Daniel stepped out just as the noisy yipping dogs pulled up and Ray-Sivullik brought them to a halt and raised his hand in greeting.

"Helloooo! Here I am!" and jumping off the skids and called to his dogs, "Settle down boys, a good days job." And walked to them to check the harnesses and pat his lead dogs head.

"Hello Ray! Did you have a good journey?" called Daniel.

"Yes it was good. The new snow made it smooth and we made good time."

Daniel said, "Come in and warm up, I'll put the kettle to boil. Are you hungry?"

Ray smiled and said, "I could eat something. Let me tend to my dogs then I'll be in. We can unload your supplies later." Ray set stakes in the ice and put his dogs on lead lines, gave them all a fast meal of fish and jerky cakes and got them settled down before going to the door and letting himself in.

Daniel warmed up the stew and put bowls and spoons out on the table. As Ray entered, Daniel was pouring hot tea into mugs and turned to offer one to Ray, who bumped off his boots and came across the floor to take it.

"Thanks, my fingers and my nose could use some heat."

Daniel slid a chair closer to the stove and said, "Here, sit down by the stove," and turned to pull a second chair over to join him.

"The stew will heat up in a couple of minutes," said Daniel.

Ray nodded as he tipped the hot mug to his lips.

Daniel smiled and said, "So. What news from the world?"

Ray answered, "A lot, actually." And launched into a description of a huge, possibly dangerous storm being predicted by the weather station.

"They see patterns that are adding up to a big storm. They don't see the storm yet, but say one's coming. Can't say exactly when. Soon, they think."

This concerned Daniel and the thought out loud, "Wonder if I'll be ok out here, if the yurt will withstand it?"

Ray shrugged and looked up at the rafters and beams, summarizing his thoughts with, "Humph."

A minute passed. Ray picked up a bowl and spoon and said, "May I?" indicating the bubbling stewpot.

"Oh! I'm sorry, of course. Help yourself," said Daniel, coming out of his thoughts back to his visitor.

After they ate, both men dressed in parkas and boots and

started unloading the sled.

Ray said, "I've brought you enough supplies to hold you another five weeks but I have to advise you that in five weeks, you had better be ready to leave here."

Daniel was a little surprised. He had expected to stay throughout October. Ray was suggesting Daniel leave before the end of September.

"Why's that, Ray?"

"Everyone is getting edgy about the weather. The winters are getting harder and colder and the weather station started to warn about this year being the worst so far with temperatures at extreme lows. Well, the town is getting very concerned."

"You wouldn't be able to bring more supplies that would get me through October?"

"Well, yes, but then what? The men with trucks won't risk driving out here during or after a huge storm. It's too dangerous for them. Their trucks are their livelihoods, they would never risk that."

Daniel was looking into the bottom of his mug, listening to Ray's explanation when Ray continued, "Here's good news…Touk wants to buy your yurt, that is if you want to sell it. He says it would make a nice summer hostel for visitors to Cape Sheridan. He could operate a summer tour kind of thing."

Daniel looked around, "Well. That would certainly save me from having to deconstruct it and ship it home to storage."

Ray said, "I'll spend the night, don't worry, I won't be any trouble, and leave in the morning."

"It's no trouble and you are welcome to stay as long as you need," said Daniel.

Later that evening, Daniel and Ray-Sivullik talked about many things. Ray described his life on Ellesmere Island and Daniel described his life in Cambridge.

Daniel marveled at how very different the two men were, yet for all their differences, here they sat in the great wilds of the Canadian outback, sipping tea and exchanging stories.

Ray left the next morning amid a great flurry of yipping dogs and shouted commands but not before he promised to tell the truckers that Daniel would be ready to leave in five weeks.

Daniel watched the sled glide off down the valley, his mind raced...*If I only have five weeks, what do I need to absolutely finish within that time?* And he stepped inside, lists of things to do already formed in his thoughts.

The next three weeks were a blur. Daniel kicked it into high gear. He knocked off the majority of his to-do list as well as several items that occurred to him as he went. Having a tight deadline helped Daniel to focus and he accomplished quite a lot.

His book had almost written itself and his paper on Pegasus was virtually completed. Another storm had come up, obscuring the sky and forcing Daniel to spend his working hours writing and his off hours organizing and packing a few of the extraneous items laying about his quarters.

By the end, Daniel was mentally drained and having to push himself physically was taking a toll.

Journal Day Seventy One.

The nights have gotten colder and I fear Ray-Sivullik's warning of a harsh winter may have been correct. Last night's temperature was -19°C, I burned more fuel than usual, and there are more cloudy nights than not.

I'm afraid my time here is limited and I expect that in two weeks, the trucks will arrive to take me back to Alert and shortly thereafter, a cargo plane, with me aboard, will lift off and away and then I will find myself back in Cambridge.

Why does this thought sadden me?

Two days later the weather had still not cleared and as Daniel ate oatmeal and dried shortbread and made a second cup of tea, he decided that he would pack up his telescope for shipment home. It was no use going all the way to the end of his stay…the nights were overcast and he had gathered more information than he would need for two books worth of stargazing.

It took two days for Daniel to disassemble and securely pack up the telescope and now the crates stood ready over to the side.

Daniel found that switching from night hours back to day hours took a toll on him physically. He felt like his head was full of cotton and his limbs full of wet sand.

One night after a bit of stew, Daniel lay down and fell fast asleep. When he woke it was 10AM the next morning and gazing up through the plexiglass window, Daniel noted the weather, while still bone-chillingly cold, had cleared and the daytime skies were a bright sort of white-blue.

It was time to take what might be Daniel's last walk in the wilderness. He washed, dressed, and ate a hearty bowl of oatmeal with brown sugar, hardtack brown bread and apricot preserves.

Daniel felt like a new man. The sleep had done him a world of good and he was ready for some fresh air. He grabbed a bottle of water, his camera, stuffed a protein bar in his pocket and opened the door to the outside.

What a beautiful day!

Daniel headed for his beloved foothills. There was one place he wanted to visit before leaving and that was where a rock cliff seemingly rose out of the earth, straight up to a flat plateau before giving way to the mountains behind it. Daniel thought the view from there would be fantastic and the pictures absolutely marvelous.

It took two hours to make most of the climb but to Daniel's surprise he made it without too much trouble.

And there is was, the sheer wall of rock that created a giant platform halfway between the foothills and the mountains beyond. *Just another meter and a half, just another dozen or so steps.* Daniel hiked himself up a little incline and with effort managed to grab onto a wide, flat stone. As he was about to stand up, the stone wobbled, causing Daniel to lose his balance. It then tipped over, hurling Daniel straight down, his feet scrabbling for a footing and his fingers grasping at anything, at everything as he fell into a hole that opened up under him without warning.

Daniel fell at least eight meters straight down and landed with a terrible jolt in a heap among stones, dirt and snow that had come down with him.

It knocked the wind out of his lungs and the sense from his head and it took some time before Daniel was clear about what had just happened. He stiffly unwound his limbs, checking to see if anything was broken.

Daniel fought to clear the fog that was closing in on his consciousness. *I feel dizzy and about to pass out...no...don't faint...breathe,* he commanded himself.

He lay among a pile of rocks and dirt that had come down with him and deeply filled his lungs once, twice, and felt his eyes start to clear and heart rate start to smooth out, not pound so hard against his ribs. He automatically reached for his touchstone but it was gone. He groped all around his neck looking for the chain, a sharp panic in his mind, and found nothing. *I've lost my stone!* As Daniel groped around the ground a sharp pain in his shoulder stopped him cold. *Catch your breath and look for it in a minute.*

As he lay recovering his senses, Daniel gazed up at the point where he fell through the ground. The opening was a bright white hole above his head. Daylight streamed through the opening to spotlight Daniel along with a few meters beyond, into darkness.

"Bloody hell," *I'll never get out that way. Too high up.*

Daniel started to get up, his head throbbed, his back stiff and his knees very sore. Slowly he wriggled himself into a sitting position and rubbed at his knees. He winced as he touched his left knee. *Must have banged it pretty bad, it's going to bruise but I don't think it's broken.* Gaining his feet, Daniel found he couldn't put all his weight on his left leg and a dull ache ran from his hip down to his foot.

"Owe!" *At least it's not broken.* "Owe!" In a controlled panic, he scanned the lighted area where he shakily stood looking for his touchstone, and checking again to see if it was around his neck or caught in his clothing. *Oh, damn, it's gone.* His edginess slowly replaced by foreboding. *This is not good.*

Surrendering to his fate, Daniel gazed around trying to make out his surroundings. *How big is this? Ooh, hope no wild animals live in here.*

As his eyes adjusted to the dim light, Daniel started to get a feel for where he was.

He could just make out the stone walls that surrounded him. They were rough and jagged and had a sort of dull luster that appeared and disappeared as he turned his head or shifted his weight on his stiff legs. The stone was black or so it seemed in the far darkness of the cave.

That's right! Daniel through, *I grabbed a torch before leaving home today.* And reaching into an inside parka pocket, extracted a small Maglite torch and switched it on.

The black stone in the walls sprang to life and dazzled with a deep hidden brilliance.

Daniel caught himself gape-mouthed and staring with wonder and thought to touch the stone so took a tentative step forward. His aching body responded enough to remind him that he should mind his steps and Daniel picked his way slowly across the rock-strewn floor.

As his hand rested on the black stone, a tingling sensation, like that of an electrical shock, shot up his arm.

He pulled his arm back. *Wow! That was odd.* And put one finger back onto the stone to test if it would happen again. This time his hand tingled. *Better watch this.* Almost without thought, Daniel picked up a small shard of the stone from the floor and dropped it into a pocket then stood where he was and looked around.

Daniel moved the torchlight up the wall to the ceiling and steadily around the walls that surrounded him. The black stones covered huge areas but not the entire surface.

As Daniel moved the light around, he spotted a depression further away and hobbled his way closer.

My hip feels a little better, Daniel thought, rubbing it lightly, *but my knee still hurts.*

As he moved closer to the depression, Daniel realized that it was an opening that led deeper into the mountain. He stood still for a time thinking, *I shouldn't move too far away from the opening...can't afford to get lost...I'm not able to climb out here...maybe there's another way out...I don't think I have much of a choice.*

The opening was as tall as the ceiling and wide enough for Daniel to step through. Several paces in, the ceiling lowered and the floor dipped down at a slight angle. *Oh geeze, it's going deeper underground.* The beam from the torch threw light around the entire space, glinting off faceted stones in the ceiling. *Looks like the night sky on a dark, clear, moon-less night.*

Daniel stopped his shuffling steps and looked at the ceiling, his mind trying to puzzle it out...*it looks familiar. What am I looking at?* Nothing sprang to mind. *Oh, well,* and moved on.

The cave narrowed some more, causing Daniel to stoop so he wouldn't nick his head on the rocks sticking out of the ceiling. He took more steps, putting a free hand out on the wall to steady himself but letting his eyes scan the cave along with the light.

Daniel didn't see the loose pile of rubble on the floor until it was too late. He stepped on it and it crumbled under his weight causing his foot to slip straight out in front of him making him fall to his rump. That force was enough to break the floor away, sending Daniel down a steep slide further into blackness.

Oh bollocks, bollocks, bollocks, oh bloody hell!

Daniel's eyes were blinded in the dark. He was marginally aware that he was still clutching the torch and that he was rolling downhill rather quickly. As his mind wrestled with trying to stay in the moment, Daniel came to the end of the fall with a great thud that pushed the air from his lungs in one big huff and snapped his head back, banging it hard against a rock.

He laid still taking inventory of his body. *Again, I've fallen.*

It'll be a miracle if I haven't broken anything this time. Crap. Daniel pulled in a breath. *The air is still ok. Wouldn't that mean there's a source? A hole to the outside?* Pulling his arm out from underneath him, *Oh my head,* Daniel banged on the torch and as it flickered to full beam, he gasped in wonderment.

This part of the cave was quite large. Everywhere the torch beam touched, a thousand facets of brilliance came alive with a sort of phosphorescence that held the light for moments after it had moved on.

Daniel, hiked up on one elbow, silently slid the light around the walls, trying to take it all in. Stopping it at a particular point, Daniel peered intently. *What? What is that?* He struggled against the pain in his body to stand up all the while keeping the light and his eyes fixed to the spot.

The dull glow from the walls wasn't just a random bunch of rocks...*That looks like some sort of symbols...*Daniel moved closer...*Mathematical symbols...*closer...*Oh, I don't believe this, it's the 3-D Euclidean Metric...*closer...*Wha...With solves for space plus time...*then he stopped and scanned the equation, working it through his mind for correctness.

Daniel pulled himself out of his study and moved the light in a wider arc around the Euclidean Metric where it touched pictures of ancient creatures, that Daniel thought may have roamed this area eons ago, and huge pieces of clear quartz, bright white in the light, that first seemed haphazard but with focus, formed the constellations of the northern hemisphere with one prominent constellation that dominated part of the wall and almost all of the cave ceiling...Pegasus.

One star in the Pegasus cluster, the beautiful, hypnotizing, orange-hued supergiant Enif, was pulsating.

Daniel thought he was imagining the rhythmic oscillations of the stone and to prove it to himself he switched off the torch for a moment. It took a second for his eyes to adjust to the total darkness of the cave but slowly, as his eyes stared through the blackness, hundreds of points of light winked to life.

Daniel was transfixed, it was all he could do to turn his head in a gentle motion from left to right, his eyes hungry to take everything in at once.

The entire cave seemed to drop from Daniel's perspective, leaving him almost groundless in the center of a dark midnight sky, surrounded on all sides by stars, constellations, planets, nebula, and a host of other inhabitants of the universe. The cave shimmered with beauty and mystery and among the indescribable breadth of all that Daniel could take in, the star Enif continued to pulse.

Daniel started to feel lightheaded as if he would faint and thought to sit when his knees buckled and he went down, losing consciousness as he dropped.

Daniel landed, face down in the snow. He was barely aware of what had happened. The cold on his face and the blinding white light in his eyes sobered him for a brief instant, long enough for him to wonder if he was outside and how did he get there, before surrendering to blackness as he lost all understanding and passed out.

In his fog, Daniel heard voices.

"Found him blacked out in front of his yurt."

"What do you think happened?"

"I don't know but he was barely breathing and was cold to the touch. I wrapped him and brought him here."

Ray had brought Daniel, wrapped in furs, to the Atsanik Inn and he and Touk had bundled Daniel into bed and packed hot rocks around him.

Both men were standing next to the bed talking when Daniel started to gain his senses. At first, he was confused as to where he was but shortly realized he was in his old room at the Atsanik and then recognized Touk's voice.

"Ahh. Here he comes," and to Daniel, "You're safe and warm and are to sleep. We will talk later."

Daniel nodded, offered a weak smile, and closed his eyes.

When he opened them again, he saw Touk sitting in the chair by the window and when he stirred, Touk spoke to him.

"Did you sleep well? How do you feel?"

"Like I've been asleep for days, my bones are stiff and I ache from head to toe...otherwise I'm fine." Then added, "I sure am glad to see you, Touk, thank you."

Touk got up and came to the bedside, "I'll go get a bowl of soup for you, I'll be right back and then we can talk. Lay still. Be still. Everything is fine."

Ray-Sivullik had arrived at the yurt a day before the truck crew was scheduled to pull up, thinking to help Daniel with the heavier or more difficult tasks of preparing to leave. Ray also wanted to run his dogs again before the long harsh winter set in.

He found Daniel a few paces from the front door, face down in the snow, and had tried to revive him. Having no luck, Ray wrapped Daniel up on his sled and turned the dogs for home. He and Touk had gotten Daniel upstairs and into bed, where Daniel had been laying, near coma, for two days.

Touk was very concerned for Daniel but felt better when toward the evening of the second day, Daniel started to moan and mumble in broken sentences. It was then Touk knew Daniel would be all right.

That was four days ago. In the meantime, all of Daniel's belongings, except for his rucksack, now stowed in his room, had been packed and moved to the storage hanger at the Alert airfield, waiting further instruction.

Tonight, the three men sat in Touk's kitchen sharing a meal of black bean stew.

"Honestly, I don't know how I got to my yurt," Daniel said. "I had gone for a hike up into the foothills and had fallen through the snow into a cavern."

Touk and Ray glanced at each other then back at Daniel.

Daniel was idly moving the stew around in his bowl, his brow knitted in thought. "The walls are covered in obsidian and embellished with symbols and pictures and advanced theoretical equations relating to space and time. Everything in painstaking detail and made from clear quartz. I wish I had gotten a picture of it."

Daniel's attention was momentarily taken by his stew and he smiled, a bit embarrassed, as Touk pushed a small basket of brown bread toward him. Daniel took a hunk of bread but didn't seem to know what to do with it. He tore a small piece and put it in his mouth and chewed.

"The most elaborate part of all were the constellations…Andromeda, Capricornus, Pisces, but brightest of all, Pegasus." Daniel held his arms out wide, "It dominated the ceiling!"

Daniel fell silent and the three sat quietly.

Touk spoke first, "My family has lived here for generations. There has never been talk of caves or ancient writings. You may have hit your head and dreamed about your stars."

Daniel was about to protest but the looks of doubt and sympathy on Touk and Ray's faces made him stop. It did sound a little crazy. He decided not to press it any further.

"You may be right."

The men sat mostly in silence for the rest of the meal and when Touk offered to make a pot of tea, Daniel turned it down.

"I think I'll go upstairs and get some sleep. I have an early start in the morning and need to finish packing up."

Daniel stood, filled his hands with dinner dishes and cleared them to the sink.

Turning to Ray, "I owe you my life and can't thank you enough."

Ray smiled and said, "Oh, it's ok. Write kind words about Alert in your book," and added, "Safe travels."

Touk said, "I'll see you off with a hearty breakfast. Have a good sleep."

As Daniel climbed the stairs to his room, a blizzard of thoughts shot through his mind. *I'll check my Pegasus data against what I remember from the cave walls...What is obsidian's resonant frequency?...Look closer into Enif, will it go supernova soon?...What does it all mean?...What is the message?*

Walking In Space

Stories always have a beginning so it is only proper to start telling this story where it all began.

In the year +2105, the Earth had become so very polluted; its air full of particulates, the water fostering a host of unknown pathogens, and the soil almost dead. The small changes in the climate that had been chronicled a mere ninety years before went unchecked as arguments about causes and who were at fault raged on. Some even denied it was anything to be concerned with at all. But slowly, insidiously, temperatures across the globe changed and set off a chain reaction that struck at the heart of nature. Food crops produced less and less, fruit trees produced small and stunted fruits, and the oceans were almost decimated. In growing panic, agriculture and commercial fisheries did what they knew best. They threw more pesticides, fertilizers, and fishing nets at the problem, all the while reaping the short-term benefits of rising profits from inflated pricing and gaining patronage among governments, forcing more regulations in their favor.

At about the same time, science was moving in a new direction, making minute advances in the study and creation of robotics, specifically in the replication of human parts. At first, the technology produced synthetic hands, arms, legs and eyes and while that was good for humanitarian purposes, there was more. As time moved forward, so did the advances into the integration of robotics with human biology. It became possible to replace a human's failing parts with those born of technology and eventually, synthesize whole new systems that not only gave humans new life, made it possible for them to have an advantage over the 'lesser', fully mortal humans of the time.

By the year +2253, the story was well underway. Food shortages caused hording, a rise in crime, and a swift devaluation of currency. Humans were dying by the score. Harmful bacteria and fungi ran rampant. Mutated insects and pathogens appeared. The remaining humans were in a panic, unsure which way to turn and watching helplessly as many more died as a result of human foible.

Science responded by building their biological robot systems more able to adapt to current conditions. Bot-eyes could see clearly in low light reducing the need for nuclear energy. Bot-muscular systems used less organic nutrients to operate at peak efficiency, reducing the need for frequent food intake. Whole systems such as arms, attached via electronics to the human nervous system, required no organic substances at all.

In the year +2715, what was left of the world was at peace. Maybe that statement should be clarified.

Because of the decimated state of the planet, and by this it is meant food shortages, pollution, unchecked disease, rampant poverty, reduced population, and crime, the world as a whole, moved through a couple hundred years of turmoil. There were civil wars, 'interventions', and general unrest among countries and between countries.

Globally, small para-military groups sprang up to claim their fair share, gangs roamed unchecked and more victims died.

The wealthy and the 'haves' built fortresses for themselves against the cruel outlanders. Their way of life came to resemble that of ancient feudalism protected by high walls and technology.

Through them, communication survived, as well as history, knowledge, and the continuing science and advancement of bio-technology.

Eventually the outlanders and their violent ways petered out leaving a handful of survivors who had managed to escape the terror and violence of that period.

The remaining factions of humanity, albeit by a higher type of moral hording, conceded the failure of individual governments in their unwillingness to accept original responsibility or to take quick and decisive action to quell the first vestiges of unrest and move to fix the issues. They vowed to work together from that point forward and formed a union, calling it the New United Earth Federation.

Under the tenets of NUE-Fed, as the New United Earth Federation had affectionately become known as, mankind became focused on current events. Oh, the Earth was still polluted and food production was at its lowest, but science had worked, in its own way, to solve some of the problems plaguing the Earth.

Basic food sources, like grains, legumes, vegetables, and some fruits, had been green-housed and supervised closely to ensure a high return of sustenance but also to produce a seed culture that would promote sustainability.

Fish farming was successful on a small scale so was still considered experimental.

Crime and violence had been eliminated. The need for weapons and walls was no more.

What was left of Earth's dwindled population breathed a collective sigh of relief and moved forward to solve problems and share in every gain.

After a few years of differing solutions to the soil, air, and water problems, frustration finally led the scientists to announce their limited findings and to predict a very real future...if true solutions were not readily found, Earth may only last another one hundred and twenty five years.

As expected, Earth's population became very concerned and then, after all the facts had been studied, became very determined to work through it.

Additional ecological studies and testing were carried out but reaped little results. The abuse heaped upon the Earth had taken a serious toll. The only reasonable solution was for humanity to leave the planet alone to see if it could recover in its own time.

The call to technology did not go unheard. NUE-Fed wasted no time, creating the Center For Enhanced Biological-Robotic Integration, whose mission was to create a perfect interface, a perfect union, if you please, of robotic technology and human biology. The purpose was to create a high functioning, high performance human being capable of long distance space flight, who would be sent out into space, immediately, to look for Earth 2.0. A habitable Earth-like planet somewhere close, somewhere that mankind could then migrate to, leaving the Earth to repair itself, if that was possible.

That was one hundred years ago. And this is where *my* story begins.

Work to integrate robotic technology with human physiology began immediately. Taking the advances that had happened to date, that is to say, building upon the vast storehouse of successes in the field up to that point, should have been a simple task.

Synthetic parts were already in production. Eyes that could register color and accurately transmit images to the brain. Arms with fully articulated hands and fingers moved and worked in conjunction with the nervous system. Automated hearts that beat regularly, slowing for sleep or beating a bit faster in excitement. All of this was a wonder in its own right, but not enough.

The more complex systems of the human body proved much more difficult to even replicate, let along improve upon.

One small example of a time-consuming roadblock was the work to automate the anterior pituitary gland. The small team focused on this aspect could not mechanically reproduce the gland's natural production of even one hormone, let alone the six required for proper function. And this problem was only one of many. There are countless organs, glands, hormones and cells in a human body all working together, like a well-rehearsed orchestra, to keep the body functioning. Integration of synth-parts was a nightmare.

Independently, space travel, previously only fantasized about in science fiction, had taken on an air of urgency. The possibility of putting a half-robot half-man into long term space flight was getting closer with every new idea.

The spacecraft's mission would be to carry its bot-human through the galaxy to another Earth-like planet, or planets, deploy a shuttle, do some 'science', and possibly travel back to Earth.

Really quickly.

Scientists worked long and hard to make their gains against a clock that would not stop ticking, marking the dwindling amount of time humanity had left in its occupancy of the Earth. The clock now showed that only twenty-five years remained to them.

As technology became more serious, huge advances were made and cosmic (forgive my little pun) assumptions postulated.

Like the complexity of the bot-human, the spacecraft was a myriad of intricate systems that needed to work together, without failures, for a sustained amount of time.

Volumes of advanced mathematics were produced that proved the possibilities of velocity over time and weight right down to the friction that neutrinos, space dust, and even cosmic rays would cause against the ship's hull, adjusting the fuel calculation to account for it.

What a beautiful thing it is when all of mankind is of one mind. In this case, the outcome was spectacular. A real triumph of innovation and problem solving.

The final outcome, the grand product of humanities denial, pain and guilt, anger and bargaining, dejection, accommodation, reconstruction, belief and hope is…me.

I am CRIS9. I am a Cybernetic Robotic Intelligent System. I am nine of fifteen. And in a way, I'm also one of one. I am the only female bot-human assigned to this mission. My contemporaries, the other fourteen bot-humans, are male. Let me explain how this came to be.

When the cosmic-clock showed there to be twenty-five years left, precisely it was indicating when the Earth would not be able to support human life any further.

NUE-Fed created a time-line that gave five years to the final designing, configuration, building, and training of the bot-humans that would pilot each of fifteen space ships being concurrently built on the same time-line. They dubbed the mission Juggernaut One.

Some of us thought the designation of 'One' was rather ironic, as if there could ever be a mission 'Two' or 'Three'. I think someone at NUE-Fed just liked the way it sounded. You know…snazzy.

At the end of those five years, the fifteen craft would be launched out into the galaxy, in diverse directions, to seek out Earth-like planets. Some far, some farther, some only on a guess, but each were allotted nine years, maximum, to complete their missions and either return to Earth or continue on outward through space, searching for other, maybe more desirable Earth-like planets.

This left a scant eleven years for the total deportation of Earth's existing population along with everything they would need to survive. In that one act, humankind would leave Earth, probably forever. But I'm getting ahead of myself.

The process of infusing humans with technology had started with men and maintaining a high level of success, scientists and technicians didn't see any reason to change their methods. That is, until one among them, a Doctor Herschel, recognized that females, 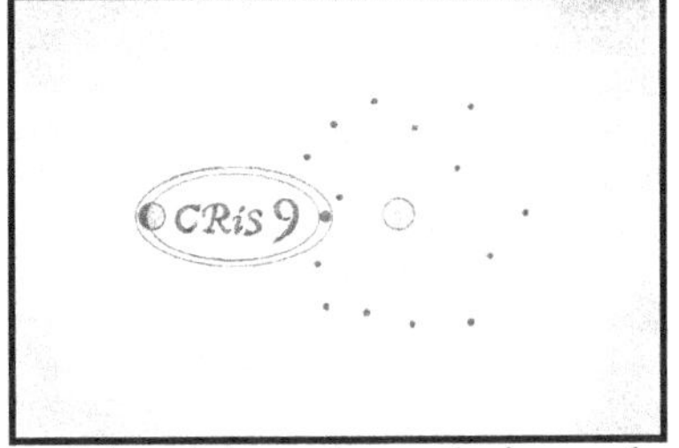 in general, possess a higher degree of intuition than their male counterparts. This fascinated Doctor Herschel enough so that she started developing a female bot-human version to join the males. Unfortunately for Doctor Herschel, her work on the female prototype took too much time. Female physiology is more intricate than male, more delicate, and much more subtle. It required a great deal of attention to detail and a commitment to time that just couldn't be given at that moment. Time was in scarce commodity. Doctor Herschel finished her work, and with great care and detail, but was forced, by the time constraint, to revert back to the male protocol in order to complete the work as originally scheduled.

I am that female, CRIS9. My techno-infusion was completed five years ago. I guess that makes me five years old. Funny though, mentally and physically, I'm closer to thirty-eight. Stable. Not prone to fluctuations.

The transformation of my body into the well imagined integration it now is took roughly two years. Almost eighty percent of my organic self was replaced over seventy-six separate operations, with highly technical and minutely specialized 'gizmos' that basically control every aspect of my body functions. Most are made from titanium.

I have a Karawatt power source embedded between my shoulder blades. It provides a seemingly endless supply of Astatine Atomic #85 power to my system with small, monthly supplements of Tritium and anti-matter when signs of reduced vigor are noticed. There are bio-parts throughout my body: my arms and legs, my hands and feet. Many of my systems are highly sensitive to temperature and touch. Almost nothing escapes my notice. I have one bio-eye that can detect the entire electromagnetic spectrum, do a bit of photon energy analysis, and send the results to my brain.

Yes, my brain. During the ramped-up years of bio-human development, when significant findings were settled upon and the

CRIS series of bio-humans was launched, it was found, to many scientists' dismay, that there was no definitive machine that could take the place of the human brain. Nothing could track and regulate the body's dozen or so systems with the accuracy of a human brain. Although the addition of a neurobiological implant did enhance memory capabilities.

Artificial intelligence had been around for at least a century but never taken out of the most basic forms of having a robot 'walk' or 'deliver a package' to someone's front door as it said, 'Thank you, have a nice day.' It was too complicated and to a great extent, astronomically too costly to research and develop anything more complex.

Realizing this, the CRIS scientists focused on embedding the human brain with tiny receptors that would receive data and impulses from the bot-systems situated throughout the body, perform a cursory analysis and package the data for consideration. The male CRIS bot-humans are predisposed to take the resulting data and apply analytical or logical reasoning to form a conclusion.

I, on the other hand, while still employing analysis and logic, am able to apply my innate intuition when it seems appropriate. I consider this to be an edge; it gives me something extra, and makes my decisions and thinking slightly better...like having a bigger toolbox with all the basic tools as well as some of the newer gadgets available.

It took three years of intensive mission training to come up to speed on every aspect of ships operation and maintenance.

One by one, as the CRIS series models became fully functional, they were paired with their spacecrafts. I was very excited when it became my time to begin training. I heard chatter from one of the earlier CRIS's, CRIS4, that training was intensive and the instructors fairly unforgiving. I couldn't wait.

I remember, vividly, the moment I stepped through the doorway from the briefing hall to the launch field and laid my eyes on my ship for the first time. I was so deep in wonderment that my breath held and words would not come for minutes.

The ship was very large and stood tall and sleek against the gray-brown sky. Its hull covered with gravitational helical pressure sensor appliqués forming the most beautiful patterns that captivated and held my imagination. Here and there, observation windows dotted the surface allowing viewing from any direction. The retractable solar sails were unfurled and their delicate-looking gold and silver mesh of collector strands glinted in the bright

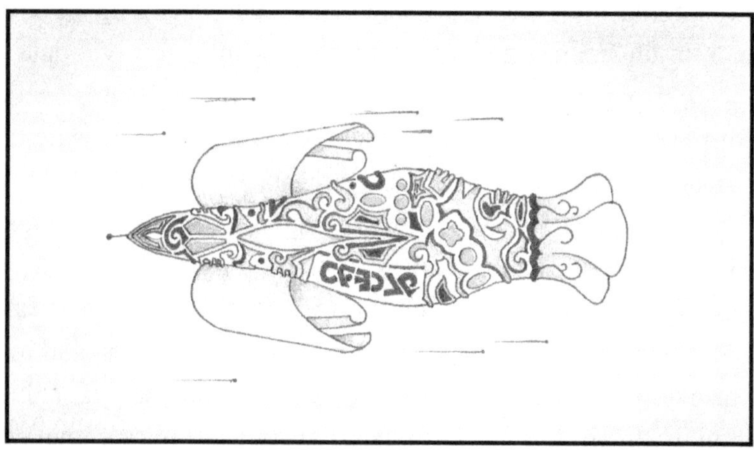

daylight and emitted glimmers of refracted light, dispersing rainbows across my retina. The sails reminded me of dragonfly wings. Translucent gossamer. I immediately fell in love and when asked what name would I choose, it took but a moment for a name to come to me ~ Harmony.

I read a story once that equated Harmony to Growth and New Beginnings and the associations that word held for me now were almost romantic.

The ship was to be my home and my companion for a long time and I felt it would be a good and successful union. Intuition? Perhaps. But at the time I felt it to be so much more.

Training was, in a word, unsympathetic.

My days started early and ended late. I was either in a classroom, performing hands-on, or doing self-study research. I think I liked the hands-on training the best. It took place on-board Harmony and included every system in its entirety starting from the look and feel of the panel or display, through its wires, circuits, wireless transmitter/receiver ports, its power source, analytical collector/reducers, memory, redundancies, and the 'how' and 'why' of its internal configuration. Work included tracing each system through its schematic and locating each component and its network throughout the ship.

Then it was on to individual systems. The power-thrust-maneuver system, life-support, connectivity, and all the other systems it would take to carry me out to the cosmos on my mission.

My enthusiasm never wavered and as the training progressed so did my confidence. I felt good. I felt ready.

The closer launch day approached the more calm I became. At first this mystified me and I wondered what might be wrong. Shouldn't I feel excited, panicked?

I spent several hours in contemplation before the reason became apparent. I was calm because my whole situation – being the only female CRIS, the import of the mission, the intense training, everything – was to me, a competition.

This didn't stem from a need to show superiority. It came

from a need to push my physical and mental self to its limits, to its fullest capabilities. I needed to see where that was. Where was the line I couldn't cross, the apex before the inevitable vertex? Really, it was a game I couldn't help playing.

Then launch day arrived.

I sat atop my beautiful ship, my Harmony, with all systems 'go.' I can barely describe the thrill that shot through my body when I transmitted, 'I am ready' to launch command and felt the thrusters rumble to life. All my sensors tingled to life, signals from my bot-self and images from my bio-self flooded my brain with graphic data and feelings. I caught myself leaning forward into the initial g-forces as if to help the ship lift up and away and smiled at my most human effort.

After breaking away from Earth's gravity and geomagnetic field, and adjusting course through the solar winds, I unbuckled my safety straps and moved closer to the large view windows in front of my command. I must have stayed there for minutes and beyond. I was roused from my imaginations by a light clicking sound from the console. It was time to set Harmony on the trajectory of her...our...mission.

Our mission path is to Kepler-62f, a super-Earth exoplanet, which lays some twelve hundred light years from Earth, out in the Lyra constellation. It's one of two possible new home worlds there, believed to orbit a red dwarf sun star through, what has been termed, a habitable zone. I've studied all the data on Kepler-62f and believe it to be a most viable commission. I place the success rate of my mission very high and am committed to bringing it to fruition.

Allowing for small variations in the initial trajectory

calculations, Harmony will easily sustain the 73_8 Kilogrids of speed per time quad to make the journey in 2.8 Earth years. After one Earth-week of travel, I mastered the technique of unfurling the sails to tap into the vast reservoir of dark matter using it to thrust forward, shaving off vital minutes.

Upon arriving at Kepler-62f, the mission required a standard orbit around the planet be achieved and infrared array data taken continuously until the entire globe was scanned and mapped. From that, I would determine how Earth-like 62f was but more importantly, could it, with effort, sustain human life. I was confident it would. However, if the data proved 62f to be less close to our desired model, well, then it was off to Kepler 62e, the next best choice.

I reviewed my mission parameters with regularity, wishing to commit them to memory but more to my desire to think about how to enhance any of the steps it contained. For instance, if 62f passed the initial suitability studies, I would place Harmony in stationary orbit, suit up, and shuttle down to the surface to begin the pre-colonization process of atmospheric enzyme "seeding" to hasten the production of oxygen and "planting" generically modified non-arthropod invertebrates in 62f's soil to begin the initial formation of micro- and macronutrients. Increasing the fertility of both oxygen and terra firma would facilitate the creation and purification of water, and as everyone knows, solid ground, air, and liquid water is "life as we know it."

By my calculations that took into account the number of shuttle trips required to transport equipment and supplies to the surface and the work required to organize, setup, test, and implement each of several dozen systems and seventeen stations in strategic locations across the planet's surface, I would have everything up and operational in four Kepler-years.

Of course, the calculation could not account for unforeseen circumstances or unusual working conditions but I figured a pad of twenty percent, or seven point one Kepler-months to allow myself "wiggle room." I was comfortable with that.

When the tenth station was brought online, I was to send a series of affirmative messages to NUE-Fed command ensuring the positive outcome of my mission. Any one of those messages would signal the beginning of Earth's migration. Each message code data would be embedded on a cluster of photon particles and aimed at Earth taking it some measure of time to reach there. It was the most advanced communication method to date and expected to work, without degeneration, across the light years to its target receivers.

I would stay with Kepler-62f to monitor and maintain the bio-processes and await the arrival of the first group of Earth humans.

In the mean, I would prepare, program, and launch three probes that would conduct searches in differing directions. One past Vega, one to fly past Messier 56, and the third to travel on and on to NGC6745, a fascinating, irregular galaxy on the other side of Lyra.

I think the three probes were a sort of insurance set up by NUE-Fed to hedge its bets, to use an archaic idiom, in an attempt to counterbalance the entire Juggernaut One project in case of unanticipated failures.

It didn't matter. My Kepler-62f mission was bound to succeed, but I would launch the probes notwithstanding. It was protocol.

Since my bot-self required little sleep, or nutrition, or dietary intake, and I quickly formed a daily maintenance schedule and a general ship's health check sheet, I was left with many hours between sleep cycles that I filled with reading, or meditating, or music, or thinking, or star gazing, or sometimes, nothing at all.

One of my most favorite activities, the one that excited me with anticipation, was space walking. I would suit up and go out through the mid-ship hatch and steadily make my way to the bow being mindful to check the condition of the sensor appliqués as I went. I knew full well that checking the condition of the sensors was not why I was out there but it looked good on the log sheet, "All grav heli sensors checked and operational." I was out there for one purpose only. Making my way to the bow, I would tether myself to the ship in such a way that I could tuck in next to a solar sail strut anchor and sit, facing into the flight trajectory, facing forward, and watch the tiny dots of distant starlight move slowly past and would listen to music playing on the vid-system through my headset. My favorites included The Mahavishnu Orchestra, B.B. King, Eric Clapton, Pink Floyd, and Leonard Cohen, although there are a host of others, these are my first picks. One time as I sat "outside" for what seemed like hours, my album of choice was Carmina Burana by Carl Orff, specifically playing "O Fortuna" several times through before letting the music continue its course to the end.

Several times over the progress of the mission, status communiqués were to be sent back to NUE-Fed command. At first, I tried to keep them pithy, sending short terse lines like, "Mission successful to date." Period. But as time went on, I wrote longer more elaborate missives thinking that if it were me on the receiving end, I would want details. I even had the nerve to sign one, "Wish You Were Here" and laughed as I hit the "send" button. What were they going to do? Discipline me?

I did run into one problem that required a tremendous amount of my time to remedy. More accurately stated, the problem ran into me.

The data stream from two of the portside thermal registers went into a sort of frenzy, as if they were starting to short out. Routine tests done a week earlier had shown that two of the ultraviolet sensors embedded in thermal Reg1727D were weak with the possibility of failure noted as one hundred and thirty two hours out, so it wouldn't have been unusual that the two thermal registers were to be replaced.

I supplied my tool belt, suited up for the task, and made my way across Harmony's hull to the register's location. However, what I found when I got there was a bit of a conundrum.

Atop the registers was a bluish-black blob of viscous substance that, at first, I was afraid to touch, even with the tip of a tool.

I went back inside, procured a specimen jar, returned to the registers, and cleaned every minute quantity of the material off, saving only a sample and flinging the rest of it away from the ship, back into the space from which it came.

After looking at the goo through the Analytical Microscope, I found it to be teeming with microbes. Although made mostly of carbon and lacking a definitive cell structure, I determined it wasn't anything too concerning but included a mention of it, as well as a diagram and chemical makeup list, to NUE-Fed in a follow-up communiqué.

After that, life went on much like it had done for months. Sleep, maintenance, read, monitor, eat, study, repair, meditate. There's something to be said about the mindlessness of routine. It frees your mind. It reduces stress. It brings you into harmony.

One of my favorite shipboard relaxations is to sit in command with my feet up on the console and just look out the windows at the great beyond while music plays throughout the ship's audio system.

I was doing exactly this, lost in the vastness of time, when several console lights blinked to life. Focusing on the panel, I saw that they were all from the hyper gravitational grid at the bow and indicating the approach of something in Harmony's path.

I typed queries to the analytical sub-comp and zoomed the telescopic lens to bring the object or objects into close focus. It appeared to be a cloud – fluffy and serene.

These particles possessed a luminescence, which was not typical of space-dust, and were all moving in straight lines, together as a group, and at the same relative speed. I clocked their radial velocity at 29° Rads per second/per second…this dust was moving.

All pertinent shipboard systems were brought up and activated. Audio, visual, thermal, electromagnetic, infra, you name it, it was recording this event. My first interest was for the safety of Harmony so I ran a dozen fast comps that would tell me if the speeding luminescence was capable of damaging the hull or worse, penetrating it. There was still time to maneuver her out of harms way if needed.

Something odd occurred. All data analysis confirmed the 'substance' existed, it was visual to my eyes and to the spectrum converter, but it had no…essence. It wasn't dust with fluorescence. It was specks of light. Literally. Millions, nay, billions of specks of light.

I sat in command watching the anomaly advance and could not think what to do so I kept recording the event and watched.

As the tiny dots of light sped past Harmony, it was like being in the most intense light show ever imagined. The dots were moving so fast they appeared to leave light trails in their path. Just moments before the cloud surrounded Harmony, I punched up The Mahavishnu Orchestra's album The Inner Mounting Flame, strapped in (just in case), and dimmed the lights in command.

The show lasted a scant forty-eight point six seconds but it was quite an experience. I'll never forget it, and neither will NUE-Fed because I copied all data recordings to them once I settled back into my routines.

During slow times, when I'm unenthused about entertaining myself, I'll play back the recording of the luminescent anomaly and it always makes me smile.

The next few months were notoriously predictable. But that was ok. I was starting to ramp up on the Kepler-62f Pre-Arrival process sheets. Arrival to 62f was approximately one month out and one of the major check items was a complete, extremely thorough shuttle maintenance and test. From stem to stern, New Beginning would be ready and able. I could feel my excitement and expectation start to bubble up.

I kept busy and focused and completed the Pre-Arrival check sheets two days early. I spent those two days as lazily as I could. I knew full well that once I reached Kepler-62f, my days would be full, intense, and non-stop for several months. My inactivity consisted of putting my quarters to right, one last slow walk through the cargo bays to assure myself that my shuttle trips would be efficient, and sitting in command with the lights low and the music loud.

Timing my sleep cycle and wake-up routines to coincide with Harmony's arrival at Kepler-62f was easy enough, but I was too excited to sleep much or take nourishment so opted for a cup of hot tea. Well, I call it tea but really, it's a concentrated concoction of macronutrients that tastes rather bitter when it's cold, so I heat it to approximately 100-deg. F and then think of something else as I sip at it.

I arrived at command a few quads early so made myself comfortable and started all recorders and began scanning all the sensor data.

Harmony approached the designated coordinates and slowed to come to a stationary position some number of parsecs from the planet from which several hours of observation were to take place.

The minutes clicked by. Harmony's programming completed and we sat motionless in the Lyra constellation, soft blinking console lights, the faint sounds of the ship in autopilot, and me, staring out through the big windows at…empty space.

I was momentarily dumbfounded. Where was Kepler-62f? There had to be something amiss with the coordinates. Certainly I was just slightly off course and with little adjustments, could soon be looking at 62f and not the nothing I now saw before me.

I got very busy verifying Harmony's trajectory from Earth to 62f, overlooking nothing, checking it from Earth to 62f and from 62f back to Earth.

The equations stayed true. Kepler-62f should have hung in the dark empty cosmos just there. Fifth planet of five in the Kepler-62 system orbiting 62a, its K2 dwarf star…waiting for my arrival.

I felt adrenaline shoot through my organic self and took it as a signal to dig in, to troubleshoot the issue, to find the answer.

Hours passed. I looked at everything Harmony had recorded throughout her journey. She was true, her direction and speed perfect. I could find nothing irregular.

After completing all the investigative checkouts, I was forced to conclude that Harmony performed as expected and we were where we should be.

I was mentally exhausted. I tucked into my command chair and let my mind clear and my physical self relax while I sequenced Mozart's Violin Concerto No.3 and turned the volume very low, barely audible. I sat like that for at least two hours, occasionally shifting my legs and leaning first to the right and then to the left. I thought about the experiences of my voyage, I reviewed every detail no matter how minute, turning it over and over in my mind.

Then it came to me, an inspiration from the universe itself: the cosmic light show from seven months earlier. It was the only unexplainable circumstance that occurred in an otherwise predictable mission.

I mused about the small photon anomaly, the tiny specks of speeding light that delighted me so. I brought up spectral-electro-analysis and programmed a map-back. My intuition told me that I already knew the answer and my curiosity would test out.

A few, long resigning moments later, analysis returned its verdict. The billions of photons, when reversed back along their path to establish their starting point, indicated that they were once the red dwarf star, Kepler 62a. Logarithms 'guessed' that the red dwarf went supernova…over eight hundred and thirty Earth-years ago. Apparently going unnoticed by the primitive space scouting telescopes of that time.

So. Why am I telling you all of this? Well, I had read a very astute quote once, by George Santayana, a Spanish philosopher of some time ago. 'Those who cannot remember the past are condemned to repeat it.'

I can remember my past. I only strive now to tell my story, to leave a record.

My mission to find Earth 2.0 among the Kepler planets ended in failure. It would be of no use to return to Earth since its time is finite. By the time of my arrival, it would already be in the throes of its final death and I could be of no help.

My Tritium power supplies and my scant nutrition, as well as Harmony's ability to stay fully functional should give me at least seven more solar years, maybe longer if I economize.

So.

The only choice is to move forward.

Who knows…I may encounter other travelers out here who may be searching for something new, something marvelous, something of imagination. I may even find what *I'm* looking for.

Without Borders

Music drifted over the air, its volume turned down low, matched only by the dim lights and the occasional table candle whose low flame threatened to gutter out whenever anyone passed by causing the slightest of air disturbance. The vid-screen on the back wall flickered its presence, its volume turned off.

Amid the soft music and dim light sat Alexandra 'Alex' Martin and Paul Jacobs. They arrived an hour ago and had been sitting at the bar sipping their drinks, contemplating their dinner choices.

"Today was a tough one," Alexandra said as she put her glass back down on the condensation soaked napkin in front of her. "Upgrading that main thruster is going to take a bit of engineering dexterity."

Paul said, "We made a good start but I think we'll have to modify the RXT housing in order to get the casing to fit properly."

Alexandra nodded. "Think you're right. Should probably figure that out first before we push forward with the heli-scope retrofit."

Paul sipped at his drink and something on the vid-screen caught his attention. "Hey Mack! Turn that up, please."

Mack Powell, tending bar tonight, owned the joint, Mack's Bar & Grill as well as the Over-Niter Motel two doors down. "Sure thing, Paul," and reached for the vid-screen's remote. A second or two later the volume was audible and the freshly made-up face on the screen was saying...

"...third report this week. This latest sighting comes just days after the Larkspur incident of last week when a couple living in the west end reported waking up in the middle of the night to see pulsating lights and hearing a light whirring sound coming from a large object suspended in the sky outside their bedroom window." [cut to a snippet of the original interview] "It was so scary. It was so big. I thought they were going to abduct us!" [back to the studio] "It looks like the large flying object is back. We have the up to the minute report for you. Kaylin?" [cut to Kaylin standing outside a residence with a nervous looking couple] "Exactly what was it you saw?" The man spoke, "About ten o'clock tonight, the wife and I were sitting on the back patio having a brew when all of a sudden this big lighted thing swooped outta the west and hovered over a house on the next block. It was huge, and dark, with lights all around its outline, that's how we knew it was so big. And we knew right away that it was a UFO. A bright light shot out of the bottom of the thing and that's when I told the wife to go get the cam cuz we're going to photo that thing and get famous."

Paul almost snorted his drink sip out, he was laughing out loud at the man on the vid. "Do you believe that? What a messed up dude."

The report continued... "Is that the picture you took?" The man held up a dark photo that had a few blurred smears of white in the top right corner. "Yes, by the time the wife got back, the UFO was leaving, but that's it, right there," pointing to the blur. [back to the studio] "Military sources are denying any knowledge of a UFO in our skies and suggest that the brew drinking couple may have fallen asleep and dreamt the whole incident. Continued attempts to find someone from Calib Military Base to speak with us have been futile and we have made numerous requests for an interview with Flight Command General Hayvitt that so far, have been rejected. He must feel very secure up there on top of Nova Darnith Mountain, shrouded in super secrecy. Many folks here at the station are wondering what the military is hiding and if..."

Mack hit the damper button and the sound from the vid-screen cut off. He looked over at Alexandra and Paul and said, "Some folk will say anything to be on the vid, others are just plain slow."

Paul turned to Alexandra and said, "What about you, Alex. Believe in UFOs?" and snorted in mirth while shaking his head in disbelief.

Alex looked pensive as she answered, "I'm not sure what to think. There are hundreds of these reports of sightings and supposed abductions from all over the country. There must be a shred of truth in them somewhere. Either that or it's a case of bizarre hysteria that maybe only affects mostly odd people who drink brew every night."

Mack was leaning on the bar just a few feet away, following the conversation.

Paul, still smiling mischievously jutted out his chin at Mack and said, "What about you, Mack. Have you ever seen a UFO?" He then sniggered as he picked up his drink. "You must have at least one story from your thirty years in Flight Command."

Mack reached below the bar and snagged an ice cube with a pair of tongs and in one fluid movement, tossed the cube up into the air to have it land with a plop and a tiny splash into Paul's drink, looked Paul in the eyes and said, "Oh, I have lots of stories. Some you wouldn't believe. But I can tell you the sky is filled with unexplained things and my recommendation to you is this: when you're up there, flying around feeling like you're on top of everything, keep your eyes and your mind open."

Paul responded, "Oh my eyes are open alright. I've logged over twenty-eight hundred hours of flying time – all with my eyes wide open and not once did I see anything that could even remotely be mistaken for a UFO. Lots of big birds but no UFOs."

Alex was watching Paul as he spoke and noticed a look of defiance creep across his face. She had seen that look many times in their twelve-year friendship. Usually he was easy-going, didn't get too rattled over things but when he thought himself right, that his opinions were trusted and true, he would stick by them no matter what. Hence the look. She thought to touch a nerve.

"So how do you explain all the sightings of flying disks and what about all the folks who swear they're being abducted and subjected to terrible experimentation?"

Paul signaled Mack to set him and Alex up with another round. Alex quickly looked to Mack and motioned that, no, she didn't want another drink.

This changed Paul's mind about another shot of hard liquor and he said, "Mack, I'll take a brew instead." He turned his seat to address Alex and said, "I can't explain something that has never happened. Maybe it's like you said, it's a form of mass hysteria, only without the mass. More spread out."

Mack put the ice-cold brew down in front of Paul then spoke, "I don't believe Command is covering anything up. That would imply wrongdoing or incompetence. There are things better left unsaid, that's all." He wiped idly at the bar with a damp towel, and continued, "There's already a great number of kooks who, for whatever reason, think they've seen UFOs. Can you imagine the unbearable number of them that would surface if the military came out and said, 'Yes. The skies are sick with UFOs and there's nothing that can be done about it.'" Mack paused and looked at Paul, who was considering what Mack had just said. A slight smile pulled at he corners of Mack's mouth and he added, "Now. What'll you have for dinner?"

"The usual for me," said Paul and quickly added, "You mean to tell me that there *are* UFOs and aliens flying around our skies and you have seen them?"

Mack was ringing up the grill order, a bloody meat sandwich for Paul and a veg plate with extra cheese for Alex after she said, "Me too," to Mack's query. When he finished pushing buttons on the auto-menu, Mack turned back to the two friends.

"I'm telling you that there are unexplained 'things' all around us. That just because you haven't seen aliens doesn't mean they don't exist." And before Paul could respond, Mack said, "I'm gonna go make your dinners," and turned to make his way to the kitchen at the rear of the bar leaving Paul and Alex watching him go.

Alex spoke first, "I think he knows something he's not saying. He's retired military. He has to have seen something. Wonder what it was."

Paul tipped his glass to take the last small taste and set it back down on the bar. "His Top Secret special clearance probably forbids him to ever talk about anything he's seen or done during his career. Alex, what if there are UFOs in our skies?"

Alex was idly watching the now silent vid-screen. She turned to Paul and said, "Then why haven't we seen them?"

The question just hung in the air between them until Alex changed the subject. "After we eat, let's shoot a round or two of Carom to see who buys dinner tomorrow. I want to be home early tonight. We have an early start in the morning and I want to study up on the engineering notes for the new thrusters."

"Okay," said Paul, "You're on. Two outta three wins a meal."

By the time Paul arrived in Flight Bay 9 the next morning, Alex was already immersed in the removal of the worn out thruster apparatus on the port side of her OS-37 Red Wing.

Paul and Alex have been partners on the Red Wing since they had flown it through its test flights and modifications to this final configuration of stealth and exospheric reconnaissance capabilities. Their insights and test flight feedback was invaluable to Red Wing's development. Alex suggested it be named OS-37 Red Wing because of its Orbital Stealth abilities and its agility, that reminded her of a blackbird she once observed diving and turning in pursuit of a tasty insect.

"Hey! Hello," Paul called out as he approached the craft.

"Morning!" replied Alex with a fast smile, before returning her attention to the bolt she was trying to wrench free from its position.

"How long have you been here?" asked Paul.

Alex gave a little grunt as she exerted one last pull on the torque bar gripping the bolt. It did not move. "Just long enough to get up here and start messing with this stubborn bolt!" Dropping her grip on the tool she said in a slightly frustrated tone, "Gonna have to get the power tools out."

As Alex climbed down from the lift, Paul was busy donning

his work overalls and looking at the schematic of the new thruster. "This shouldn't take too long. We should have this and the additional recharge unit installed by mid-day."

"I figure the upgrades and mods should be completed by mid-week, and test fires and docs the day after. We could be flying by the weekend."

Alex was standing at the workbench trying to decide which tool she would try next when the sound of approaching footsteps caused her to look up. Paul casually leaned against the bench and watched the two cadets make their way through the Bay to stand at attention twenty feet away and wait for recognition from Alex who now stood facing the two young men.

"Do you have something for me?" asked Alex.

The taller of the two stepped forward, "Yes Major. You and Captain Jacobs are to report to Flight Commander Tourick's office as soon as possible."

Alex glanced at Paul, who merely shrugged a bit to signify that he had heard what was said, then looked back at the two staff cadets.

"Tell Commander Tourick that we will report in ten minutes."

The cadet thanked Alex and nodded to Paul before turning on his toes and striding out of the Flight Bay, closely followed by the other cadet.

Ten minutes later, Alex and Paul were being ushered into Commander Tourick's office.

Tourick stood up from his desk, smiling pleasantly at the two pilots and came around, entreating them to take seats in the conference area of the office.

Alex took the cushioned chair by the window and Paul sat in the wooden straight-backed chair opposite.

Tourick lowered himself down onto the couch as he was saying, "I've called you here to talk about a special project I want you both to be involved with. We'll be joined in a minute by General Hayvitt and Colonel Miers who will brief you to the particulars."

A soft knock on the door preceded a staff cadet who entered with a tray holding a coffee pot and several mugs. As the cadet was leaving, he stepped back from the door as the General and the Colonel entered, then quietly left, closing the door behind him.

Alex and Paul stood to attention but were waved to ease by General Hayvitt. "I trust Commander Tourick has told you why you're here?"

Tourick spoke, "Only that they're to be involved in your project, General."

"Okay," said the General, "So. First a little background information is necessary."

The General filled the next half an hour with a brief history of the military's knowledge and involvement with alien extra-terrestrial spacecraft and the like. Apparently the military was not only aware of alien UFOs, but had been aware of them for nearly forty years. As General Hayvitt spoke, Colonel Miers provided a steady stream of papers and photographs to corroborate everything Hayvitt was saying.

Alex leaned forward, listening to the narrative and looking intently at the proffered evidence. Paul, on the other hand, was almost stunned numb with each, more detailed revelation.

The military, along with top government officials, including a very influential Senator and at least one Aide to the President, knew that UFOs had been making regular appearances in their skies, although no one knew the exact purpose of their visits.

News stories were always full of accounts of scary abductions by squirrelly, little green beings that performed all kinds of experiments on their captives. Those stories were probably made up or hallucinated at best.

Four years ago, one of the alien craft had a mechanical failure and crashed in a remote area of the Pastalle Mountains out past the Senical Valley. Their compatriots, if any, must have rescued the pilots and crew, because the badly damaged craft was empty. There were traces of biogenic material so it was assumed any crew that may have been on-board must have been taken off. The craft was recovered and studied to understand the alien's command of inter-stellar travel. It was revealed that from the gained knowledge, a proto-type trainer had been built and from that, a more developed ship followed.

Studies of the piloting consoles and access panels and hatches, and simulations as to what physical form these beings must have, yielded a surprising conclusion…they look very similar to ourselves.

This revelation almost made Paul laugh out loud but he quickly reached for his coffee mug to cover his reaction.

The General pushed on, "Without question, you two are the most advanced pilots in Flight Command."

Tourick added, "You both will be reassigned to this project. It's a Top Secret special assignment for an undetermined period of time. You will be transferred almost immediately to General Hayvitt's command. Any questions?"

Alex spoke, trying to disguise the nervousness in her voice, "We start immediately?"

Tourick said, "That's right."

Alex added, "Sirs, what will happen to my Red Wing?"

Tourick was ready for her question. "I've assigned a maintenance crew to complete the upgrades you and Captain Jacobs have started. It'll be tested for accuracy and because I know how possessive you are about your responsibilities, Major, your Red Wing will be waiting for your safe return to my command."

Paul asked, "Sirs, if I may, what exactly *is* this project?"

Colonel Miers answered, "Yes, well, first of all you will be briefed into a Top Secret level classification. Amid the many details of the clearance is one particular directive: you are not to talk about the project with anyone not directly associated with the project. After your briefing, you'll be assigned to Level 6 where you will begin a three-month training period. Within that time you will become proficient on the operations and piloting of the proto-type alien craft, which we've dubbed Bug Hunter."

Tourick cleared his throat and shot the Colonel an incredulous look but said nothing.

Colonel Miers, a bit embarrassed, said, "It's a weak name for such an important project, but the men started using it early on and for morale purposes we let it stand."

Paul and Alex exchanged glances but remained silent.

Miers poured another mug of coffee and continued, "We expect you to aid in the further development of Bug Hunter's successor by contributing your expertise and offering valuable insights."

General Hayvitt interrupted, "Well, I think that's all for now. You will be fully briefed at 0700 tomorrow. Remember, nothing leaves this room. Colonel?" Hayvitt got up to leave and the Colonel busied himself with scooping up the papers from the table and stuffing them back into their folder before jumping up to follow Hayvitt to the door.

After exchanging terse pleasantries with Commander Tourick, the General and the Colonel left.

Alex and Paul had been standing at attention until Tourick motioned them to relax as he said, "You have the rest of today to clear your belongings and organize your workstations down on Level 2. Tell the Flight Bay Sergeant to expect a communiqué from my office. You will both report to Level 6 at 0700. Wear your flight suits and good fortune in your new assignments."

Alex and Paul replied in unison, "Thank you, Sir," and stepped from the office out into the hallway.

Paul spoke first and in a lowered voice said, "That was some meeting. Half of what I heard was unbelievable. The other half was fantastic which is almost the same."

The two walked to the lift at the end of the hall in contemplative silence. Paul waved his hand over the call light until it brightened and stood back looking at Alex who had a concerned look on her face. She was deep in thought.

After a short moment, she turned to Paul and said, "After we clean up our Flight Bay, let's meet in my quarters for a cuppa. We've got things to discuss."

Three hours later, with all the chores done, Alex and Paul were seated at her kitchenette sipping hot tea.

"A Top Secret clearance is like having a gag order slapped on you. It's very hard not to just talk when I think of something to say," said Paul.

"I know what you mean. We'll have to be aware of ourselves from now on." Alex pushed the Ketose closer to Paul, who smiled his thanks then dropped a tablet of the sweetener into his mug.

Alex continued, "At least the question of alien visitors has been answered."

"I'm telling you that I almost fell out of my chair. Forty years they've been coming here?" he asked rhetorically. "It seems odd that in my lifetime and my father's late lifetime, no one I know has *ever* seen a UFO. Those stories have always been confined to the scandal sheets and used for low entertainment."

"I guess the saving thought here is," Alex sipped her tea, "no abductions."

Paul said, "You know, I'm very excited about Project Bug Hunter."

Alex laughed and Paul continued, "Can't wait to see the alien ship and the proto-type that inspired it."

Alex said, "This is so technologically advanced. My mind is crammed with questions… How do the engines work? What kind of fuel does it use? How fast can it travel? What's its range?"

"I can't wait to get a look at it," Paul said. "All we can do now is speculate. Guess we'll have all our questions answered tomorrow. And more."

Alex said, "We have a steep learning curve ahead of us, that's for certain. But it's very exciting!"

"Looking forward to it," added Paul, then continued, "Are you ready for dinner? You're paying by the way."

The security briefing took over an hour but finally Alex and Paul were shown to Section J. The view, when the heavy outer door was pushed open was crammed with workers, consoles, cables, lights, and movement. And right in the middle of it sat the alien flight simulator, Bug Hunter.

Alex and Paul were introduced to their flight trainer,

Commander Peretz, who would train and test the pair on all known flight systems, and Technician Noland, who would guide modifications to the systems based on any input they provided, as long as it fit within the twelve-week training period.

Almost immediately, Peretz launched into a complete overview of the simulator. It was a large oval-shaped space with pilot and co-pilot seats facing the same direction and surrounded by instrument panels full of blinking buttons, switches, and signage. There was an instructor's seat behind the pilot's consoles, situated in such a way as to observe without interface. There was no canopy to this cockpit as it was only a training station.

Commander Peretz addressed himself to both Alex and Paul, "My training plan for you will be straightforward. You will receive individual as well as team instruction. The simulator may be a little rough at first. We've managed to translate about eighty percent of the alien craft and incorporate those findings. However, the remaining twenty percent is still unknown. Part of your duties will be to observe and test that twenty percent and provide ideas and feedback as to function and operation to Technician Noland, who has been assigned to you throughout your training period."

Noland stepped forward to shake hands and introduce himself by saying, "I've heard that you both are the best in your field. I'm looking forward to working with you."

Peretz continued, "Any questions before we begin?"

Alex spoke, "Yes, Sir. Will our assignment to this project conclude at the end of the twelve week period?"

Peretz answered, "No, Major, the twelve week period is necessary for two reasons. You will learn to fly a full-scale prototype based upon your simulator experience and you will help complete the final interpretation and integration of the heretofore, unknown systems. You will be briefed to extended mission status when your training is nearing completion."

Peretz smiled and waited a moment for any further questions and receiving none said, "Shall we get started?"

Paul clapped and rubbed his hands together and smiling with excitement said, "Yes. I can't wait!"

The next ten weeks were the hardest and most rewarding that Alex thought she had ever been through. Her days started early and were filled with reviews of previous lessons, introductions to new systems, flight sims where nothing went wrong, flight sims where it seemed that everything went wrong, and on-going studies of schematics and diagrams. She and Paul were a good team. Each trusted the other and each grew exponentially in their newfound expertise.

At the conclusion of week eleven, they were given a night off and immediately headed for Mack's Bar & Grill for a few games of Carom and a cheeseburger.

Mack saw them come in and smiled his big smile. "Welcome back to Level 1! You've been missed!"

Paul said, "We've been busy."

Mack tapped two glasses of draft and set them down in front of Paul and Alex, saying, "Welcome home." And leaning closer, "I hear Level 6 is pretty swanky. Having fun up there?"

Alex and Paul froze. They never mentioned Level 6 to anyone, so how did Mack know?

Mack gave a short laugh then asked if they wanted anything to eat.

Paul said, "Yes, we're both gonna have cheeseburgers with slaw, hold the onions, please."

Mack nodded and walked toward the kitchen.

Paul turned to Alex and in a hushed voice asked, "How would he know we were assigned to level 6?"

Alex said, "I don't know. Don't forget that he's retired military. Still in the pipeline, I guess."

Mack came back with napkins and utensils, saw the blank looks on both Alex and Paul's faces and said, "I know things. That's all."

It was enough to unsettle Paul and make Alex a little uncomfortable. They ate their dinner, shot three games and called it a night.

Week twelve was all testing, testing, and more testing. Commander Peretz was determined that his charges were to be at one-hundred percent readiness and that Technician Noland picked their brains clean of any ideas or suggestions they still had – no matter how big or how impractical they might seem.

And on the fifth day of the twelfth week, Major Alexandra Martin and Captain Paul Jacobs were officially certified as pilot and co-pilot of all things related to Project Bug Hunter.

Commander Peretz stood in front of the full compliment of technicians, engineers, support persons, and mechanics to make that announcement and the entire Section J sent up a jubilant cheer and loud applause that lasted at least five minutes.

"We've all worked hard to see this mission through and I'm thanking each and every one of you for giving me your best. But no one has worked harder than Major Martin and Captain Jacobs." Peretz smiled and turned to applaud the two pilots standing to his right. When the cheers and joy making in the room settled down,

Peretz spoke to Alex and Paul.

"If you'll come with me, we have a briefing with General Hayvitt and a few others, in about ten minutes."

When Peretz, Alex, and Paul entered the meeting room, General Hayvitt and Colonel Miers were standing and talking softly with a Major General.

Alex eyed the Major General's nametag. Evensten. Major General Evensten. She remembered the name from memos and orders but this was the first time she could recall seeing a face to go with the name.

Introductions occurred and Colonel Miers mentioned that they would be joined by one other, Senator Richmont, who was running a few minutes late.

As the small group was finding their seats around the table, the door pushed open and a harried little man blew in. "My apologies for my tardiness. Security misplaced my Visitor's Pass and... well... some trouble later... here I am." Glancing around the table, his eyes lit on Alex and Paul and he made a beeline for them.

"Major Martin, Captain Jacobs. I'm Senator Richmont. So happy to make your acquaintance. Congratulations on your well deserved accomplishments." Shaking hands and grinning the whole time.

Alex and Paul smiled their thanks but otherwise didn't speak to the Senator, who turned and busied himself with finding a seat, when once found, wriggled back and forth to get comfortable.

General Hayvitt started the meeting. "I needn't remind anyone that this project and the ensuing mission remains at Special Top Secret level and that any information pertaining to it is not to be discussed with anyone not associated. Do I have everyone's acknowledgement?"

Hayvitt made a point of looking each of the attendees in the eye to elicit a response.

Around the table were, "Yes," "Of course," and "Yes sirs."

Hayvitt continued, "Special Clearance personnel are fully aware of the history and current situation concerning UFOs in our skies. Instead of taking a 'Wait-and-See' attitude, our government had the foresight to begin preparing to meet any alien visitors, or invaders, on equal ground, so to speak. Project Bug Hunter is just a step along the way. A very good step and a very important step that has provided an historic way forward."

Hayvitt nodded at Colonel Miers who tapped a few buttons on his tablet causing the room lights to dim and a three dimensional hologram to appear above the projection pad embedded in the center of the table.

The hologram, slowly rotating to offer full views to each participant, was of the Space Station Aurora, originally launched ten years ago, but routinely expanded and upgraded to keep it state of the art. It orbited the planet several miles above the exosphere and fell under the purview of Flight Command.

Hayvitt picked up the hand control and pressed a button. "We've made several significant modifications to Aurora and in fact, are busy with a couple more based upon research done on Bug Hunter and feedback provided by Major Martin and Captain Jacobs during their training."

Hayvitt said, "Sirs, if you will observe..." then casually picked up his glass and took a sip of water.

Paul thought, *what a ham going for a dramatic pause*.

The Aurora hologram slowly started to change its shape. The

center pod split into two halves and moved outward. The hatch doors on Pod C opened and projectile-like apparatus extended outward. Other sections rotated to form fins and angled thrusters. By the time the Aurora had completed its metamorphosis, it resembled a futuristic space jet with a dull black poly-fiber-looking covering stretched smoothly against its subtle angles all along its width and length.

No one spoke. Everyone sat staring at the depiction.

Alex's mind was racing. *Hayvitt mentioned that an alien craft had been recovered four years ago. Is this what it looked like? Are those thrusters? Where's command? I didn't see a view port anywhere.* Her rapid-fire thoughts were interrupted by the sound of Hayvitt's voice.

"Meet our Stealth Trans-Galactic Cruiser. Mechanical details are not required for this meeting so I will move on with a brief mission overview." Taking a deep breath, Hayvitt pushed on, "Our cruiser, by design, closely resembles the type of UFOs entering our space. We've done this so as to blend in and not be noticed by our visitors. We intend to deploy a Spatial Positioning Device, an SPD, that will be attached to the outer hull of an alien's ship and remain undetected as it sends a tracking beacon back to our instruments. This will allow us to track the ship as we stealthily follow it back to its origins where we will observe their world, build intelligence, look for weaknesses, and return home. At that time, we will develop a defense strategy based on the new found intel and, as always, act accordingly. Questions?"

Paul slightly raised his hand while saying, "Yes Sir. Just one question at this time... When do we start?"

Phase II of Bug Hunter Project started at 0600 the following day. Peretz met Alex and Paul at the lift and escorted them to Section N where they were to work and quarter for the next four weeks.

"Let's grab a coffee from the crew's kitchen in Bay 1 and have a fast meeting in the conference room just there," said Peretz pointing at a little fridge/coffee pot area along the wall and a glass walled room five steps further along.

The conference room held a half-round table and roughly twenty chairs. The table was close to and centered on a massive white screen wall and could be used by an instructor or a small group of trainees. Today, it was used as an informal meeting table that would serve to prop up coffee mugs.

"This phase of your training," Peretz was saying. "will augment what you've already mastered and push you a little farther into alien territory…figuratively and literally."

A moment passed in silence as Alex and Paul passively watched Peretz tap the screen on his tablet, searching for a specific file. When found, Peretz continued, "You will learn about the details of the mission starting with the ship's flight configuration and handling, the Spatial Positioning Device, alien language and symbols, the type and quantity of surveillance we expect, and your duties upon your return, which by the way, will include a massive debriefing from Technician Noland."

That last comment made both Alex and Paul laugh a little and Alex said, "Tech Noland is nothing if not single-minded."

Paul added, "It was pleasant to work with someone as knowledgeable and as nice as Noland. It made his focused get-to-the-point questions easier to take,"

Peretz nodded and continued, "First we'll tour the facility. You'll get a look at your ride up to the Space Station. We've modified a Red Wing. It's a little bigger and less agile but will shuttle you up with no problem."

"Would love to pilot, Sir, if that would be okay," asked Alex. "I'm getting anxious from missing flight-time."

Peretz replied, "Don't see why you can't pilot the shuttle, Major," and tapped a brief comment to his outline notes before going on. "Several briefings about alien language and the symbols they use will be held. You will feel that you're learning to speak a foreign language and indeed you will be. It will be difficult because it's unlike any language we know and," Peretz tapped the table with a finger, "because your time to learn it is finite."

Paul spoke up, "Has speech recognition software been built or a word look-up application been developed? I'm thinking that if we concentrate on key words and semantics first, language nuance could be layered on as we go."

"Good observation. I believe your instructor has taken that into account and has compressed the lessons to fit schedule but ask about detailed word help after you've got a look at his teaching tools."

Peretz took a swig of his coffee and looked at his tablet screen. "While trailing the alien craft back to its home world, you will be tasked with collecting and recording certain data. Training of these requirements and those systems will be provided in brief. It's my belief that you will have more time to review the language and symbol interpretation and the surveillance requirements once you are deployed."

Peretz paused to look at Alex then at Paul. Both were ready and attentive.

"Any questions, so far?"

Paul shook his head.

Alex said, "Not so far. Everything you've said has been very clear."

"Good. I've asked Commander Jenston to join us," and turning to look out the glass wall, noted the Commander standing just there chatting amiably with a worker who was dressed in a flight suit. When Jenston glanced up, Peretz raised his hand and nodded and the Commander stepped to the door.

Alex and Paul stood to alert and shook hands upon introductions.

Peretz followed with, "Commander Jenston is in charge of this phase of your readiness training and the launch of the Stealth Trans-Galactic Cruiser. I leave you in very capable hands and with a first class team." Extending his hand in salutation added, "Your mission will be a great success and I look forward to seeing you on your safe return."

Smiles and thank you's later, Peretz collected the now-empty mugs and let himself out of the meeting room.

Jenston faced Alex and Paul. "Shall we begin?"

Both Alex and Paul were issued communication tablets for their four-week use. The tablets were loaded with their tightly controlled schedules and study references. They could use them for written or verbal virtual communication, called V-comm by casual users, and for access to Section N's vast library of specs and tools.

Training was intense but amicable and geared to helping the pilots learn as fast as their capabilities would go punctuated with ample periods of review and hands-on.

Alex was pleasantly surprised when she found, at the end of week three, she could understand and converse in rudimentary alien, recite the entire propulsion system of the Cruiser, and trace five of the seven control systems from the command chair back through their wiring schematics to their point of origin.

She was very pleased with Paul's progress, too. He had excelled in the maintenance and repair of all the Cruiser's major systems, testing himself on speed and accuracy as a matter of course. When they sat together for a meal or were on an exercise break, they brought each other up to date and fell into a sort of banter that tested each other's knowledge.

While pacing on treadmills one day, Alex tested Paul, "Okay, what's a VTS?'

"VTS is the Verdin Transitive Scale of flight speed... of space flight speed... represented by a scale of VTS1 through VTS9 with each increment result multiplied by 35.75 to reach the next subsequent VTS speed measurement." Paul looked at Alex and smiled his I-know-I'm-right, smile at her then asked her in return...

"What is the top-most VTS as recommended by the systems guide?"

Alex answered without hesitation, "VTS6. That's approximately 180,000 VTS per Vector and pretty damned fast. Next question."

Paul smiled wide, "Are you going to follow that recommendation?"

"Probably not!" This caused them both to laugh out loud.

Commander Peretz and Commander Jenston accompanied Alex and Paul, along with other launch team members, on the shuttle ride up to the Space Station.

Taking up a stationary position along side the Space Station, the command was given for the station's transition into its hidden Stealth. Alex, from her position at command, had an unobstructed view of the metamorphosis and watched wide-eyed and in amazement as minutes clicked by. Paul watched the station and listened to the comm unit as a composed voice, from Calib Command Center, named the transformation stages as they unfolded.

No one on the shuttle spoke.

The four-day hands-on training when smoothly. Peretz and Jenston observed and offered helpful information to enhance Alex and Paul's already stellar accomplishments, and added their insights to already learned tactical and surveillance techniques.

By the end of day four, it seemed that everyone was more than satisfied with the training results.

Commander Jenston addressed himself to the little group, "I and Commander Peretz, as well as all of the support members will be boarding the shuttle for return to Calib Field within the hour. This will give you several hours of quietude before your launch. Upon launch, you will maintain mission parameters and be under the no-comm command, so I will wish you speed and accuracy and a welcome return at the designated time."

Jenston shook their hands and departed through the storage bay to the shuttle air lock followed by the miscellaneous techs and trainers who added their hopes to the leave taking chat as they, too, departed.

Commander Peretz was the last to leave, "You've done well,"

he said, "You are ready."

Paul said, "I feel ready and excited to get going."

Alex leaned against her command chair and said, "This morning when I thought about the last sixteen-weeks, I became momentarily overwhelmed, almost to the point of numbness. We've been through so much, had so much new information thrown at us, and frankly, Sir, I am so very proud of what we've accomplished in such a short time. And I want to thank you, Commander, for guiding us," Alex smiled at Paul, "and guiding me, to this point."

Peretz said, "Couldn't have been an easier task and entirely my pleasure." And stood for a brief moment looking at them with fatherly pride before adding, "Smooth voyage." And stepped away.

Paul took his seat and monitored as the air locks snapped and the shuttle drifted away before it fired its engines and steered a course back to Calib Field.

Alex stood behind Paul's chair watching the shuttle recede into the distance. "Do you hear that?"

Paul came to alert and strained his hearing. "No. Hear what?"

Alex said, "Silence."

Following procedure, Alex maneuvered the Cruiser to a position into the shadow of the moon where they were to maintain cover until the arrival of an alien craft that would signal the start of Phase III of the mission. The Cruiser had maintained position for three days.

Alex was sitting quietly in command monitoring the console for notice of an approaching ship. Paul had just completed his scheduled rounds of the Cruiser's secondary systems, putting each one through a diagnostic test, and now stepped through the bulkhead opening.

"All systems passed diagnostics with flying colors. We're ready to go. Any signs of the bugs?"

Paul had taken to referring to the aliens as bugs and for the most part, Alex let it slide but she gave the aliens more credit than she would for a mere insect. Hadn't they been involved in galactic, or further, space travel much longer than they? That had to take a level of intelligence far above that of a bug.

"No sign yet. The Object Position Velocity monitor sounded about an hour ago but it was only a stray meteor and a small one at that."

Paul said, "I'm starting to get anxious to get going. I guess I'm not too good at waiting."

A small light on the console started to blink accompanied by a faint audio sound. Alex tapped a command sequence on her panel and a large console display screen blinked to life. The OPV showed a small dot and followed it as it traced a straight line that when extrapolated, came within two vectors of the Cruiser's position.

"Looks like our wait is over," said Alex as she focused on the OPV display. "That's a G Class ship. Large. About our size. Slowing its approach."

Paul took his co-pilot's seat and buckled in. Busying himself with displays and checks, said, "All systems ready. Spatial Positioning Device ready in... 5... 4... 3... 2... 1. SPD ready. Subsystems check."

The alien ship slowed to a halt some five vectors from the planet and held its position for about ten minutes.

Alex and Paul silently monitored the ship's bearing.

"Be ready to fire the SPD on my command," Alex whispered.

Paul moved his right hand, lightly placing his index finger on the launch button.

The split second the alien ship started its progress closer to the planet, Alex called out *"Now"* and Paul pushed the button. Both watched the console and within seconds the SPD relayed its first click, indicating that it had successfully attached itself, in an undetectable manner, to the alien craft and was sending clear signals back to the Cruiser.

"Okay. Now we wait for the aliens to depart our space and we fall in behind to trail them to their home," said Alex as she reached to lower the audible beep the OPV console was making. "I'll take the first watch."

Paul said, "This may take a couple of hours. I'll make us a bite to eat but call me if something comes up." And he rose to leave command.

The wait wasn't that long. Paul had whipped up a couple of sandwiches and a pot of coffee and brought them up to command. They were just finishing when the OPV signaled rapid movement.

"Looks like our visitors are leaving," said Alex.

Paul checked his monitors and said, "Ready when you are Major," and clicked displays and pushed console buttons fine tuning his readiness.

As the alien craft sped past, Alex gave it a lead of twenty-five vectors and pulled the Cruiser out of the moon's shadows and fell in behind. The pursuit was on. The SPD sent strong, clear signals indicating that the craft was on a straight course through the galaxy.

Paul said, "Would be nice to have an idea of where we were going or how long the trail is."

"Well, Peretz speculated that it could take weeks so we should prepare for the long-haul."

For the next few weeks, Alex and Paul busied themselves with standard duties around the Cruiser. Systems were monitored and routine maintenance performed. They divided the time spent in command watching the little dot on the OPV console move steadily on and ensuring that all devices were accurately recording their data streams. In their down time, they played Montrist, an ancient game of strategy and conquest, to pass the time.

Today, Alex sat in her command chair, one foot hiked up so that her chin rested on her knee, and looked out through the view window at the stars that hung in a part of the galaxy she had never seen. The look on her face was soft with far-away thoughts. *These stars are so bright. Is there a biography of my journey to an alien planet, here? Wouldn't that be something… a book about an alien world, a real alien world. The scandal sheets would have a field day! Weeeel, maybe not. Don't think Flight Command would like that.* Alex's thoughts slowed and silenced as she relaxed into the quiet.

A low audible alarm brought her to attention. The alien craft had changed speed. It was slowing to a crawl but maintaining.

Alex flipped the ship's comm, "Paul, better come forward… there's been a change."

As Paul came through the bulkhead entry, Alex said, "I've located a position where I think we can sequester and still monitor."

Paul glanced at his console and reported, "The aliens have started to chatter. Probably sending data to their command. I've got the channel recording, now."

Alex said, "Turn the volume up, and let's eavesdrop."

The sound that filled their ears was so foreign. Alex's ears almost couldn't take the high-pitched staccato and asked that Paul turn it back down. They listened for a minute and managed to pick out a familiar word or two, recognized from their training.

"Successful observations," "Planet not full," and "Water," were the words first used.

Alex said, "We'll maintain this distance and monitor their comm to make sure we stay undetected. We'll pull comm copies every fifteen minutes and evaluate what their chatter is all about."

"Aye-aye," said Paul, giving his attention over to his console.

"I'll be right back, I'm going to stretch my legs and get us some coffee. We're in for a long session, now."

Paul nodded and Alex ducked out through the bulkhead, returning about fifteen minutes later with mugs of hot coffee and a quart of water.

The pair sat sipping their drinks, listening to the alien chatter and piecing together sentences to shape the content of their broadcasts. Thirty minutes passed. Another comm segment was added. Sixty minutes passed. Two more comm segments were added.

"Are you positive about that last translation?" asked Alex.

"Checked it twice," said Paul. "It clearly states... 'Should ready the fleet and prepare to move within... within,' hold on," said Paul as he flipped pages in the language manual. "'Within sixteen weeks,' that's confirmed." He sat looking at Alex, whose mind was racing through possible scenarios.

She held her comments until an ideal plan formulated in her mind. "We'll stay stealthy and commence planet observations and surveillance as the mission dictates. We'll continue to record and translate their comm and see where we stand in a day or two. I think we have at least that amount of time before our next move."

Two days later, with the alien planet specifications recorded, Alex and Paul met over all the data collected to date.

It was a dense planet at 5.514 G's per AU, rotated slowly around a central star, contained an N_2O_2 Argon atmosphere, had a population in the tens of billions, and an inordinately large military strength that stood at almost four to one when matched to the civilian population.

"Looks like a huge military force. Why would they need a force that large?" asked Paul.

"Good question. It's way out of typical proportion. They'd be better off spending their resources on cleaning up their badly polluted planet. How are they sustaining themselves?"

Both sat looking at their tablets until Alex broke their concentration, "Do we have a compilation of their comm translated?"

"Yes, it's posting now. Should be on your dock in a second."

Initially, the aliens had registered a huge spike in communication as they neared their planet, however, the last few hours had been quiet, giving Alex time to mentally walk-through different strategies that might be needed.

"I want to move the Cruiser closer. Take some terra-maps. Find a good location, please."

Paul responded, "What about here," pointing at a satellite moon close by. "We can park in the shadow but still conduct reconnaissance."

"Perfect."

One hour later, Alex had analyzed the maps and spotted what amounted to at least four flight bases, each one with ten huge military transport craft parked in neat formation. A closer look revealed that there was a massive amount of activity surrounding each base indicating that the aliens were getting ready to move.

Alarmed at the new data and aware that time was slipping away, Alex made another decision.

"I think we should cut our surveillance operations and return home almost immediately."

Paul nodded at the idea then said, "Do you think we should blast out a base or two, or maybe cripple their communication, or try to disable their capabilities before we leave?"

Alex looked at Paul's face and noted his seriousness. "That did cross my mind but I had to dismiss it after thinking of the consequences. We could do real damage but on a small scale which would alert them to our presence. Then we'd be on the run back to our world, because they would chase us. No... " Alex paused and pulled in a breath, "the best use of the sixteen weeks we may have is getting home as soon as possible, warning Flight Command, and preparing for what may be an alien invasion of our home world."

Paul said, "I can have the systems ready within the hour."

Alex smiled at him and touched his arm and said, "Then we leave within the hour."

Alex maneuvered the Cruiser through the satellite's shadows until they were fifteen sectors away from the planet, moved out into the flight path and accelerated up to VTS 8^2, far exceeding the normal speed range, making a bee-line straight for home.

After flight operations had been settled into a steady navigation, Paul eased his hands from his console and sat back in his chair. "At this speed, we need to keep a close watch on the engine thrusters. At first sign of overheating or over-arcing along the fuel converters, reduce speed."

Alex said, "Noted. I'll set an alarm to signal if any changes in those systems are detected."

Paul said, "I understand the need for haste but not at our expense. Wouldn't do to float around out here without power."

Alex smiled at her thoughts, *Free floating in an alien look-alike craft and having aliens try to rescue them. The absurdity of the situation was laughable.* "At this speed, we'll cut our travel time down to less than half and I'm counting on the Cruiser to do it."

When not attending to ship's duties or their own sleeping and eating maintenance, Alex and Paul busied themselves with clarifying the myriad of alien data that had been collected.

Both worked on language interpretation while Alex took the lead on geo-spatial mapping and classifications as Paul engrossed himself in planet analysis. When they pulled their heads up from their work, their conversations were always energetic and contained newly discovered facts or serious conjecture involving possible events and outcomes.

"We need to digitalize everything into proto-packets and prepare to send it to Flight Command," said Alex.

Paul looked up from his tablet and watched as Alex stood up, stretched her back, and step away from her chair.

She turned to face Paul and added, "I've decided that when we reach the halfway mark back to our point of origin, I'm going to break protocol and transmit every bit of the alien information and our observations and speculations to Flight Command."

"I'm glad to hear you say that," said Paul, "I've been feeling uneasy that you and I are the only ones to have this information and are at a disadvantage to do anything about it."

"We're agreed then," said Alex as she visibly relaxed the muscles in her shoulders that had become tense at the prospect of an argument with Paul. For all his bravery and daring, he always observed direct orders, protocol, and mission objectives and Alex was sure she was going to have to rigorously defend her decision.

"Thank you, Paul," was all that was needed. "We reach sector 87.2e in fourteen hours. Can we be ready at that time?"

Paul took a moment to size up where they were against where they needed to be and then spoke, "I think that all of the data can be fully compressed and into proto-packets in about... ummm... five hours." Then looked up at Alex, expectantly.

Alex smiled and said, "Perfect. Now how about a cuppa?"

It took just under fifty-six minutes to send the massive proto-file of alien information to Flight Command. Then there was silence.

Alex and Paul sat in command monitoring their comm screens.

Paul said "I know it went through because a receipt was logged."

"I'm sure they're busy with trying to de-encrypt the message. They're weighing a proper response," said Alex as her mind raced on, *Breaking protocol is a disciplinary offense... this silence is making me second guess my decision to send the data... wish they would respond one way or the other.*

She didn't have longer than a few minutes to wait when an audible beep on the comm screen signaled an incoming message.

Sucking in a tight breath and holding it, Alex leaned closer to the screen, as did Paul, to read the communiqué...

>>> Cursory inspection of surveillance data has triggered massive preparatory measures...

>>> Excellent work Major Martin and Captain Jacobs...

>>> Upon return arrival, you both will be assigned to speed-train six pilots in the operations of trans-galactic cruisers...

>>> With the time allowed, will be ready to meet and vanquish the enemy in their own space...

The comm screen held its position on that last blinking dot for what seemed a very long time.

Paul turned to Alex and said, "Well, at least we're heroes."

The comm screen beeped again...

>>> We've located the alien planet on our star grids... it is in a small solar system located in the Kalos Quadrant of our galaxy commonly referred to by its inhabitants as... *Earth*.

Part Two

Holiday Series Introduction

It all started in 1993 when I wrote my first holiday card letter. It was all the rage at the time to write a nice letter telling your friends and distant family members all about your exploits and misbehavings of the previous year. It wasn't uncommon to receive these letters from other friends and family members and at one point, it was almost expected that a tell-all letter was included in every card that was sent out. Forces help you if you didn't send one of these letters, why, the risk was that you were to be thought of as uncaring!

At that time, actual cards were still in vogue and had been for at least two generations prior to mine. The addition of a letter was just the fancy twist of the time, seeing that almost everyone had a personal computer in their homes with fancy printers and software that formatted envelopes with addresses. You could buy pretty holiday printer paper, too, complete with pictures of Santa's head or maybe a beautifully decorated tree, blazing with colored lights with a silk Angel on top.

Every year prior to 1993, I had handwritten a nice note customized to the recipient and happily signed the card with good wishes for the holidays and beyond. I knew the destruction of handwriting had been ongoing for at least ten years prior to my arrival to the holiday card scene and by 1993, thought to take the electronic plunge and typed up a nice letter to include in my greeting cards that year.

I worked furiously over that letter. I wanted it to be happy and uplifting and strove to exclude any of my going-ons that might bring down the whole idea of holiday joy for any of my family or friends. After all, it was Christmas, wasn't it? A time for joy? A time for cheer? So I left out the parts about colleagues being laid off, unemployment driving inflation, my mortgage company inflating my insurance payments, the cost of living going up and up, and anything in general that would spoil the joyous holiday mood.

I was very proud of my first holiday letter and with great pleasure, printed out lots of copies, glued one copy into every card, deigned to actually sign my name in ink, and sent about forty-five of these gems out into the season's mail.

Some months later, I came upon this letter, filed somewhere on my home computer, and snapped open the file, eager to read the world's best, newsy holiday letter ever written! Oh, gack. What I read made me a bit ashamed to have sent it out. It read like a simple-minded face-cram full of barely disguised self-pity and thinly veiled egomaniac dribble. I vowed right then never to send out one of those letters again. My first and my last. I swore it. And have gladly kept to my word all these years.

Well, lucky you! For the next fifteen years, I sent stories to my holiday card recipients. I thought to keep the stories to one page so as not to bore anyone too much. I still glued them into cards and still signed them with ink before mailing them out, and know that for some, the reading was well received. There are eleven of them included here, in this humble compilation, for you. These stories still make me smile, unlike the dreaded Christmas Letter of 1993.

Enjoy! N. K. Hart

Suddenly

To suddenly find oneself in the midst of an unfamiliar setting was a bit unbalancing.

Turning to the right, my eyes wandered to the horizon. At first, there was nothing other than sun dappled riffles and a flock of

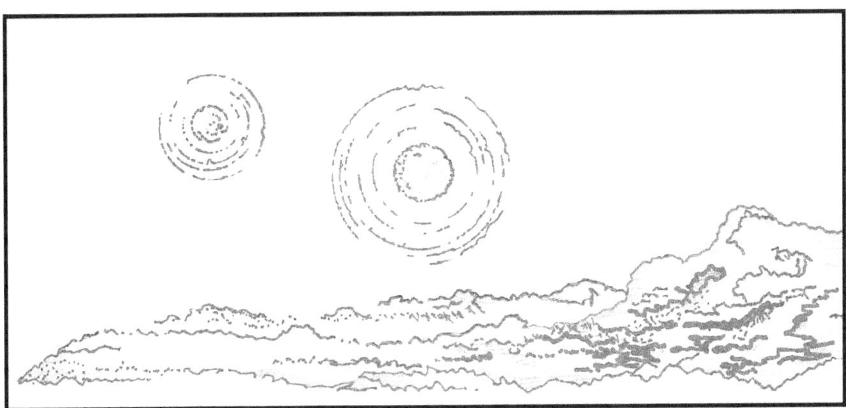

sea birds fighting for a chance to dive into the center of a school of squid that had wandered too close to the surface. That price was always too high. A warm gentle breeze against my face prompted me to suddenly turn and look in the direction from which I had just come.

You took my hand in a reassuring gesture, and, dropping it after a moment, indicated that we should continue onward. Further ahead in our direction of travel, I could just make out shadows that moved in the late summer heat and imagined that they were living beings worthy of momentary curiosity.

We continued our journey for what must have been some measure of time because the colors of our surroundings softened in the fading light. What was our destination? I can't seem to remember what plans might have brought us here.

We do not speak for long periods. It is considered bad manners to converse without the advantage of looking full in the face of the one you are addressing, and there was urgency in our pace. My questions could wait.

The warmth of the day and the weariness of the journey are relieved in the coolness of the night and the security of darkness. Overhead, the stars move quickly out of view and the soft indistinguishable sounds pricking at the peripheral of my conscience dared to move closer to my awareness. We may have slept. It is very hard to draw differences between what was and what now is.

At dawn, the lingering thoughts that link the three realities together have always left me with the vague feeling that some of the pieces had been arranged and that they no longer represented the whole truth but rather, an over-dramatized hieroglyph. I study your face for some hint of the future and can clearly see the lines that your thoughts must have left behind when the sun rose and the sounds retreated to the shadows.

Momentarily, we found ourselves at the edge of a precipice that presented a panorama view of a landscape that was wild and sharply focused.

This was it. We were sure that this was it. Joy overwhelmed us and as we tightly held hands, stood side by side, gazing heavenward at the two moons that had risen in the eastern sky. How lucky we must be to have reached what others clearly have missed.

Suddenly the train appeared out of nowhere and flattened us where we stood.

Where Has Time Gone?

We're not really sure when it happened. Cast out of time, not able to reenter. In the beginning it was easy to mark time by feel. All we had to do was imagine that a few minutes had passed or that the day had just completed and agreement was immediate and final.

There was really no way of telling if any of these events actually occurred, but the agreements drove the conviction that we were right in our reflections. Then small variances began to creep in. It was hardly noticed at first; surely others must have experienced occurrences such as these, although we could not be sure.

We filled the ensuing void with discussions of culture, we played word games and laughed at the variances we produced. I can say with some certainty that it was a relief and more than a bit exciting to discover that we had not yet conducted a thorough deliberation on the concept of transcendency and set upon it with vigor. All the while, we waited for time to return. We were consumed with questions of where time had gone, why had it left, and when would it return, all the while assuming that it was time that was displaced, not us. Discussions would last for... for what? for days?

It was during lengthy discussions on myths that we first noticed that variances in the void began to appear. Like small tears in the fabric, these variances began to enlarge and distort allowing brief glimpses of what was beyond. At last we connected the discussions of mythical stories with wider variances in the void. This was extremely exciting! With a fever unmatched in recent memory, myths and concepts such as Hercules, Helen of Troy, Jason and the Argonauts, the Three Sisters, Heaven's Angles and other worthy legends came before us, were summarily discussed and dismissed at lightning speeds. It was only when we touched upon the last legendary figure on our list that things began to happen.

Almost as soon as we uttered the opening words to what promised to be the piece de resistance to the anthology of mythological men and beasts that the very air seemed to rip apart filling the space around us with a blinding white light. We shielded our eyes and held on to each other as we felt the firmament under our feet fall away. With a thud that momentarily knocked the wind out of us, we fell to the ground and opened our eyes. How could this have happened? What power of the universe held sway over time? For as sure as we found ourselves in our warm undersea hideaway, we are also as sure that it was the discussion of the last legendary figure, Santa Claus, that brought us here…

Who Am I

Some of you may not know me. It's for you that I arrange ink on paper and attempt to place light where there is darkness. Yes. Let me consider for a moment how I shall accomplish this…

I consider myself complex; a creature of many facets and interests. I am an artist. I have composed many hours of drama and suspense, have enjoyed the work and have been as surprised by the final scenes as any of you might be.

I am a warrior and have fought valiantly upon the fields of honor. I meet the enemy full face and without fear for I fight for home and hearth and honor.

I have spent endless summer afternoons considering the realms of inner and outer space and plan to journey there in the near future. I am available for consultation on the myriad of issues surrounding the subject. I am a mathematician and have calculated forces and angles enough to resolve difficult problems that enable me to surmount gravity and distance. I can accomplish great leaps while expending sparse amounts of high cost energy.

My prowess is to be envied by all who have observed me in action. I sometimes think that I might have been an Olympian if I had even the least bit of spare time. I am quite agile and think very quick on my feet.

Some might hint at immortality, and while I blush at these thoughts, I humbly beg their pardon and remind them that I am, after all only a superior creature capable of much greatness but certainly subject to the same rules of astral plane as other living creatures. My immortality is ensured by tales of my conquests and lasting accomplishments.

I am master of concentration. My hunting skills and patience is beyond measurement and I always hit my mark.

Have I mentioned that I am famous! There are many stories written about me, some are written in the most delightful books, most of which are true and some of which have pictures.

I have been mistakenly called aloof and loner, when in fact, I am a creature of warmth and sensitivity. I have a sophisticated, highly refined sense of humor and can be seen quite often smiling to myself over this or that.

I have always loved being in the company of those who love me and will freely spend my time among them.

I am sure you must know me by now. I am like no other,

because you see, I am The Cat.

The Struggle

Once upon a time when the world was stilled by the blanket of winter, there walked a giant of a figure, capable of striking terror into all those who came within its gaze. Small groups of men under the cover of darkness and unseen by anyone, would slip into dark alleyways to discuss what could be done about the giant. What would it take to rid the world of such a monster? Who would save them from this horrible fate?

Plans slowly began to take shape. The giant's predictable wrath made it too dangerous an adversary to confront in town, and too much for the locals who were understandably demoralized by their dark dilemma. It would have to be done by an outsider. A lone man, a cold man. Several of the town elders, having contacts reaching beyond the town borders, would quietly make queries of subordinates in the north, and to the east. The quest for a champion would begin with the gray light of morning.

Days turned into weeks with no word from distant sources and the reign of terror from the

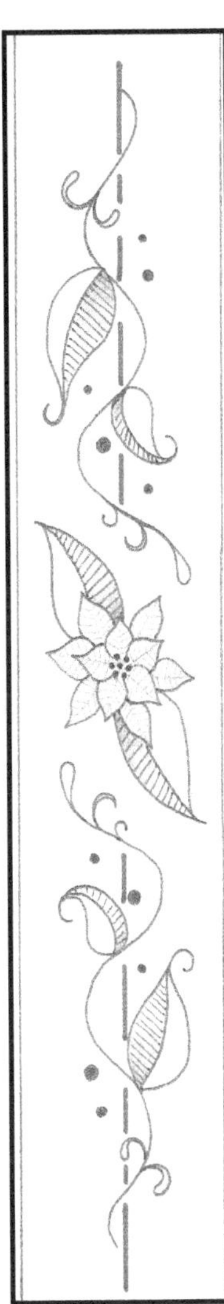

giant continued unabated. Townspeople were routinely plucked from the streets, their screams lasting several seconds before being muffled and then stilled. I myself can remember running blindly through the night, my lungs burning from the labor they performed in an effort to escape into the shadows. Food stores were seized, farm animals too. It was to the point where there wasn't enough to last through the dark winter unless something was done. Our cries for mercy went unheard.

Then one day, a stranger came into town. He was tall and perhaps of medium build but when asked later to describe him, all that could be remembered were his cold steel-gray eyes. The townspeople were afraid of him. He filled us all with fear and yet he was empty inside. Meetings were held to exact the price of the deed. Regardless. Whatever final amount was agreed upon would be paid without haste and the work would begin soon afterward.

This man walked among us for a time. Observing. Calculating. Waiting. At first we watched closely expecting a sudden end to our problem but soon wearied and returned to skirting the main roadways and hiding our small insignificant selves from view.

And then it began...

We were brought to the scene by the sounds of inhuman wails of agony that split the winter air. Rushing forward, the ones in the front were crushed backward by the force of the two adversaries as they shuffled and wrestled and knocked one another from one side of the street to the other. Through the mist, one could see muscle and sinew straining to gain the advantage and hear the punches falling again and again against their marks. A heavy body slam into the Grange Hall on the corner brought the brick walls down with a deafening crush and a blinding cloud of dust, obscuring the view. But it was the light from the pale winter moon, which cast its rays downward, that outlined the lone figure emerging from the rubble.

As he strode forward under the moonlight, the evidence of the battle was obviously about him. Torn red shirt, black boots scuffed and caked with blood, and face bruised and dirty, the white of his beard turned brown by the dust swirling about him. But through it all, it was his bright smile that clearly conveyed to everyone present that he was the winner that night.

The figure strode past the observers, boarded his vehicle, and sped into the winter night. In hushed tones, the townsfolk would talk about this for years afterward never really understanding what had taken place.

Santa, In One Act

THE PLAYERS

Santa, a moody somewhat fat and obnoxious man
Many Santas, making up a chorus
The ghosts of several children

ACT ONE

[The stage is arranged as a living room with a small, framed door on the left and a massive fireplace on stage right. A garden can be seen in the background through large windows flanking a set of French doors. The winter sky is lit only with a few bright stars and the full moon. A blanket of snow has settled on the evergreens. Two overstuffed chairs are present in the room, one is just inside the doorway and the other is arranged in front of the fireplace. There is a sideboard located along the wall on stage left. There are books and newspapers spread out among the furniture and on the floor. A glass stands half empty on a small table next to one of the chairs; a dark bottle can be seen there also. A roaring fire is seen in a massive stone and brick fireplace at stage right. The room is lit dimly by the glow of the fire.]

[A group of Santas, enter from the door at stage left and begin to sing.]

MANY SANTAS CHORUS   We are fat and show well fed
Let us mount our broken sled
We will fly above your head
Pelting you with bits of lead.

[Santa chorus exits stage rear.]

[A large man enters through the door on the left and makes his way across the room to the chair by the fireplace.]

SANTA, "There had *better* be a fire made up. I'm cold and my feet are tired. Where's that brandy I left here, oh, yeah, here it is. Hrrumph."

[There's a sigh of relief heard as Santa drops his weight into the chair.]

SANTA, "Rosario! Rosario, where are you?!! Damned help is never around when you need them. Probably off somewhere complaining about how hard the work is. Rosario!"

[Santa takes a long drink from the brandy bottle. When finished, he pours enough into the glass to fill it up again and finishes by taking another long drink from the bottle. Sitting back into the overstuffed chair, and still grumbling about his difficulties, Santa falls into a deep sleep. Soft snoring sounds can be heard just above the crackling of the fire.]

[Enter the ghosts of several children who begin to walk around the prone figure of Santa.]

CHILD ONE, "You are so mean. Christmas is almost upon us and you have forgotten us again. You should be getting ready; instead we find you here doing nothing!"

CHILD TWO, "We waited so long for Christmas to come, but you broke your promise, it never arrived and we're now dead."

[Sounds of torment are heard rising and lowering in the background.]

SANTA, "I have been working my whole life for you and what have I gotten in return? Nothing! What do you want from me"?

CHILD THREE, "We want you to keep your promises."

CHILD ONE, "Just look at the condition of the world; you did this! Filled with broken promises and dreams killed by your thoughtless actions!"

[The group of Santas reenters from the set of French doors at the rear and begin to sing.]

MANY SANTAS CHORUS   We are fat and ride in sleds

> Will drop gifts upon the heads
> Of children running fast in dread
> Look out world! We're men in red.

[Santa chorus exits stage left.]

SANTA, "It's not fair to blame me. The world is in its state not due to me, I am innocent!! And I am tired! Go away, leave me alone!"

[The sounds of torment rise to a fevered pitch as the children turn their backs on Santa and leave, one by one, through the door on stage left.]

[Santa wakes up with a start. Looks around and lets out a long breath to relieve the stress.]

[The group of Santas reenters from stage left.]

MANY SANTAS CHORUS   When returning to the shed
> In time to brace our comfy bed
> We will have shouted and have said
> Look out world! We're not dead.

[The Santa Chorus exits.]

[Santa takes another long drink from the brandy bottle, slowly rises from his chair and walks to the French doors. He stands for some minutes looking into the darkness before opening the doors and calling out to an unseen figure in the darkness.]

SANTA, "You there! Ready my sleigh. It's time for me to leave."
[Santa steps out through the doors and is gone.]

Ho, Ho, Ho

"Ho ho ho, my ass!" **And that's a direct quote.**

ATNAS DERIT

The sound of the alarm clock pierces the darkness. A hand reaches out, fumbling against the headboard, and a crashing sound ensues. This has little effect on the alarm clock, which continues to ring in spite of the fact that it is now wedged between the bedpost and the wall. The light snaps on and the ugly awareness that the day is starting before it should, makes its way through the fog.

Slowly swinging the legs out and over the edge of the bed affords a small lift to the upper body, which twists to face the rest of the room. Half pushing and half pulling manages to finish the job of sitting upright.

Rubbing the sleep from the left eye makes things more faded. Rubbing it from the right eye makes the view seem as if it were underwater.

Leaning forward to the point of falling, the weight shifts from sitting to a kind of precarious balancing act on a pair of spindly legs and creaky knees. Being careful not to move too fast does not prevent falling in reverse and sitting down abruptly and making a dull plopping sound. The arduous process would have to be repeated at least once more.

Slowly, slowly moving on until the furnace switch is located along the corridor wall. Which direction does it go for heat? Was it up or down? Without glasses it's impossible to tell, although it'll be clear soon enough. Clanging metal noises from below indicate that the furnace is trying to start up. It'll be some minutes before heat from the floor registers is felt this far up in the house. The bed seems awfully inviting and warm, maybe just another 15 minutes. But no, must press on.

Back through the corridor, barely moving, one foot in front of the other, an inch or two with each step. In what must have been close to an eternity, the distance between the bed and the bath finally shortens. Another light snaps on, this one more glaring and harsh than the first.

With eyes squinted almost shut, a hand moves over the fixtures to find the hot water spigot and spins it to the right. That's cold! It always takes too long to warm up. Leaning forward but bracing creaky knees against the washbasin cabinet, two hands come together to form a bowl and catch the now tepid water. In one seemingly quick movement the water is splashed upward into the face, wetting the beard in the process. As the fog fades away, things come into focus and the surroundings become more friendly.

With a familiar spring coming back into each step, dressing is quickly accomplished and the stairs are easy and few. A fast breakfast of muffins and coffee and it's out the door for a brisk start of the day. But before leaving, one last look in the mirror to adjust the red cap and to pinch red into the cheeks. Leaning forward for a closer look, the reflection of the calendar hanging on the opposite wall almost stops the heart from beating. Why, there was no need to get up today at all!! It's December 26th!

Up The Chimney

'Twas the quarter before Christmas and all through the workforce there were shocked and unforgiving faces frozen in disbelief at what they were hearing from top management.

"Because we have been unable to demonstrate financial stability during the last three fiscal quarters, and having been largely unsuccessful in finding entrepreneurial financing or other forms of support, we will be forced to cut back on amenities, staff, production, delivery schedules, and customer support."

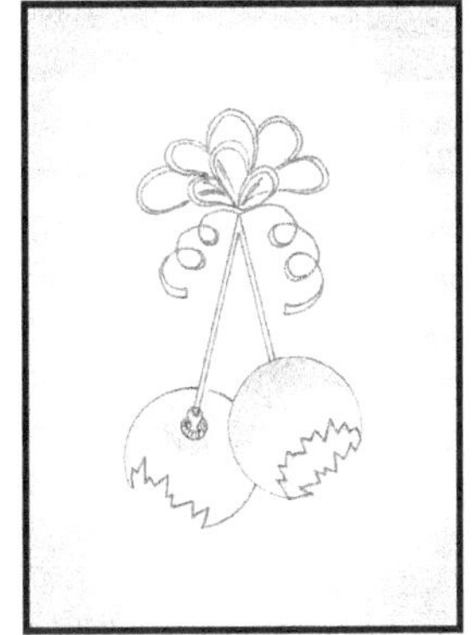

The resulting outbursts were almost deafening and I, myself, could only hear those closest to me and watch the man in the unkempt red suit at the podium mouthing words that I could not hear. I fancied that he offered apologies and opined explanations that had words of sympathy sprinkled throughout, but I knew better. The words would be hollow and without meaning. And even though I could not hear them, I knew what he was saying. "Poor customer reviews, untested products, too many problems, long lead-times, slow turn-around." It would go on like this for another two hours before we heard the second shoe hit the floor with an audible thud.

Mr. Claus continued, "In order for at least some of the work to continue, certain cuts will have to take place immediately. There will be a 45% reduction in workforce that will occur within the next two days. Many positions are being eliminated, and the names of those being let go will be given to the supervisors at the conclusion of this meeting. Supervisors will inform affected staff by the end of today's shift and those being displaced, or downsized if you will, will report to HR to complete all appropriate paperwork. Your unemployment insurance will be adversely affected if you do not report to HR and sign these papers! So please follow the instructions!"

The next two days were filled with rumors and innuendo. First there was talk that the Lotta Joy Toy Company was going to buy out Santa Incorporated and that all share holders would receive a generous buyout package as well as job offers but this quickly dissipated when the newspaper hinted that Lotta Joy Toys was also in financial trouble. You could almost find the story under all the bad news of other layoffs and quarterly loss statements that led the headlines. It was said that Santa Inc. was talking about moving operations further south to take advantage of cheap Eskimo labor but this too diminished, along with other hopes, within days. I think the last straw for Clancy O'Pal were the rumors he heard and that he himself repeated, that told of management hiding the real facts and figures from the workers, that if we all knew the real story, we would be sure that Santa Inc. was going to ruin. In a very short amount of time, it would only be a case of the last elf to leave making sure the lights were all out.

Most of the survivors from the initial layoff were still in shock when another round of layoffs occurred. This time, management wasn't so nice. Elves were taken aside as they were showing up for their shifts and hustled out with no regard for seniority or years of service. Another 32% were let go. This put the shop down to an operating efficiency of 23%. Who could actually produce anything running at 23% efficiency? Management actually said that the remaining departments would be combined into one big partnership and that our continued hard work would prove to potential customers that we still had it. Under my breath, I asked what 'It' was, only halfway wanting to hear the answer.

The late shift was eliminated and the remaining shifts were scaled back to the point where they could not function in a quality manner. Everyone was angry and focused that anger at the line supervisors who were in just as much or more fear for their jobs as anyone else. If there were ever an area between a rock and a hard

place, the supervisors were in it up to their ho ho ho eyeballs. Workers and management were drawing lines and daring the other to step over it. Attitudes and opinions flew in all directions, workers called in sick, meetings were held, and the reindeer broke out of their paddocks and flew off into the stormy night.

The hard cold point of no return had been reached: there was no product, no delivery system, customers had gone elsewhere, and the last deadline had passed. There was nothing left to do but wait for the final quarters returns and the New Year because Christmas has been canceled.

Santa's Echo

After last year's devastating breakdown of Santa, Inc.'s management and operations that precipitated an extremely hostile takeover by a relatively new Santa company based in Fredonia, Big-Hot, You-Want Toys, the whole environment could be summed up with one word: chaos.

The elves that were left after the horrendous and painful lay-offs were faced with a terrible mess of broken and unlabelled parts, partially assembled toys, missing inventories, lots of boxes of unknown things, and a whacking bad attitude. They began by trying to straighten out the work areas and organize the parts for the operation processes. Supervisors talked with new management about the on-going need to work with labor, communicate freely, and to understand what was most needed in order for the team to pick up and continue. Management was reminded that labor had just watched their friends get the axe and that it would take a bit if time to recover from the severely depressed morale that was much in evidence. Management responded by holding a company meeting where they promptly told labor "Get over it and to get to work".

The new Santa was pretty pleased with himself for being able to manipulate the old Santa, Inc. into a state from which they couldn't recover (he had friends in the shipping and transportation industry) and for acquiring the half-dead company at such a bargain. He immediately started installing all his friends in all of the highest positions around the

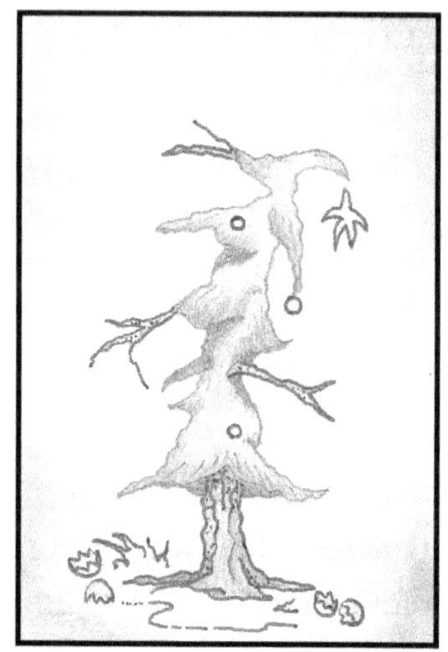

company and even felt so good about his affairs that he let down his guard and let loose with some of the meanest things ever heard. No one escaped his acerbic 'humor'. In the boardroom, he made Mrs. Claus the goat by commenting that "She was out back sweeping the porch like a good little girl." That always got a laugh.

Some of the elves seemed to "get over it" and actually started to "buy into it" as evidenced by their apathy and short memories. It was almost as if they had all developed A.D.D. within the last few months. Unbelievable. When reminded about the bloody lay-offs, most could not recollect clearly the events and could only remember some high level situations and only in hazy nondescript terms.

With Big Santa in charge, and all his crones in seats of secondary power, it wasn't long before new rules were in place. Part assemblies were being subcontracted out to fourth-world countries. Painting would not be done by hand any more; that took too much time. Only the less expensive inventories were stocked, everything was done by machine, and the elves took a devastating wage cut to stay employed. The VP's would position themselves at vantagepoints and yell "Hey, look over there!" while 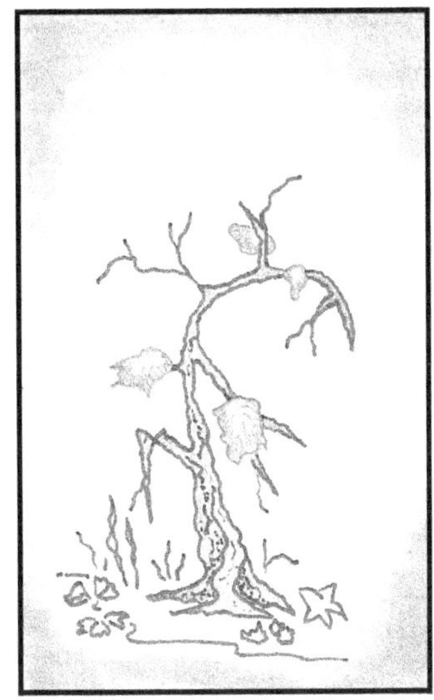 pointing at something insignificant. While the elves were straining their necks to see what was supposed to be happening, paid thugs would disassemble common areas, such as the lunchroom, and cart the cabinets, tables, and chairs out to moving vans. It was rumored that Big Santa was cannibalizing the Company.

Other elves, who remembered the true spirit of Christmas, formed a rival toy company and were determined to retake Christmas.

Santa Answers Your Letters

Ho,

There's this whole thing about walking barefoot in grass. This so upsets me that I am forced to abandon my boots and pinch my toes together in such a way as to pluck out several blades of it at one time. I do this until I feel better or until my toes are stained green.

Have you ever noticed that no one ever stalks Santa?

I guess I'll have to go to the mall this week to finish my shopping. Most of the stores are going to offer a discount if I use their credit system, which I won't. I don't want to discuss the point with a smiling little cashier, either. One of them recently asked me if I was interested in purchasing a thong panty for 40% off. I felt like saying, "Have you even seen my butt-end?" Spare me.

After my complaining about gastrointestinal difficulties, my doctor told me to cut back on the cookies and milk. This is going to be very easy because I haven't had a good homemade cookie in years. All I get anymore are the generic store brands and they taste of cardboard and grease. And whose bright idea was it to leave cookies and milk out for me anyway? For crying out loud, I'm an adult! How about something more substantial like a nice salami and cheese with mustard on French bread or a nice hot meal for a change. A New York steak and baked potato with sour cream and butter with a big piece of apple pie would do, oh so, fine! And a cup of hot designer coffee - a double decaf half-caf with foamed skim milk - to go!

What's up with stringing colored and blinking lights all over your house? If you have to do it, try being a bit more creative. I was over a place once that had so many lights on it that it actually made a humming noise. All I could think was that the Electro-magnetic field generated by all of those lights was probably causing goiters all over the neighborhood to pop!

Yeah, but after it's all been said and done...

I'm still in love with Christmas.

- S.C.

Christmas In The Swamp

The swamp was especially humid for the month of December. Oppressively humid. But the swamp, humid or not, is my home, and I have left it only once in the past month, making sure that it was for a short period of time, and no longer.  How else would I have known about the new neighbors and the feast they brought with them?

I was crawling along the shore one day when something brushed past my peripheral vision. Not sure of what it exactly was, I made up an explanation that almost fit the apparition. A Shar-Pei, perhaps? I decided to investigate and followed along the edge of the reeds taking care not to make any sounds. As I approached the small clearing at the edge of my property, I saw it. Yes, it was a Shar-Pei, and it was alone. Well, not for long.

Asking ourselves where had that dog gone off to, we decided to take a walk around the swamp and try to call him home. It was getting to be late afternoon but we thought that if little Mao Ji was going to be home that night, we had better start searching.

There was something spooky and very mysterious about the swamp and around twilight, things started to happen. As we moved deeper into the fetid bog, we found small torn bits of red cloth strewn about as if they had been torn from the body of a fleeing person. Darkness descended quickly and fear choked my throat, but thinking of my poor dog, I continued calling out in soft whispers. What was that! We froze in our steps, and although we couldn't make it out exactly, it sounded like distant choral rhythms followed by a low growling voice that sent chills up our spines. Occasionally, there were the sounds of vicious animal fights and birds squawking as they flew blindly into the night. We're so frightened that we crouch down in the tangled roots of a Banyan tree to hide from the night and pray for daylight.

We're lost. Dammit. And we've given up hope of finding the dog alive. Stumbling out into a small patch of soggy ground, we discover what looks to be a recently occupied encampment. The horror! There is a tattered tent and a worn out but well used camp stove simmering a pot of meat stew. Oh no! is this our Mao Ji? Horrified at the scene, we flee and manage somehow to stumble back to our home.

I love my swamp. I love everything about it! While on a leisurely crawl back from the small clearing at the edge of my property, I came upon three small creatures playing within 100-yards of each other. An American Short-haired Cream Tabby was the first, a nice little crunchy tidbit. Ah, it went down smoothly! The next was a Yorkipoo. What a cute little bite that was; no dog show for that little pup! The last treat was a Shar-Pei, but I've got to tell you, it was a bit like swallowing a massive cotton ball. I hacked on that one for fifteen minutes. Geesh.

It took a day to calm down and realizing that the local law enforcement wouldn't care too much about the fate of one dog lost in the swamp, we decide to take matters into our own hands and set a trap. By sheer willpower, we make our way back to that unholy encampment, set the trap, and hide in the distance. After many silent hours, and just before dawn, we hear a bone-snapping sound accompanied by an inhuman wail. Petrified, we held silent in the dark and waited until light to move from our hiding place among the reeds. At first light, gathering our courage, we slowly approached the trap, pulled aside the Spanish moss, and discovered, to our utter amazement, that the snap trap was empty except that the spring mechanism was tangled with sleigh bells.

Author's Note…Originally written in 2004 but since, expanded into a really cool story titled Swamp's Edge that has been included here in this collection.

About the Author

N. K. Hart was born in up state New York, moved to California as a grown child and has lived in the Bay Area ever since. After an illustrious career in the tech field, NK studied horticulture, design, and began writing suspense thrillers, humor, and sci-fi stories as an expression of an active imagination.

NK has been in love with stories and storytelling since early childhood. Forays into fiction have included The Innocence of Power, a modern day suspense thriller, and Up The Crime Ladder, a humorous look at the sometimes-complicated lives of Henchmen.

When not writing, NK creates high relief ceramic tiles and lives in Morgan Hill California with a very nice and wonderfully smart cat named Awesome.

www.ingramcontent.com/pod-product-compliance
Lightning Source LLC
Chambersburg PA
CBHW071933130726
47908CB00015B/371